D0408548

# LORI WICK

## *Donovan's Daughter*

*Lori Wick*

**HARVEST HOUSE PUBLISHERS**
Eugene, Oregon 97402

Scripture verses are taken from the King James Version of the Bible.

Except for certain well-established place names, all names of persons and places mentioned in this novel are fictional.

*Cover by Terry Dugan Design, Minneapolis, Minnesota*

DONOVAN'S DAUGHTER

Copyright © 1994 by Lori Wick
Published by Harvest House Publishers
Eugene, Oregon 97402

ISBN 0-7394-4148-5

**Printed in the United States of America.**

*This book is
dedicated with love to my nieces,
Jessica Wick, Julie Kolstad,
Katharine Arenas, Johanna Wick,
Barbara Wick, and Mary Wick.
I praise God for each of you,
and pray that you will grow
in the grace and knowledge of
our Lord and Savior, Jesus Christ.*

# About the Author

Lori Wick is one of the most versatile Christian fiction writers in the market today. From pioneer fiction to a series set in Victorian England to contemporary writing, Lori's books (over 2 million copies in print) are perennial favorites with readers.

Born and raised in Santa Rosa, California, Lori met her husband, Bob, while in Bible college. They and their three children, Timothy, Matthew, and Abigail, make their home in Wisconsin.

## *Books by Lori Wick*

**A Place Called Home Series**
*A Place Called Home*
*A Song for Silas*
*The Long Road Home*
*A Gathering of Memories*

**The Californians**
*Whatever Tomorrow Brings*
*As Time Goes By*
*Sean Donovan*
*Donovan's Daughter*

**Kensington Chronicles**
*The Hawk and the Jewel*
*Wings of the Morning*
*Who Brings Forth the Wind*
*The Knight and the Dove*

**Rocky Mountain Memories**
*Where the Wild Rose Blooms*
*Whispers of Moonlight*
*To Know Her by Name*
*Promise Me Tomorrow*

**The Yellow Rose Trilogy**
*Every Little Thing About You*
*A Texas Sky*
*City Girl*

**English Garden Series**
*The Proposal*
*The Rescue*
*The Visitor*
*The Pursuit*

**Contemporary Fiction**
*Sophie's Heart*
*Beyond the Picket Fence*
(Short Stories)
*Pretense*
*The Princess*
*Bamboo & Lace*

## Willits Families—1881

Alexander Montgomery (Willits' doctor)

Marcail Donovan (Willits' schoolteacher)

Cordelia Duckworth
Sydney Duckworth (Cordelia's grandson)

Allie Warren

The Austin Family
Husband—Dean
Wife—Kay
Children—Marla
Daisy

## Santa Rosa Families—1881

The Riggs Family
Husband—Marshall (Rigg)
Wife—Kaitlin (Katie)
Children—Gretchen
Molly
Donovan

*March 25, 1881*
*Santa Rosa, California*

*Dear Marcail,*

*Happy Birthday! It's hard to believe that we're not together on your nineteenth birthday; it's the first time I can remember our being apart. You know my love and prayers are with you and Father. Let me know what the two of you did that was special. Tell Father I hope he baked you a cake!*

*Rigg sent your birthday box in plenty of time, so when you read this, you should be able to write and tell me if the dress fits. I know all-white is impractical, but you look so pretty in white.*

*The girls talk about you constantly. I tell them that you'll come to see them when you can. Donovan is growing like a weed, and I so wish you could see him. The girls were nowhere near his size at this age. I think he's going to rival Rigg before he's done. And speaking of Rigg, you can't believe the joy in his face when he holds his own little son. God is so good, Marcail.*

*I just couldn't resist writing to you on your birthday. Write back soon and catch me up on all the news. I don't know about you, but it feels to me as if you've been gone for three months, not three weeks.*

*Love, Katie*

April 6, 1881
Visalia, California

Dear Katie and Family,

*I love the dress. It's beautiful and fits like a dream. Thank you so much. I've been saving a white ribbon, and now I have a dress with which to wear it. From whom did Rigg order the dress?*

*I wanted to take my time to tell you about Father's gift to me, but I'm so excited I can't wait. Father told me I could start taking the special studies class with my teacher, Miss Wilkins, and get my teaching certificate. It means staying after school every afternoon, but I should be done by mid-summer and be able to apply for teaching positions this fall!*

*I can hardly believe it's true, Katie—I'm finally going to be a teacher! It's what I've prayed for and dreamed about for as long as I can remember. I think it was hard for Father when I told him I did not want to be married right away, but after he took some time to get used to the idea, I could see he was going to wholeheartedly support my decision.*

*I think his change in attitude might have something to do with his watching me tutor. He can tell I love to teach. I'm not sure if he can understand that it's not the same as having my own class, but I am really enjoying it. Mitchell, the little boy I tutor every afternoon, has a crush on me and tells me he's going to marry me. Renee, the little girl I teach, is just the opposite. She resents my presence, and I have to coax nearly every word out of her. Please pray for both of us.*

*Give Rigg and the girls my love, and kiss Donovan for me. I've found a pair of matching dolls for Gretchen and Molly, but I'm not going to send them. I'd rather bring them when I can visit, to see their faces when they open them. I might hold onto them until Christmas.*

*I wish I could tell you I'll see you soon, but with my studies intensifying, I just won't be able to get away. I hope this finds you all well.*

Love, Marcail

Dear Marcail,

Well, summer is upon us. The weather is hot in the extreme and all the grass in Santa Rosa is already brown. Every window in the kitchen is open as I write this letter.

Rigg's mood has been nothing short of nonsensical tonight. He keeps coming through the kitchen and giving me messages for you. The last one was that a man was here, a doctor, seven feet tall, and he was asking for your hand in marriage. Honestly, Marc, he certainly can be outrageous when he makes up his mind!

Business picked up at the mercantile, and I was able to order a new rug for the girls' bedroom. You remember how worn the old one was. I know Rigg hated to see it go since it had been his grandmother's, but Molly's foot catches on the loose threads time and again, and I'm afraid she's going to hurt herself. I cut them, but I can't seem to stay ahead of it.

We painted your bedroom a soft peach color. It really brightened things up. Wish you could see it. (That was a hint, in case you didn't catch it.)

I'm glad your studies and tutoring are progressing well. We're praying for you, Mitchell, and Renee. I have every confidence you'll have your certificate in record time. I'm so proud of you. Write me soon.

Love, Katie

June 17, 1881
Visalia, California

Dear Katie,

I stood at Miss Wilkins' side today and watched her sign my teaching certificate. I can't really explain the way I felt, except to say that I was excited and scared all at once.

I knew that the Lord would want me to trust Him, as you trusted Him so many years ago the first time you taught in Santa Rosa without Mother's help. I loved the schoolhouse there, and I love thinking back to your gentle way of teaching; so often you reminded me of Mother. I think she would be thrilled with the decision I've made.

I don't believe for a moment that I would be receiving my certificate if you hadn't been such an encouragement to me. Thanks, Katie, for all you've taught me, and for being the pillar of love and strength you've been in my life.

Love, Marcail

*July 25, 1881*
*Santa Rosa, California*

*Dear Marcail,*

*I prayed this morning about the perfect teaching position for you, and then found myself asking God to open the doors here in Santa Rosa. Then I realized that I was trying to help God with your life, and I was not trusting.*

*This letter is to inform you that I've given you over to the Lord and His tender care. Here are some verses that I know you love and have shared with me in the past. As I read them this morning, I found them a real comfort. Thanks, Marcail.*

*Isaiah 55:8,9, "For my thoughts are not your thoughts, neither are your ways my ways, saith the Lord. For as the heavens are higher than the earth, so are my ways higher than your ways, and my thoughts than your thoughts."*

*All my love, Katie*

*August 12, 1881*
*Visalia, California*

*Dear Katie,*

*I've received letters from three school boards who have seen my credentials and want to hire me. Father and I talked and prayed before finally deciding on the school in Willits, which is only about five hours from Santa Rosa by train.*

*I'll be coming through Santa Rosa on August 25, on my way to Willits. I can't stay any longer than the train does, but if you're at the station around 10:00 a.m., we'll have a few moments.*

*The conduct and dress code laid down by this school board is very strict, but I think that's part of the reason Father liked it; that and knowing how close I'll be to you and Rigg. I know he wants peace of mind over how I'm being cared for.*

*Father can't get away to come up with me, but he asked me to tell you he's planning on coming to Santa Rosa for Christmas, and we'll all be together then. If this won't work for you, be in touch. I won't write again before I leave, but don't forget to write me once I get to my new home. Thanks for all your prayers.*

*Love, Marcail*

# *prologue*

*Santa Rosa, California*
*August 25, 1881*

Marcail Donovan waved from the window as the train pulled away from the Santa Rosa station. Her sister, Kaitlin, brother-in-law, Marshall Riggs, and nieces, Gretchen and Molly, all waved furiously in reply. Her nephew, eight-month-old Donovan, sitting comfortably on his father's arm, was too busy working on the thumb in his mouth to notice his aunt's departure.

When the train station was out of sight, Marcail settled back against her seat with a smile and a sigh. How good it had been to see them, however briefly. It was an unexpected blessing amid numerous blessings of late from the Lord.

If Marcail had had the luxury of time, she would have loved to stay and visit, but knowing her teaching position awaited her further up the tracks was enough to keep Marcail's mind from how deeply she missed her family.

Marcail suddenly thought of her father, Patrick Donovan, and again she smiled. It wasn't every girl who had a full-time father for the first nine years of her life, saw him only occasionally for the next ten years, and then had him come back into her life to stay when she was nearly 19.

It had taken some weeks, but father and daughter had become close. At first Patrick had struggled with the fact that his little girl was now a grown woman, and there were times he had treated her like a child. But he was always swift to apologize when he saw the disappointment in her eyes. He soon saw that her manner of life, and the loving way she responded to his affection and counsel, showed that Marcail was level-headed enough to know what she wanted.

And what Marcail wanted was to teach school. Patrick's first reaction when she expressed this desire had been enthusiastic, until she informed him that she was willing to travel anywhere in the state to acquire a position.

"Wouldn't you like a teaching position here in Visalia?" he'd asked her in some surprise.

"Yes, I would. It would be wonderful to teach close enough to live here, but if nothing is available, then I'm going to look for a position somewhere else."

Marcail could see that her words surprised her father, and she did not push the point. She also did not tell him that she felt it was time to be on her own. Marcail knew that if he was totally against the idea of her teaching elsewhere, she would drop the subject, but as she hoped and prayed, he came to her a few days later and told her to follow her heart.

And follow her heart was just what Marcail did. She began submitting her resume whenever she found a school board advertising for a teacher, and in a surprisingly short amount of time, several responded.

Marcail had been careful to consult her father on all the correspondence she received, and in just a matter of days, Patrick advised her to take the job in Willits. It was a long way from where they were now living in Visalia, but not too far from Katie and Rigg. And with the strict code of dress, Father was certain the townspeople would be upright and moral.

Marcail had plenty of time to grow nervous as the train drew ever closer to her destination. She had prayed for most of the journey and worked at overcoming her anxieties. There was so much she could panic over if she allowed her mind to wander; little things, like living alone for the first time, taking care of all her own finances, and being the sole authority in the classroom.

Marcail had known responsibility for numerous tasks over many years. She had always risen to the occasion and seen to every need, but she suddenly found herself asking, what if something entered her world that was beyond her control? What if she became sick or the schoolhouse burned down?

Marcail realized she was working herself into a fine frenzy and immediately prayed for calm. It was true that any of those things could happen, but worrying about them would change nothing. *If* and when the time came to handle any and all disasters, she knew the Lord would lead and guide her to His good work.

She was completely calm by the time the conductor called Willits as the next stop. As the town came into view, however, Marcail's heart began to pound once again. This time there was no fear, only excitement.

# *one*

---

Marcail peered through the window as the train pulled into the Willits station. There was nothing unusual or remarkable about what she could see of the small town, but the fact that it was her new home made it, along with the moment, a thing to be treasured.

The train came to a complete stop. Marcail stood in the aisle, her carpetbag in one hand. As she stepped forward, her heart beat against her ribs so hard she was certain the fabric on her dress was moving. She glanced down at her simple black gown with the long sleeves and high collar, and suddenly found herself hoping it would hold up under the censuring eyes of Willits' school board members.

There were a few other people disembarking with her at the train station. Marcail, wanting to soak up every person, every nook and cranny of this small town, smiled and greeted anyone who met her eyes.

Her letter of introduction, held firmly in one hand, said she was to locate a Mr. Stanley Flynn. He was, the letter explained, the local banker. Because Marcail's only piece of luggage was her one overstuffed bag, she carried it in one hand and the letter in the other.

More than one shop owner stepped to the boardwalk in front of his store as she passed, and Marcail took time to smile and greet each one. She didn't tarry long, however. Her desire to meet Mr. Flynn gave her a singleness of purpose that took her swiftly to the door of the bank and over the threshold. Once inside the small building, Marcail approached the single clerk who stood behind the counter.

"May I help you, miss?" Marcail noticed he was very businesslike, his speech and manner proper in the extreme.

"Yes, thank you. I'm looking for a Mr. Stanley Flynn."

"May I tell him who is calling?"

Feeling much younger than her 19 years, Marcail gave her name and watched the bank clerk walk to a private office at the rear of the building. She looked around admiringly at the elegant surroundings of the compact room, taking in the gleaming woodwork. She thought she detected the faint odor of linseed oil.

Moving to the windows that looked out over the street, Marcail spotted a cobbler shop, hotel, dry goods store, and what appeared to be a doctor's office. When she heard footsteps behind her, she turned with a ready smile. A man was approaching, his smile cordial but his eyes watchful. He extended his hand to Marcail, who was well aware of his scrutiny. She was quite conscious of the fact that she looked like a girl on the threshold of womanhood, and not a woman fully grown. But Marcail was confident of her ability to teach, and in her posture and the very tilt of her head she unconsciously relayed just that.

"Miss Donovan, it's a pleasure to meet you." Stanley Flynn must have liked what he saw because his manner became very solicitous, his smile genuine.

Marcail smiled in return. "It's a pleasure to be here, Mr. Flynn."

She might not have been so confident or ready to smile if she could have read the banker's thoughts, the first of which was that she was beautiful. The second was that she looked innocent enough to be malleable. It would be some time before Marcail would find out that she was Willits' ninth school teacher in three years.

□ □ □

Ten minutes later Mr. Flynn put Marcail's bag in his buggy and drove Marcail to her house. As they appeared to be headed out of town, he explained that the builder of the schoolhouse and teacher's home, some 30 years before, had not liked how noisy children could be. It had been his opinion that the school should be located on the outskirts of town. Since he had supplied most of the funds, the town had acquiesced.

Willits was larger now, and the last houses on that end of town were within sight of the school. Still, a small group of trees on the town's side of the school gave it a very distinct feeling of isolation. Marcail spotted one small farmhouse in the distance, but she asked no questions concerning the owner. She was much too captivated with her first glance at the small house into which Mr. Flynn was now leading her.

Mr. Flynn did not tarry. Only five minutes passed before Marcail saw him to the front door, waved to him after he was back in his buggy, and shut the door. She turned back to the room, her hands going to her mouth, her eyes sparkling with pleasure. This was her house, her own little home! And some 50 feet away was the schoolhouse where she would start work on Monday.

Marcail's gaze roamed the room with pleasure. It couldn't have been more perfect if she'd designed it herself. The main room of the house was spacious, with a kitchen in one corner. The one doorway led to a small bedroom. It was a house intended for one person, holding only two kitchen chairs at the table and a rocking chair near the stove.

Marcail moved into the bedroom. The bed she found was very small, but then so was she, making her feel that everything was all the more perfect. The curtains on the window and the quilt on the bed were both a soft, sky-blue plaid.

After throwing the curtains back to let in the sunlight, she went to work unpacking her single bag. She hung her other two dresses and put her undergarments in the drawers of the small dressing table. Her entire outer wardrobe consisted of three dresses—one brown, one dark blue, and the black one she was wearing.

She set a few of her personal books on the nightstand, and put the others on the bed to be taken to the school. A picture of her mother as a young girl went on the dressing table, as did a picture of herself and her siblings taken in Santa Rosa. Marcail smiled at the homey touches.

She stopped before the mirror that hung opposite the bed to check her hair. She was not accustomed to wearing it up because of its length and thickness, but her hairstyle and the dark-colored clothing were all a part of the stipulations set down in her contract.

The last item Marcail removed from her bag was her Bible. She sat on the bed and held it in her arms, and then prayed aloud in the stillness of her home.

"Thank You, Father, for bringing me to this place. It's more wonderful than I could have dreamed." Marcail didn't speak again, but sat quietly and dwelt on verses from Psalm 46: "Be still, and know that I am God. I will be exalted among the heathen; I will be exalted in the earth. The Lord of hosts is with us; the God of Jacob is our refuge."

# *two*

Marcail spent the next hour inspecting every inch of the schoolhouse. It was spotless and well equipped. She had brought along a few of her books and stood for a long time just looking at the way they sat on her desk. The platform in front of the blackboard, on which her desk sat, was raised about eight inches from the rest of the schoolroom floor. Marcail, whose height and frame were so diminutive, was very pleased.

After she finished at the schoolhouse, she went home to make out a complete list of all the supplies she thought she might need. She was eager to take a walk into town. The schoolhouse and her home sat on the west edge of the community. A quick scan out the schoolhouse window had earlier confirmed that the only visible structures beyond were the small house and barn that she had spotted on her arrival.

It didn't take long for Marcail to reach the houses of town, but the shops were a bit further. She was flushed from the weight of her dress, as well as the warmth of the day, by the time she reached a storefront that said Vesperman's General Store above the entrance. The building appeared to be half the size of Riggs' Mercantile in Santa Rosa, but once inside there did not seem to be any lack.

Marcail's eyes took in pins and measuring cups, fly traps and thread, composition books and soap flakes, eggbeaters and blotters, cookie cutters and bibs, fabric and shoes, checkerboards and muffin tins. She chose a basket near the door and began to shop. Not until she was near the candy counter did Marcail meet the proprietor. He was a smiling man with a sandy mustache, who introduced himself as Randy Vesperman.

Marcail liked him instantly. He answered all of her questions and informed her that his children, Erin and Patrick, would be in her classroom Monday morning. The friendly sparkle in his eyes confirmed that she had made her first friend. He encouraged her to take the basket in order to carry her purchases home.

Marcail's next stop was the bank. The tutoring she had done in Visalia for the two children who, for different reasons, were unable to attend the schoolhouse, allowed her to come to Willits with something of a financial cushion. She spent a fair amount in gaining supplies for the next month, but with the exception of a few coins to get her by, she deposited the rest into a savings account.

It soon became obvious that the townspeople knew who she was. Several people approached her in the bank. One couple, the Whites, introduced themselves and their children, allowing Willits' new schoolmarm to meet two of her students.

Marcail was moving toward the door when it opened and a woman of immense proportions, both in height and width, swept in. She was dressed in black crepe, and Marcail felt instant sympathy for her mourning. It took her a moment to realize that the woman was not going to let her pass, causing her to finally look up into her eyes.

"You must be Miss Donovan." The voice was cold.

"Yes, ma'am," Marcail replied and swallowed hard. The woman had the hardest eyes she had ever encountered.

"I am Cordelia Duckworth," the woman said, as if this explained everything. "I trust that Mr. Flynn made you aware that I'm expecting you for lunch tomorrow?"

"Yes, Mrs. Duckworth. I was planning on it."

"Well, see that you are. I'll finish your interview then."

Mrs. Duckworth moved toward the teller without giving Marcail a chance to reply. Marcail left feeling a bit dazed. Interview. The woman had said interview. Marcail wondered suddenly if the teaching position was really hers.

The basket was now starting to weigh on her arm. Turning toward home, she intended to reread every bit of correspondence she had received from the Willits school board.

❏ ❏ ❏

Dr. Alexander Montgomery closed and locked his office door before heading toward Rodd's livery. Rodd always kept his horse, Kelsey, in exchange for free medical services. But considering that Rodd's wife had had four babies in the last four years, Alex sometimes wondered who had gotten the better end of the deal.

Kelsey, a rather high-spirited bay gelding, was more than ready to escape the confines of his stall. Alex could tell that he was ready for a run, but was careful to keep the animal on a tight rein until they were past the houses in town. Ready to heel his mount into a gallop, Alex spotted a lone, darkly garbed figure walking ahead of him on the road.

She moved to the far edge of the road when she heard the horse approach, but Alex had the impression that she would not have even looked at him if he hadn't stopped beside her. It took him an instant, even after she stopped, to figure out who she was and where she was headed.

"Hello," Alex called cheerfully. "You must be Miss—"

"Donovan." Marcail supplied the name and tried to see the man addressing her. The lowering sun was directly in her eyes, and even squinting didn't give her a clear view of the rider. Having switched arms so many times while carrying the basket that she now held in both hands, she was afraid to lift her hand to shield her eyes for fear of dropping her load.

"I can't really offer to give you a ride, but why don't I drop that basket on your doorstep?"

"Oh, that's all right. I'm almost—" Marcail stopped midsentence because he was already bending low from the saddle and taking the thick handle from her grasp.

"I'll just take this ahead for you. It was nice meeting you, Miss Donovan. By the way, I'm Dr. Montgomery."

Marcail did little more than raise her hand in a gesture of thanks before the rider was once again on his way. She continued her walk, knowing that if she passed that man on the sidewalk and he didn't speak, she would have no idea who he was. Well, no matter really. He was a doctor, and Marcail knew she would have to be dying and then some before she'd have anything to do with him.

# *three*

By the time Marcail climbed into bed that night she was very tired, but not discouraged. She had searched through her documents, and beyond her being listed as one of the school board members Marcail could not find any mention of a Cordelia Duckworth. There was nothing to indicate that she would be interviewed once she arrived. As much as Marcail wanted to stay in Willits, she trusted that if the door closed in this small town she was already coming to love, God had another teaching position for her elsewhere.

Marcail was able to blow out her lantern with a peaceful heart. Having eaten only a light supper, she fell asleep dreaming about the bread she planned on baking the next morning.

❏ ❏ ❏

At 11:30 Saturday morning, having finished her baking earlier, Marcail started out for her luncheon appointment. Feeling as though Mr. Vesperman would welcome her inquiry, she stopped and asked for directions to Mrs. Duckworth's home. He was more than happy to oblige, but Marcail caught what she thought might be pity in his eyes. She prayed that her imagination was working over-time.

Following the directions she was given, Marcail headed through town, passing businesses she had seen only from a distance. When she met people on the street, they were friendly, and Marcail found herself hoping she would be able to stay. Mr. Vesperman had told her that she wouldn't be able to miss the Duckworth house, since it was as far to the east of town as the schoolhouse was to the west. It was set apart and seemed all the more grand as the ground rose to meet it. Marcail had to move up a slight incline to the front steps.

The Duckworth house was an imposing structure, and Marcail felt rather intimidated as she approached. The sensation intensified after knocking on the massive front door. Marcail began to feel like a child waiting to see her teacher. She scolded herself over groundless fears.

As she might have expected, a servant answered the door. Marcail was led toward the rear of the house to an elegant dining room. She paused on the threshold, her head tipped back to take in the massive chandelier that seemed to fill the ceiling. The sound of a sharply cleared throat brought Marcail's head around.

Mrs. Duckworth was already seated, and with a regal nod of her head, bid Marcail to enter. She did so and took the chair being held for her by a nervous-looking man-servant.

"You are very prompt. I like that," Mrs. Duckworth declared stoutly. Several more servants joined the first two, and the food began arriving. Before Marcail could think twice, her plate was filled with a sumptuous piece of roast beef and all the trimmings.

Marcail watched as her hostess picked up her fork. She was about to follow suit when the interrogation began.

"So tell me, Miss Donovan, are your parents living?"

"My father is."

"And your mother, did you ever know her?"

"Yes, she died when I was nine."

"Siblings?"

"Yes. One sister and one brother."

"Older or younger? Do they have families? Tell me about them."

Marcail took a breath. "They are both older. My sister, Kaitlin, is the oldest. She's married to a man named Marshall Riggs, and they live in Santa Rosa. They have three children. My brother is also married. He and his wife, Charlotte, live in Hawaii with their two children."

Mrs. Duckworth ate while her guest answered questions, but Marcail, not knowing when the next question would come, did nothing more than hold her fork in her hand.

"And this is your first teaching assignment; is that correct?"

"Yes, ma'am. I've been a private tutor, but I've never had my own school."

"And you understand the terms of the contract, that your clothing and conduct *must* be above reproach at all times?"

"Yes, ma'am." Marcail watched her hostess take another bite of food and thought this might be the only chance to ask a question. "I'm a little confused, Mrs. Duckworth. I didn't expect to be interviewed. I thought the job was already mine."

"The job of teaching the town's children is yours," the older woman answered without hesitation. "I am interviewing you, however, to see if you are suitable to teach *my* grandson. Right now Sydney is with his parents, but he lives with me much of the time. He's a delicate child, and they simply do not understand him. I usually hire private tutors to see to his education, but I thought it might be time for him to try the classroom again. And since you are the person at the head of that classroom, I must make certain you are sensitive to Sydney's needs."

A small warning bell was ringing in Marcail's mind. "I'm not a teacher who plays favorites, Mrs. Duckworth. If Sydney does his work and is respectful to my authority, we'll get along fine."

Unfortunately Mrs. Duckworth did not appear to have heard her.

"You haven't told me about your father, Miss Donovan."

Marcail blinked at the change in topics, but was willing to accommodate nevertheless.

"For years he was a missionary to Hawaii, but now he's a pastor for a small church in Visalia."

"Is he remarried?"

"No."

"And you, Miss Donovan, are you looking for a husband?"

"No, ma'am. I want to teach school." It sounded like a platitude even to her own ears, but it was the truth. "I'm not saying that I'll never be married, but I don't wish to be now, and probably not for quite some time."

"You understood that your conduct is to be *above* reproach?"

"Yes, ma'am. The contract was all very clear to me." Marcail's voice was losing some of its congeniality after being questioned time and again over a matter she felt was settled.

Marcail glanced in front of her to see that her plate had been removed. She hadn't had a bite. Setting her fork down, she leveled her eyes on her hostess. She watched as Mrs. Duckworth looked at her own soiled napkin and then to Marcail's empty place setting. To her credit she had the good grace to look momentarily ashamed.

Marcail would have loved to ask what her little game was, but she knew the question would have been disrespectful. When dessert was offered, the young guest declined, and not long after, thanked her hostess and went on her way. As far as Marcail was concerned, the interview was over.

Marcail would have been surprised to know that Mrs. Duckworth watched from the living room window until she was out of sight. The older woman was torn between consternation and admiration. Consternation because Miss Donovan wasn't going to be as easy to manage as she hoped; admiration because in a very respectful way she'd stood up to her, and that was something few people had ever done.

# *four*

Marcail spent the rest of the day in the schoolhouse preparing for Monday morning. Her mind was never far from her luncheon with Mrs. Duckworth. However, each time she felt her worries assail her, she prayed and asked the Lord for wisdom.

Marcail was writing her name on the blackboard, her last job before heading back to her house to prepare some supper, when someone knocked and entered.

"I really thought they were exaggerating. Well, it wouldn't be exaggerating because that means something gets bigger. What's the opposite of exaggeration, when you really mean something is small?"

Marcail stared at the round, pink-faced young woman in the doorway and smiled. "I'm afraid I don't know. Maybe if you tell me what they were exaggerating about." Marcail was beginning to think she'd walked into the middle of a bad theater performance.

"Your size. I mean, they said you were tiny, but I never dreamed . . ."

Marcail couldn't help but laugh. The other woman was talking again, so she tried to control herself.

"And here I thought we were going to be good friends,

but being with you is only going to accentuate my size."
The talkative visitor moved closer.

"Your hair is really black, isn't it? I mean, *really* black,
and mine is so blonde it's almost white."

Marcail laughed again, and the rotund blonde smiled
also, thinking the new schoolteacher was just wonderful.

"My name is Alice Warren. But you can call me Allie
because we're going to be friends."

"I'd like that." Marcail smiled a genuine smile. "My
name is Marcail Donovan, and you can call me Marcail,
since we're going to be good friends."

"Marcail." Allie tested the word on her tongue. "Do
you spell it with a *k*?"

"No, it's *M-a-r-c-a-i-l*, but the *c* is hard."

Allie beamed. "I like it. It suits you." Allie's face turned
to a sudden frown. "But I don't think Alice suits me. I've
always pictured myself as a Mirabelle." She finished this
last sentence with a dramatic sigh.

"Mirabelle?" Marcail bit her lower lip to camouflage
her smile.

"You don't think so?"

The smaller woman shook her head apologetically,
and they both laughed.

In the space of the next few minutes, Marcail discovered that Allie's family ran the sawmill at the other end of
town. She had two older brothers, both of whom were
the bane of her existence, or so she proclaimed.

They talked for the better part of an hour before Allie
jumped up with a hand to her mouth.

"I completely forgot why I was here. Mother wants
you to come to dinner after church tomorrow."

"Oh, I'd love to. Thank you."

"Good. I'd better go now. By the way, how old are
you?"

"Nineteen."

Allie sighed. "I'm 20. Do you think we'll ever find husbands?" She sighed again and flew out the door. She'd have returned to hug Marcail if she could have read her thoughts.

*I don't need a husband, Allie—not when I've found a friend like you.*

◻◻◻

Church was not at all what Marcail expected. The building was fairly large and packed with people. They sang good hymns of faith for most of the service, but not a word of Scripture was read, even during the short sermon. Marcail wondered if this was something out of the ordinary and not the norm. She certainly hoped so.

Marcail met just about all of her students that day, and by the time she emerged from the building, she was certain the Warren family must have left without her. They had not.

Marcail exited the building to find Allie standing with two well-built, good-looking men. She approached with a smile, and as soon as she reached them Allie said something outrageous.

"Marcail, these are my brothers, Logan and Mallory. I believe they are about to make absolute fools of themselves where you are concerned."

Marcail's gaze flew to the faces of the men flanking their sister, but they didn't seem to be the least put out by her remark. Both of them smiled as though Marcail were a dream come true, and reached at the same time to escort her to the wagon. Allie pushed their hands out of the way with an unladylike snort and took Marcail's arm herself.

"Just ignore them, Marcail, or we'll be here all afternoon deciding who is to help you into the wagon."

The boys were on hand to see the ladies into the rear seat, and Marcail soon learned that Allie was right—her brothers couldn't seem to take their eyes off her.

With both men turning to look at her every few minutes, the ride seemed to take forever. Their actions caused Marcail to stop and think of how few young women she had seen in church that morning.

Allie's parents had gone ahead of their children, so dinner was nearly on the table when the young people arrived. Mr. and Mrs. Warren were gracious, hardworking people, and they welcomed Marcail into their home as if she were a long-lost daughter. But when the dishes were passed and everyone began eating without a prayer of thanks to God, Marcail began to wonder if there wasn't something very important missing from the lives of these dear people.

Allie and Marcail took a walk after the meal. Marcail was greatly relieved to escape the interest of the Warren boys. It wasn't that she found them repulsive; they were nice-looking and seemed very kind. But their quiet watchfulness was beginning to unnerve her.

"How do you fill your days, Allie?" Marcail asked her new friend.

"I keep the accounts for the mill and help Mama around the house. I know she likes my company, but she is so anxious to see one of us marry and make her a grandma that it seems that's all I hear."

"So you don't really care that much if you get married?"

Allie was quiet a moment, and Marcail apologized for intruding.

"You didn't intrude, Marcail, but I'm not sure a girl like you can understand what it's like for me."

"I don't know what you mean by 'a girl like me.'"

"I don't know either. It's just that the girls who have no desire to be married are the ones all the boys chase, and girls like me, who really want a husband and family, can't seem to draw anyone's attention."

"I guess it does seem that way at times, Allie, but I believe that if God wants a person to be married, then He shows that person exactly whom they're to marry, and when."

Allie stared at her new friend uncomprehendingly, and Marcail knew that all she'd just said was completely foreign to Allie.

The subject of marriage and God was dropped for the time, but Marcail asked God to open the door someday. She wanted to introduce Allie to the Man, Jesus Christ, who would change her life forever if only she would let Him do so.

# *five*

On the first day of school Marcail had the worst attack of nerves she'd ever experienced in her life. The coffee she drank made her feel sick to the stomach, and when she burned the piece of bread she was going to eat, she decided to go without.

Too excited to stay home, she was over at the schoolhouse an hour before the children were expected. There was no need to ring the bell when the time came because the children were already on their way. Marcail rushed to the door when she spotted the first group heading toward the schoolhouse.

Mr. Flynn had given Marcail a list of whom to expect. She noticed that Sydney Duckworth's name was not on the list. Without him she had 19 students, the youngest of whom was seven and the oldest 15.

Marcail introduced herself to the children as they entered the classroom, and then requested their first and last names, even if she'd met them the day before. She told them to take any seat for the time being. They did as they were told, but each and every one turned in his seat to stare at the new teacher. Marcail felt compassion for them. Up to the time she was ten, her mother and then her sister had been her only teachers. When that changed she clearly remembered how worried she'd been about the new instructor liking her.

"Good morning, class," she greeted her students once she was in front of the blackboard. Marcail smiled at them with sincere warmth and felt her heart melt over some of the shy smiles she received in return.

She proceeded to tell the class a little bit about herself before asking each student to stand and introduce himself again. From that point forward, the day flew. Marcail could hardly believe her eyes when the big clock on the wall read 3:00.

A few parents came in wagons to claim their children, and two students had horses they had stabled for the day in the small barn out back. Most walked, however, and Marcail stood at the door until they were far from view. She stepped back into the room and stood smiling at the little signs that clearly showed children had been there: a crooked chair, marks on the board, the globe on the floor.

"Thank You, Lord." She whispered the words. "Thank You for a wonderful day."

❏ ❏ ❏

Marcail had been teaching school for ten days with no sign of Sydney Duckworth. It wasn't hard to figure out that Mrs. Duckworth had decided against sending him. Even though Marcail would like to have met him, she had other things on her mind, specifically, the lunchbox social scheduled for the next day.

When Marcail got up on Saturday morning she had already planned what she would put into her basket to be auctioned. The proceeds went to the school, and Marcail was determined that everything be perfect.

She found a small-handled basket in the cupboard,

and after lining it with a yellow linen hand towel, she began to fill it with the lunch she had prepared. All the women of the town, married or single, were encouraged to attend and bring their baskets. The auction would start promptly at 10:30, so all baskets could be auctioned off in time for a noontime picnic for the entire town.

Marcail used a little piece of string and paper to label her basket. She held the paper for just a moment and stared at the name. Miss Donovan. She felt a little thrill each and every time she wrote it.

Not certain where the auction was to be held, Marcail left the house a little early. She should have known not to worry since the noise from people gathering in the town square could be heard from 300 yards away. From a distance it sounded as if all 296 of Willits' residents were in attendance.

Marcail greeted the families she knew as she made her way to the blanket Mrs. Warren had laid out for her family. Allie was the only one seated, and Marcail joined her.

"Hi, Marcail. Is your basket all set?"

"I think so. What's in yours?"

The girls traded baskets, and then exchanged compliments and conversation until a good-looking, dark-haired man walked by. Marcail's gaze followed him as he passed.

"Handsome, isn't he?" Allie sounded almost smug.

Marcail laughed over being caught looking. "Yes, he is," she said with an unrepentant grin. "Why haven't I seen him before?"

"Oh, he keeps to himself. Some say he's still mourning his wife. But she's been gone for over four years."

"What's his name?"

"Dr. Alexander Montgomery," Allie answered and chattered on, but Marcail caught little of it. Her mind was conjuring up a man bending from the saddle to relieve her of her basket, his manner solicitous, his voice kind. But a cold feeling had swept down her spine on hearing the word "doctor." His good looks and the previous kindness he'd shown her were overshadowed by his title. Marcail knew that if they met and talked she would be cordial, but past experience told her she would never be completely at ease in his presence.

More thoughts on Willits' doctor were cut short when the auction began. The women carried their baskets and hampers forward and joined the crowd around the stand.

Mr. Flynn from the bank was the auctioneer, and the first basket belonged to Mrs. Warren. It was customary for the woman whose basket was on the table to step forward to the platform during the bidding. Mr. Warren knew his job and bought his wife's basket. It went for a good price and that seemed to get the ball rolling. Baskets and coins were exchanged amid a backdrop of laughter and great fun.

Marcail's basket was one of the last to be auctioned. She moved toward the platform and took the hand offered her as she stepped up. Her eyes briefly met those of Dr. Montgomery's before he released her hand and she turned to face the audience.

There was a moment of silence that caused Marcail to become a shade nervous. What she couldn't know was how she appeared to the townspeople at that moment. She wore her dark blue dress with the white collar. Her black hair, braided and then wrapped into a fat bun, shone in the sunlight, and the young, vulnerable look she sported on her beautiful face was enough to stop the men of the town dead in their tracks.

"Well now," Mr. Flynn said softly, as though shouting would spoil the moment. "Most of you have met our new schoolmarm, Miss Donovan. Let's give her a grand welcome to our small town by bidding high on her basket."

The bidding started at two bits, and Marcail smiled when it swiftly went to 40¢. There seemed to be four young men bidding—the Warren boys and two men Marcail did not recognize. She felt her face flame when her basket went over a dollar, and the crowd began to cheer with each accelerated bid.

Mr. Flynn didn't yell *sold* until the bidding stopped at $2.75. Marcail had never heard of such a high bid for a lunch basket. She moved in a state of shock and once again felt the doctor's hand before suddenly being grabbed by someone and nearly pulled from the platform.

"Take it easy, Rowie." Marcail heard the smooth tones of Dr. Montgomery's voice. "You've won the basket fair and square; there's no need to pull her arm off."

"Sorry." The young man apologized but did not relinquish his hold on Marcail's arm.

"Do you two know each other?" Again the doctor spoke.

Marcail could only shake her head as she stared first at the doctor and then at the burly stranger who held her arm in a possessive grip.

"Miss Donovan, this is Jethro Kilmer. Rowie, this is Miss Donovan."

"How do you know her?" Rowie's jaw suddenly jutted forward, and if Marcail had recognized the signs of jealousy, she would have backed completely away from this squarely built man who had bought her lunch basket.

"She's my closest neighbor, Rowie. You know I live past the schoolhouse." The doctor's voice was once again honey smooth, and the younger man calmed visibly.

Marcail was given no chance to thank Alex for his help before she was pulled across the grass to the area where everyone had placed their blankets. When Rowie stopped to look around, Marcail gently disengaged her arm.

"Which blanket is yours?"

"I was sitting with the Warrens."

Rowie's head spun around so quickly to face Marcail that she thought he might have hurt himself.

"You like one of the Warren boys?"

Marcail blinked at the aggressiveness in his voice. "Allie and I are friends," she explained calmly.

Again she watched him relax. She could tell he was going to take her arm again and drag her off to who-knows-where, so Marcail turned and walked with steely determination to the Warrens' blanket.

Mr. and Mrs. Warren were already seated on the blanket. Seth Porter, a man Marcail had not met, bought Allie's lunch. He and Allie were headed their way. Allie introduced Marcail to Seth, and they talked for just a few moments. Marcail immediately noted the excited gleam in Allie's eyes and the lovely blush on her cheeks each time Seth looked in her direction.

Everyone was in high spirits as they began to eat, but Marcail soon discovered that this lunch was going to be work. Rowie sat as close to her as she would allow. She did her best to keep her small basket between them. He didn't have much to say, but she felt his eyes on her much of the time. When he wasn't watching Marcail, he was looking at the other people on the quilt as though he wished they would disappear into another state.

Logan, who had not bid on anyone else's lunch, stared at Marcail also, putting something of a damper on her afternoon. Mr. Warren seemed to sense what was happening and sent his gawking son on an errand as soon as he was finished eating.

People began to mill around, and Marcail was tempted to rise also. Weighing how safe it would be to wander around town with this man, she hesitated. When Seth, Allie, and Mr. and Mrs. Warren left, leaving only Rowie and Marcail on the blanket, he spoke.

"You don't have a boyfriend back home or anything like that, do you?"

"I'm sorry, Jethro, but I don't feel that's something you need to know."

"I like it that you call me Jethro."

Marcail sighed with frustration. He hadn't heard a word she said. Rowie went on to ask Marcail a score of questions about how she liked children and housework. That he was in the market for a wife was more than obvious. Marcail decided to nip his thoughts in the bud, at least where she was concerned.

With a gentle tone, she told him in no uncertain terms that she was not in the market for a husband. Rowie looked crestfallen until Marcail told him it wasn't personal, and that she didn't want to be married to anyone. Rowie didn't push the point, but Marcail had the distinct impression that he believed he could change her mind. When they parted company later that day, Marcail did so with a prayer that Jethro Kilmer would not push her, because if he chose to, his feelings were certain to get hurt.

# *six*

Alexander Montgomery helped himself to a serving of potatoes and then passed the bowl to the young girl on his right. He was having dinner, as he did most Sundays, with his best friends, Dean and Kay Austin.

The Austins had two children, nine-year-old Daisy and 11-year-old Marla, both of whom were in Miss Donovan's class. Before the girls left the table the conversation turned to the high price Miss Donovan's lunch basket brought at the auction. As soon as the girls were out of earshot, Kay teased Alex.

"Honestly, Alex," Kay spoke in feigned rebuke. "You didn't even try to bid on Miss Donovan's basket. You can't tell me that you don't find her attractive."

Alex's eyes sparkled with laughter. "You're right, Kay, I can't tell you I don't find her attractive, but it's a good thing I didn't bid, since I had only 25¢ in my pocket."

Kay became instantly alert, an action Alex did not miss.

"Calm down, Kay, I have a sufficiency. My last three patients all paid with food, and you know when I go hungry, I land myself on your doorstep."

"Well, just see that you do!" Kay spoke the words with a gruffness she didn't feel and left the table. Dean took a sip of his coffee and leaned back in his chair.

"She worries about you."

"I know she does, but I'm fine, really."

"Tell me something, Alex. If Miss Donovan's basket hadn't topped out so high, would you have been interested?"

"I don't know," the younger man answered honestly.

"Linette has been gone for over four years, Alex. Does it still feel unfaithful to you when you think about marrying again?"

"No, but sometimes I think I've lived as a bachelor for too long. I feel set in my ways."

"I can see why you would, since you're all of 30." Dean's voice was dry, and Alex smiled. Both men were quiet for a few minutes, and then the youngest Austin girl joined them.

"Do you want to see what I made, Uncle Alex?"

"Sure."

Alex took the offered picture. It was a pencil drawing of an open field of grass and wildflowers. Daisy showed real talent, and Alex's compliment was sincere.

"Thank you," she told him. "It's for Miss Donovan because I think she must like pretty things."

"Why is that?" her father wanted to know.

"Because she's so pretty," the young girl spoke in a matter-of-fact tone, as if this must be obvious to everyone.

Daisy went on her way, and Dean started to ask Alex a question but found him studying the picture Daisy had left on the table. For some reason the look on the younger man's face caused him to keep still.

❑ ❑ ❑

Marcail dropped the last of her hairpins onto the table and shook her head carefully. She massaged her temples as her hair fell out of its braids in a mass of waves down her back and to her hips. She sank into the rocking chair and prayed that her headache would go away.

Until the last few weeks she had never worn her hair up for more than a few hours, and by the time church was over and she'd eaten with the family of one of her students, her head was throbbing. She fingered a few strands and thought with regret over the way Allie had responded when she asked her to cut it. Allie had been more than willing until they had arrived in Allie's bedroom and Marcail had taken her hair down.

"I can't do it, Marcail."

"What do you mean, you can't do it?" Marcail had been truly dismayed.

"I just can't," her friend spoke apologetically. "I mean, I had no idea it was so long and beautiful. I just can't cut your hair."

Marcail had sighed. "Who can I ask?"

Allie shrugged. "I could ask Mama, but I'm sure she'll say no."

"Will you check with her anyway?"

Allie had gone to her mother then, but just as she predicted, Mrs. Warren would not touch Marcail's blue-black locks.

Marcail didn't know what to do. She had to wear her hair up in public, and there was nothing wrong with the school board's request. But Marcail was young, and Kaitlin had always encouraged her to pull her hair away from her face, letting the back hang free. Her hair curled naturally at the ends, so she never did anything but wash it and brush the tangles out.

Marcail let her head fall back against the back of the rocker. It was a depressing thought, but it looked as though she would have to wait until she was in Santa Rosa for Christmas. Then she would ask Kaitlin to cut her hair.

# *seven*

On Monday morning, the children had just taken their seats when a large black carriage pulled up in front of the schoolhouse. Marcail, having heard the horses, moved to the door. She watched as a frail boy of approximately 11 years stepped down and moved toward the school. Marcail spotted Mrs. Duckworth in the dark interior and knew that at long last Sydney had arrived.

Marcail greeted her new student warmly and felt instant pity as she looked at his pale, pinched features. He was polite, but there was a hesitant, almost defiant look in his eye that, strangely enough, made Marcail want to hold him.

Most of the children in class were familiar with Sydney, so Marcail wasted no time in long introductions. The day moved along very smoothly, and Marcail learned in no time at all that Sydney was in line with the others his age, if not ahead of them, scholastically.

Not until the afternoon of Sydney's second day in class did he show any sign of behavior beyond the ideal. Marcail asked him to come forward and take his turn reading aloud, but he told her he didn't feel up to it.

"Are you ill?" Marcail questioned him.

"No, I just don't want to."

"I'm sorry, Sydney, that you would rather not, but this is not a time when you have a choice. Please come forward and do your reading assignment."

Sydney stared at Marcail without moving from his seat.

Considering this was Marcail's first confrontation, she was very calm. "You will come up and read, Sydney, as I have instructed, or stay in your seat for the afternoon recess."

With ill-disguised boredom, he shuffled to the front. Marcail listened attentively as he read. He did an excellent job, and she told him as much, but he pouted for some time in his seat.

Marcail sat on the schoolhouse steps during recess, and for the first time had to break up an argument between two boys, one of whom was Sydney. She was almost relieved when it was time to dismiss the children and wondered if the rest of the year was going to be like today.

Marcail went straight home and stayed on her knees for over an hour in prayer for Sydney and the rest of her class. By the next morning she thought she was ready to tackle anything, but when Sydney disappeared during the morning recess, Marcail nearly panicked. One of the other children found him hiding behind the outhouse, and Marcail, not doing anything to hide her anger, made Sydney write sentences on the board until lunch.

Thursday was perfect. Marcail was not lulled into a false sense of security, but it did give her hope that Sydney could behave when he put his mind to the task. It also made the events of Friday all the more painful.

By Friday at lunchtime Marcail had corrected the older boys on more than one occasion about talking out of turn. Sydney had been the worst offender. Marcail hoped that some time outside during lunch would help and that he would come back in ready to work.

For an hour after lunch everything seemed to be more settled, but there was an anxiousness about Sydney that concerned Marcail. She turned to write something on the board, thinking as she did that she would ask him if he was feeling well. But as she turned back to the class, a rock flew seemingly out of nowhere and struck her on the cheek.

Marcail's head snapped back, more out of surprise than anything else, and she grabbed the edge of her desk to keep her balance. When Marcail looked up, her students were as still as death. She searched their faces and felt frightened over the searing pain on her own.

Marcail finally reached with a shaking hand to touch her face. She stared for a long time at the blood on her fingertips. Her voice shook as she addressed the class.

"Throwing objects in this classroom will not be tolerated. Do you understand?" Marcail didn't wait for an answer before going on, but she did notice that more than one head turned toward Sydney.

"I find, children," Marcail's entire body had begun to shake, "that I'm not feeling well. School will be dismissed a little early today."

It took a moment for the children to understand that they could leave, but within the space of ten seconds they exited the room with unusual haste.

Marcail stayed on her feet until she reached her house where she collapsed on the bed. Unable to stop shaking, she lay as still as she could for some minutes before rising and wiping her face with a damp, cool cloth. She stood before the mirror and cleaned the cut, which was much smaller than it felt. In fact, with the blood gone, it was barely noticeable. The effort of cleaning, along with the deep feeling of disappointment within her, tired her. Again she sought her bed.

Once there, Marcail curled onto her side, her uninjured cheek pressed into the pillow, and tried to pray, but she must have dozed because she lost all track of time. A sound woke her, and she sat up wondering why she was in bed during the day.

The pain in her cheek brought her thoughts quickly back to earth as someone knocked on the door. Realizing that it had been the knocking which had awakened her, she halfway hoped that whoever it was would go away before she answered. On legs that were just a little bit shaky, she moved toward the door. The person standing on the other side was Dr. Montgomery.

Marcail stared at him for five full, silent seconds before realizing she was being rude. He was the last person she wanted to see, but the least she could do was invite him in.

"Please come in, Dr. Montgomery."

Alex stepped over the threshold, and once in the room, turned to face Marcail. He didn't recognize the fact that he'd just wakened her. She was as white as a sheet, and if he'd had any closer relationship with her, he'd have ordered her immediately to bed.

"I don't wish to disturb you, Miss Donovan, but Marla Austin came by my office. When I asked why she wasn't in school, she said you weren't feeling well. Is there anything I can do?"

"No, no," Marcail spoke and took a step back toward the door. "I'll be fine, but thank you for checking on me." Marcail opened the door, relieved that this was all he had come about, and stood expectantly.

Her message was more than clear to Alex, and he moved toward the opening but paused in the doorway. Because he was not comfortable with her color or the way she wanted to be rid of him, he was on the verge of breaking his own rule about pushing medical attention on someone who was sane enough to refuse him.

"Are you sure I can't do something for you?"

"Yes, I'm sure." This time her voice was emphatic. "But thank you for stopping."

She seemed to be a little more at ease with him heading outside, and Alex, assuring himself that she looked a little better than before, went on his way. He sat astride Kelsey for a few seconds before starting down the road, wondering as he did so how she'd obtained the little cut on her cheek, and knowing in light of her almost frightened response to him that he would probably never find out.

# *eight*

Marcail spent a long time studying her Bible and praying on Saturday morning. She read in the book of Philippians, the second chapter, that she was to put others first, but one of her students had acted in violence toward her and that was not to be tolerated. Marcail knew she had to go for help and advice.

By 10:30 she was on her way to see Mr. Flynn at the bank. The scratch on her face was very small, unnoticeable really, but Marcail was quite conscious of it.

The bank teller gave her a searching look when she asked for Mr. Flynn, and she forced herself not to reach toward her face. She watched him disappear into the back office and reappear with the bank manager.

"To what do I owe this pleasure, Miss Donovan?" Mr. Flynn smiled cordially until he got a close look at Marcail's tense features.

"I have a problem I need to discuss with you, Mr. Flynn. Is this an opportune time?"

"Yes, certainly." He'd become somewhat tense himself in the last few seconds, and his movements were agitated as he led Marcail to his office. Marcail took the chair Mr. Flynn gestured toward and watched as he sat behind his desk. She was on the verge of explaining her visit when Mr. Flynn spoke.

"Is there a problem with someone in your class?"

"Yes, sir, there is."

"I hope it's not Sydney Duckworth. I can go to the parents of anyone else in town, but if Sydney's been difficult, well, you'll just have to do your best."

Marcail couldn't believe her ears, and her look must have registered her surprise.

Mr. Flynn continued: "I know I've shocked you and probably caused you to think I don't deserve my position as head of the school board. However, Mrs. Duckworth will make the town miserable if I go to her and complain."

"He threw a rock at me, Mr. Flynn." Marcail's voice reflected her mounting anger. "It hit me in the face!"

"You *saw* him do this?"

"You can't possibly be questioning my word?"

"No, *I'm* not." Mr. Flynn's voice was kind. "But please understand, Miss Donovan—Mrs. Duckworth will."

Marcail was silent for an entire minute. This was inconceivable to her.

"I guess I'll have to go to Mrs. Duckworth myself," Marcail said, thinking she had come up with a logical solution.

"I really hope you won't do that."

"Why not?"

"Because the last five times a teacher went to Cordelia and complained about Sydney, she pressured the rest of us into keeping our children out of school until the teacher quit. We've had to hire other teachers in the middle of the year. In fact, you're the ninth schoolteacher we've had in three years."

"And you let her get away with this?" Marcail was

incredulous. "Just because you're afraid she won't speak to you the next time you pass on the street?"

"I wish it were that simple," the banker's face was drawn. "You see, Mrs. Duckworth owns over half the town, including this bank. When things don't go her way, our rents go up or we find ourselves completely out of work.

"Having to wear dark clothing and put your hair up at all times is part of her belief that the schoolteacher must be a shining example to the children of town. *But*, she's completely blind to her own selfishness or the deeds of her grandson."

Marcail felt something grow cold inside of her. It chilled her to think that one person had this much power.

"You could just up and quit; others have. You certainly have grounds, but we're very pleased with your work and hope you'll stay."

For just an instant Marcail's heart grabbed at the word "quit." How easy it would be to run home to Father, but then Marcail remembered how badly she wanted to prove to herself that she could do this.

She also realized the word "quit" was not a part of her vocabulary. She shook her head ever so slightly.

"I take it that means you're not quitting. Well, I'm glad to hear it. I'll start making surprise visits to the schoolhouse every few days. I think if more than one person is watching, Sydney will be less likely to act up."

Marcail nodded almost numbly. She could see that nothing more was going to be offered to her. As Mr. Flynn saw her to the door and she began the walk home, her mind worked over the options before her. Quitting was out, but she could go to Mrs. Duckworth. However, Mr. Flynn's initial response to her predicament had shown her that such a move would cause trouble for the entire town.

Marcail was tempted to write her brother-in-law, Rigg, or her father and pour out her entire story, knowing instinctively they would show up in Willits within hours or days of hearing from her. But all her life she'd been protected, and she so wanted to stand on her own this time.

Marcail's mind played over every second of the previous afternoon, and she realized that in throwing that rock, Sydney had succeeded in shocking even himself. With that in mind, Marcail decided that she would confront Sydney on Monday so he would know where he stood, and then pray there would be no more outbursts.

"Hello, Miss Donovan."

Marcail was startled out of her musings by the sound of Dr. Montgomery's voice. She'd been so intent on her walking and planning that she had not heard his approach.

"Hello, Dr. Montgomery." Marcail's hand had gone to her throat in surprise. She tried to smile pleasantly, but as usual he made her nervous, and she was a bit embarrassed over how preoccupied she'd been. She watched as he swung from his mount to stand before her.

"How are you feeling?"

"I'm fine, thank you," Marcail replied, actually mustering up a smile.

Alex nodded and continued to watch her. He had wanted a closer look at her than his mounted position would allow, and now he was able to see that her color was much better than the day before. In fact, she was rather flushed. On the other hand, her discomfort in his presence hadn't changed in the least; she was obviously afraid of him. He wondered absently if it was just him, all doctors, or men in general.

Marcail was standing as far from him as propriety would allow, and for some reason Alex was torn between turning on his best bedside manner or laughing. The latter won out, and Marcail watched as his eyes lit with some inner amusement.

Alex witnessed the raising of her chin and knew that the voice she used to address him was one she used with her students.

"Was there something you needed to see me about, doctor? If not, my schedule is quite full, and I'd like to be on my way."

Alex caught a light of vulnerability in her eyes, slight, but nevertheless evident to him. All humor fled.

"I'm glad to see you're doing well, Miss Donovan. Please don't let me keep you."

Marcail nodded to him by way of answer and turned even before he mounted his horse. She felt his eyes on her back for some steps, but before long her mind was back on Sydney and she didn't give Willits' handsome young doctor another thought.

# *nine*

═══════════

"I'm so sorry, Miss Donovan. I'll never do it again," Sydney told Marcail with heartbreaking sincerity, his bottom lip quivering pitifully, his face nearly ashen. Marcail had been correct—he had shocked even himself.

"I'm glad to hear that, Sydney," she told him gently, "because if you do, I'm going to have to punish you severely." The young boy nodded, and Marcail reached to give him a hug. It was not the first time she'd hugged him, but for the first time he reciprocated. His thin arms clung to her, and Marcail's heart thundered with emotion.

They were the only ones in the schoolhouse, and Marcail, realizing that the children would be returning from recess very soon, knew she had to quickly say what was on her mind. Holding Sydney gently at arm's length, she began.

"I understand, Sydney, that people have days when they feel upset, but no matter what you're feeling, you must *never* deliberately hurt someone."

"I understand, Miss Donovan." Again Sydney's lip quivered, and Marcail believed he meant it. They talked for a few moments more, Sydney apologizing for the third time and Marcail telling Sydney she forgave him.

As he returned to his desk, Marcail realized that something special had happened between them. Sydney was looking at her with new eyes, and as much as Marcail regretted his action, she prayed that this incident would make a difference in their future relationship. Some of the shock over being struck was still there, but Sydney was as precious to her as he'd always been.

□ □ □

In the weeks to follow God sustained Marcail in a way she would not have dreamed possible. She was growing very close to her entire class and knew that some of the students thought the world of her. The Austin girls had even come after school one day to tell her they prayed for her every night. Marcail had been so moved she had nearly cried. She asked the girls to also pray for Sydney, and for Marcail's relationship with him.

The girls had readily agreed, and Marcail felt their prayers. There were days when Sydney was a school-teacher's dream and days when he was a nightmare, but amid the ups and downs they grew closer. Marcail was swiftly learning to take each day as it came.

Sydney had not turned into a model student, but neither had he shown any signs of aggression since the day he'd thrown the rock. Marcail suspected this was because he was becoming slightly infatuated with her.

They were able to talk with ease, but Marcail's prayers were many on Sydney's behalf. She hadn't mentioned her fears to anyone else, but she recognized the fact that he was a child who was prone to acts of violence when angered. It frightened her a little that she had no idea what had set him off the last time, but she kept an eye on him, and Mr. Flynn was making his visits as promised.

Teaching school was harder work than Marcail had

anticipated. Her sister had made it look so easy. This made the weekends a time of relaxation and recuperation. She liked to work on her lessons and bake Saturday morning. Often she would walk into town in the afternoon.

One Saturday, when the weather was beginning to turn cold, Marcail ran into Kay Austin in the general store.

"Miss Donovan," Kay greeted her warmly, "did the girls give you my message about tomorrow?"

"Yes, Mrs. Austin, they did, but tomorrow is—"

"The pie auction," she finished for her. "That's no problem because I want you to bring the young man who buys your pie."

"Oh," Marcail said with genuine pleasure, "that sounds wonderful. I'll plan on it."

Kay squeezed her arm and smiled before telling her she would see her on the morrow. Marcail thought that Mrs. Austin would never know what a relief the invitation was. Rowie Kilmer had seen Marcail just the weekend before and made it quite clear that he was going to bid on her pie. Marcail had been gracious, but in her heart she sighed and wished that he would turn his attention elsewhere.

She had crossed his path from time to time, and although he made no move to press her, he questioned her very carefully as to whether or not she'd been seeing anyone else. Her comments on the privacy of her own business seemed to roll off him like boulders on a hillside.

❏ ❏ ❏

The next morning Marcail went to church. Since the auction was to follow the service, she brought her apple pie in a basket, as did most of the other women in town.

Allie's pie was mince. She whispered to Marcail during church that it was Seth's favorite. Marcail smiled at the joy in her friend's eyes. She had missed Allie since she'd started seeing Seth, but Marcail recognized the signs of love and told Allie, in all honesty, how thrilled she was for her newfound happiness.

No social time had been planned, since the weather was cooling, but spirits were high as the bidding began, raising funds that were once again to go to the school.

Marcail's pie came up in the middle of the bidding, and just as Rowie had said, he was on hand and bidding like a rich man. It looked as if Marcail's basket was going to go high, and the young schoolmarm kept her eyes on Mr. Flynn as two men took the price over $1.00. She recognized one voice as Rowie's, and the other as Allie's brother, Logan's.

Marcail, preparing herself for an afternoon of being gawked at or pulled around, was praying for patience. A deep voice from the back of the crowd startled her with a bid.

"Three dollars!"

Marcail's eyes slid shut on a sudden rush of tears. She was barely aware of the way Mr. Flynn stuttered to a halt or how still the crowd had grown. Moments passed before Mr. Flynn declared the pie sold and Marcail turned and made her way back off the platform.

A massive hand was there to take her basket and then her hand, but Marcail didn't dare look up until the man had led her away to the semiprivacy of a nearby tree. As soon as he stopped she let her tear-filled eyes meet his, and a second later she was crushed in Rigg's arms.

Marcail didn't know when anything had felt so good. She let herself be cuddled against his chest and tried not to cry.

"I've missed you," Rigg whispered in her ear, feeling as though he could cry himself.

He couldn't love this girl more if she had been his own child, and in a way she was. He was only 17 years her senior, but she had come into his life as a nine-year-old girl whose mother had just died and whose father was overseas. Their's had been a love-at-first-sight relationship, a brother-sister type of love.

A year later he was married to Marcail's sister, and she was living with them. Not even the birth of his own three children had diminished his love for her. He'd gone into a state of near mourning when her father had returned to California and she had moved downstate to live with him.

Rigg released Marcail and tenderly wiped a tear from her cheek. There was so much they wanted to say to each other. They had just began to share when Jethro Kilmer came on the scene.

"Who is this, Marcail?" Jethro demanded unexpectedly.

Rigg only glanced at the younger man before turning his surprised gaze to his sister-in-law.

"Rigg, this is Jethro Kilmer. Jethro, this is my brother-in-law, Marshall Riggs." Marcail's voice was polite, but Rigg heard the note of longsuffering.

"Oh, he's married! Why didn't you say so?" Rowie's voice was so filled with relief that Marcail felt angry. She would probably have spouted off at Rowie if Rigg hadn't put his hand on her arm.

"It's nice to meet you, Jethro," Rigg's voice was steady. "But I'm sure you'll understand my wanting to spend some time with my sister."

Rigg led Marcail away without further explanation. Marcail was so pleased over the way he'd handled Rowie that her smile nearly stretched off her face.

"Do you need me to talk with this young man?" The question came softly to her ears as they walked. When they stopped, trying once again to steal some privacy, Marcail shook her head.

"No, but thank you. As you've probably guessed, I'm not encouraging him, even though I'm sure he would welcome any interest on my part. I'm certain he'll grow discouraged and eventually leave me alone."

Marcail grew silent then and simply drank in the sight of her sister's husband. He had seemed bigger than life to her when they first met, and even now he was one of the largest men she'd ever known. But there wasn't a mean or malicious bone in his body, and from the first he'd always made her feel loved and secure.

"How's Katie?" Marcail asked softly.

"She has a bit of a cold."

Marcail nodded. "And the kids?"

"Colds too. They miss you almost as much as I do."

They grinned at each other again, and Marcail reached to give him another hug. She explained the invitation for lunch, and as they talked they made their way toward the Austin home.

Marcail had a myriad of questions, as did Rigg. They had exchanged most of the pertinent information regarding family and friends by the time Rigg knocked on the Austins' front door.

Unfortunately, some of the joy went out of Marcail's afternoon when the door was answered by Dr. Alexander Montgomery.

# *ten*

Two hours later Alex knew with a certainty that Miss Donovan's fear was not of men in general. She was at complete ease with her brother-in-law, as well as with Dean Austin. This left only him, or doctors in general. Alex wondered why the thought was so discouraging to him.

He figured it might have to do with the fact that after 15 minutes of conversation around the dinner table, he knew that both Rigg and Marcail were believers. This made the young teacher safe enough for him to drop his guard, but no more approachable.

Alex knew that everyone in town believed he was still too much in love with his first wife to even look at another woman, but that was not true anymore. What the townspeople didn't understand was how earnestly Alex took his relationship with Jesus Christ, and in so doing, he was serious about finding a wife who shared his belief.

Without a doubt, the first criteria was that the woman be a Christian. Alex found himself thinking, however, that it certainly didn't hurt that her hair was so black and shiny it appeared blue in the right light, or that she had eyes like big brown pansies. Her eyes, along with the tiny dark mole near her lower lip, drew his attention to her smiling mouth and her beautiful teeth when he least expected it. No, none of those things hurt at all; and, added to the fact that she loved the Savior, they made her more distracting by the minute.

Alex had worked hard at not staring at her all afternoon, but surprisingly, he found himself alone with her in the living room after the dessert dishes had been cleared. Alex could almost hear her telling herself to relax. After a few minutes of tense silence, she smiled at him. It gave him hope, and he spoke, his excellent bedside manner coming to the fore.

"It was certainly nice of Rigg to surprise you today."

Marcail smiled a little wider because he didn't seem at all threatening to her at that moment. Her voice revealed her relief when she answered.

"It was, wasn't it? I don't think I knew how much I missed him until I heard his voice at the back of the crowd."

"How long has it been?"

"I saw them for a few minutes when the train stopped in Santa Rosa, but I moved away in late February. I wish Katie and the children could have come, but Rigg said everyone has colds."

"You're an aunt then?"

Marcail beamed with pleasure, and Alex sucked in a sharp breath at her enchanting beauty.

"Several times over, actually," Marcail answered easily, not having noticed the doctor's reaction. "Katie and Rigg have Gretchen, Molly, and Donovan. My brother, Sean, and his wife, Charlotte, have Ricky and Callie."

Alex smiled at her, a smile of genuine warmth. Marcail returned the grin until Alex shifted in his chair. Marcail thought he was rising to join her on the sofa. She tensed and moved a little further down the cushions, an action that Alex did not miss.

"Is it me, Miss Donovan, or all doctors?"

Marcail's face flamed with humiliation, and she stuttered an apology.

"Please don't apologize." Alex's voice was tender. "It's just that if I've done something to upset you, I'd like to ask your forgiveness."

"No, no," Marcail assured him swiftly. "You've been very kind; I just—that is—I'm rather—" The young woman came to an awkward halt and was surprised to find the doctor smiling at her, his eyes filled with understanding.

Marcail met his gaze for just a moment and then unintentionally spoke out loud. "I guess you might not be so bad after all."

Laughter erupted from Alex's chest, and Marcail's hand flew to her mouth. Her face had heated all over again, and she began to rise from her seat. Alex waved her back with his hand, still chuckling over her remark.

"Please don't go, Miss Donovan. I assure you, I'm not easily offended. I find your honesty refreshing."

Marcail eyed him carefully to gauge his sincerity. She finally relaxed back on the sofa, and they continued to talk. If Marcail wasn't exactly at ease in the situation, she found it tolerable. What she didn't know was that Kay Austin was beyond the door, hesitating before entering. She was also listening to every word and hoping that before long Marcail would find the situation much *more* than tolerable.

❑ ❑ ❑

"I can't believe how swiftly the day went."

"I can't either. I sure enjoyed the Austins' hospitality."

"I really hadn't known them before, but they're wonderful," Marcail agreed and added, "Are you sure you have to go first thing in the morning, Rigg?"

The full moon shone on Rigg and Marcail as they stood

at Marcail's front door recalling the afternoon. Rigg was headed to the hotel for the night, and this would be the last they would see of each other.

"I really do, Marc. Jeff is going to open the mercantile for me, but I've got to get back. Christmas is only about two months away, and we'll all be together then."

Marcail nodded, and they hugged one last time. She stood in the doorway and watched him walk toward town. When she finally shut the door, it was with a prayer of thanksgiving for her family, and for the way God had sent Rigg on the day she needed him most.

□ □ □

"But don't you think she's perfect for Alex?"

"Kay," her husband spoke patiently as he slipped into bed, "that still does not give you an excuse for eavesdropping."

Kay looked somewhat rebuked, but she was so excited about the little she'd overheard that she was not very sorry.

"I can see you're not at all sorry."

"I am sorry that I listened. I should have walked right into the room instead of waiting, but I'm not sorry about what I heard."

Dean frowned at his wife's line of reasoning, but she was too wound up to notice.

"You should have heard his voice. When he found out she was afraid of him, he was so tender with her. I just know she's the one."

Dean shook his head, kissed his wife good night, and turned down the lantern. Kay listened as his breathing evened out into sleep. She was planning ahead and much too excited to sleep. Alex came to lunch every Sunday afternoon; maybe she should ask Miss Donovan to join them more often. It was a delightful plan.

# *eleven*

An entire month passed before Alex saw Marcail again. It was not for lack of trying on his part, but he wanted to be careful about how often he went to the front door of her home, and there was really no other time when he ran into her. Since she would probably have to be dying before she would call on him, he knew better than to hope she would need medical attention.

On this particular Saturday morning he was a little late heading into his office in town. For the first time he saw Marcail at the side of her house. He did a double take when he saw that the tiny, black-haired woman was chopping wood, or at least making an attempt. Knowing that he was getting a glimpse of Marcail Donovan's determined personality, Alex dismounted and stood watching her.

Marcail balanced a fat log on end, and then lifted the ax in front of her, bringing it down on the log. A small piece of wood flew off as the remainder of the wood landed on the ground. Alex watched in fascination as she added the piece to a small pile of chips and started again.

Just as Marcail raised the ax again, she spotted her neighbor. She repeated the process and then stood breathing heavily as Alex approached.

"I can't believe you're doing this yourself."

"Well, I said I would," Marcail was still panting, "so I'm going to."

"And just who did you say that to?" Alex reached for the ax and tried to ignore the surreptitious way Marcail backed away from him.

"Jethro offered to chop wood for me, but I didn't think that was a good idea, so I told him I would take care of it myself. In fact, I think you should give the ax back to me."

Alex stared at her for a full ten seconds, shook his head, and began to chop. In 20 minutes he had a large stack of burning logs and a smaller stack of kindling. They worked together carrying the logs to the house and dumping them into the box by Marcail's stove. On the last load Marcail turned to thank the doctor, but found him standing and watching her from the door. With his gaze leveled so intently on her, it took a moment for her to speak.

"Thank you for your help."

"You're welcome. Will you do me a favor?"

"What is it?"

"Will you do it?" he persisted.

Marcail hesitated. She knew it was unfair of him to ask for a commitment before explaining, but he *had* chopped her wood, and she could see his desire to help was out of kindness and not selfish motives.

"All right."

"Come by my office and let me know the next time you need wood."

Marcail nearly panicked. That would mean he would be around more often. She had to make him see this wasn't necessary.

"There really is no need. I, uh, well, I mean, that is, I didn't think that you would, I mean, I really appreciate, but I don't want to bother, and I—" Marcail came to a breathless halt when she saw laughter in the depths of his blue eyes.

Marcail took a breath and tried again. "Thank you for your help, but I'll be okay now."

*You're not about to let me near you, are you, little one?* These were Alex's very tender thoughts. What he said aloud was much less personal.

"I don't want to push in where I'm not wanted, but if you'll let me, I'll just keep an eye on your woodpile. I won't come into the house; I'll just stack it by your porch when it looks like you're getting low."

Marcail's mouth had suddenly gone dry. She did not want to be beholden to this man, but she couldn't go on as she was. Every day was colder than the day before, and as hard as it was to accept his help, she didn't really have much choice.

"Thank you" was all Marcail could muster, and then she scolded herself for her rudeness. But the doctor must not have minded. He smiled at her, raised a hand in a small wave, and went on his way.

It would be a long time before Marcail knew that Alex found her delightful, especially when she stood looking very proper and composed, unaware of the strands of hair that hung in her face and the dirt that was smeared on her cheeks and forehead. Delighted, captivated, fascinated—Alex's emotions ran the gamut, and much to his chagrin, he found he could think about little else.

❑ ❑ ❑

Marcail was invited to the Austins for dinner again the first Sunday in December. As much as she wanted to, Kay had not had the courage to ask the girls' teacher to join them the week after the pie auction, and every week to follow. So on this day, she decided to pull out all the stops.

Alex was the first to arrive, and spotting the extra place setting and fancy dinnerware, he turned a curious eye on his hostess.

"Who's joining us, Kay?"

"Who?" Kay sounded much like an owl.

"Tell him, Kathleen," her husband commanded as he entered the room.

Kay turned aggressively on both men. "I happen to know that she eats by herself every evening, and I think the least we can do is ask her to join us on the weekends!" Kay stormed back out to the kitchen and left the men to stare at each other.

"I take it the lovely Miss Donovan is joining us today?"

Dean only nodded and watched the younger man. "I'm sorry, Alex, if that's a problem for you."

"It's no problem for me, Dean. I find myself day-dreaming about the next time I'll see her. However, I don't know how Miss Donovan is going to feel about *my* being here."

A moment later they both heard the knock on the front door.

"Well," Dean spoke again, this time softly, "we'll know soon enough."

Marla answered the door and stood grinning at her teacher. Marcail was just as glad to see her because the Austin girls were some of her best students. The fact that they prayed for her gave them a bond she did not share with any of the other children. They were also bright and well behaved, and looked at her with something close to adoration, which was good for any teacher's confidence.

Daisy joined them as they made their way to the dining room. Even though both girls were talking at once, Marcail didn't miss the sound of Alex's well-modulated voice. Surprisingly enough, she did not feel like running away. There was a constant supply of chopped wood next to her door, and Marcail wanted to thank him. Unfortunately her mouth went dry the moment she felt his eyes on her.

"Hello, Miss Donovan," Kay greeted her warmly. "Come in and make yourself at home."

Marcail had to clear her throat before any words would come out, and only then was she able to thank her hostess. Dean greeted her, and then Marcail had no choice but to meet the doctor's eyes.

"Hello, Dr. Montgomery," she began. "I want to thank you for the firewood."

"You're welcome. Has there been ample?"

"Yes, more than enough, thank you."

Alex had to hide a smile. Such a speech had obviously cost her, and he found the look of profound relief on her face adorable. He realized in an instant that he wanted to court this woman. With Linette, his attention had been welcome; with Marcail, he didn't know whether he even stood a chance.

Alex had sudden visions of the young men in Santa Rosa, just waiting for her to disembark from the train when she returned for Christmas. He couldn't believe the wave of jealousy that overwhelmed him at the thought.

"Dinner is ready," Kay called as she added a soup tureen to the table and everyone gathered around.

Marcail found herself next to Marla and across the table from Daisy. Alex sat on Daisy's left, and even though Marcail told herself not to, she looked at the young doctor almost constantly.

Her mind ran in two directions. One moment she found herself enjoying his handsome face, dark hair, and blue eyes, but regretting the fact that he was a doctor. The next moment she wished his features were pale and washed out, and that she found him repulsive.

Alex did not miss the way Marcail's gaze strayed to him repeatedly. He tried to squelch the hope rising within him that she might be interested, but it didn't work. When Marcail said her goodbyes, Alex did the same so they could leave together.

Marcail was looking uncomfortable all over again as they walked out the front door. But Alex so wanted to be with her that he ignored her look, took a big breath, and asked if he could see her home.

# *twelve*

Marcail's mouth was dry and her palms were wet. She felt like some type of small prey that was being stalked by a larger animal. She told herself she had no one to blame but herself, as she realized her looking at Dr. Montgomery had given him the wrong impression.

"Why don't I just rescind that question, Miss Donovan, since I've obviously upset you?"

Marcail's heart broke just a little at the dejected tone in his voice and the look of resignation on his face, but she felt she had to be honest.

"I'm sorry." Marcail's voice was soft, and Alex saw very real regret behind her fear.

"Don't be," he assured her. "It's nice to know right up front that my suit would not be acceptable." He mustered up a gentle smile intended to ease her guilt and went on his way. Marcail stood still until he rounded the house to retrieve his horse and watched as he started toward home.

❏ ❏ ❏

Alex stretched his stocking feet out in front of him and relaxed back in one of the kitchen chairs. The supper he'd just eaten had been filling enough, but he was feeling a bit empty inside. His Bible lay on the table. He reached for it, but didn't open it.

"I thought she might be the one, Lord," he said out loud in the quiet house. "I can't push in where I'm not wanted, and not until she apologized did I realize how badly I wanted her to want me. I don't know why I feel this way, Father, but I somehow think that she needs me . . . that we need each other."

Alex believed that his was the God of all comfort, but the truth was he hurt right then in a way that he'd never hurt before. Losing Linette had given new meaning to the word loneliness, and his hurt over her loss had been very real. But this was different. This was rejection.

Alex opened his Bible to the book of Genesis. It always comforted him to read the account of creation and to marvel again at the perfect, orderly way God had constructed the world. When Alex read in chapter 2, verse 18, that man should not be alone, he stopped to pray.

With a heart honestly seeking to be the man God would have him be, Alex committed his thoughts of Marcail to the Lord. He lay his own desires at the feet of a holy God and prayed that God in His timing and will would provide someone special to share his life. At the moment the only face Alex could see was Marcail's, but he trusted that God could change his heart and turn this fresh pain into glory for Himself.

❑ ❑ ❑

Marcail brushed through her hair with long even strokes as she sat on the edge of the bed and thought about Dr. Montgomery. She knew she was being silly, since he couldn't be nicer, but fears were never logical, and the truth was that she was afraid of him.

Marcail lay in bed thinking of the humble way Alex had accepted her rejection. She wondered for a moment if her fear wasn't causing her to pass up what could be a wonderful relationship. How would she know either way? She fell asleep before she could come to any solid conclusions.

# *thirteen*

---

*Santa Rosa*
*December 18, 1881*

Marcail beamed across the living room at her sister, who mirrored her look as though they alone shared a secret. They were silent for a moment, a relaxed, easy kind of silence that sisters who are also friends can share. Kaitlin was the first to break the spell.

"I can't believe how good it is to have you here. It's been so long."

"That quick hug back in August when the train came through didn't count."

"You're right, it didn't."

Again they smiled at each other. Marcail had arrived the day before. Now it was Sunday afternoon, and they'd already been to church and eaten lunch. Little Donovan was napping, and the girls were with their dad at their grandparents' farm. The house was quiet.

"You look good, Marc. You must be happy."

"I am. I mean, the job isn't without its drawbacks, but I really do love it."

"It's what you've always wanted to do, that's for certain."

"The biggest difficulty," Marcail spoke with a twinkle in her eye, "is that both you and Mother made it look so easy."

"And you're finding out different?"

"In a hurry." Marcail spoke fervently this time.

"Have there been some problems?"

"Yes, but I believe I'm handling them."

"Why didn't you write about them?"

"Because I wanted to stand on my own, and if Rigg had known about the one problem, he'd have rushed to Willits. I didn't want that."

Kaitlin looked concerned. "Were you in some sort of danger?"

"In a way I was, but the situation is under control now, at least I pray it is."

"Want to tell me about it?"

Surprisingly, Marcail did. She told her older sister all about Mrs. Duckworth, Sydney, and the town's refusal to stand up to this family. She half expected Kaitlin to be angry, both at her for not sharing and at Mrs. Duckworth's manipulation. But instead Kaitlin looked very thoughtful.

"Mother had a problem like that once."

"She did?" Marcail was astounded.

"Um hm. In Hawaii. You were probably too young to recall. One of the leaders in the village wanted his son schooled, but without the slightest bit of correction. And believe me, this boy needed to be disciplined."

"How did she handle it?"

"She wouldn't allow him into the schoolhouse. He ran home to his father, who stormed over to Mother in a fury, but she stood up to him. When he left he took not only his own son, but every child who was related to him by blood or marriage. Half the school was missing."

"What did Mother do?"

"She taught the children who remained," Kaitlin stated serenely, obviously agreeing with her mother's choice of action. "Within a week's time, all but the one boy were back in school. It took another month before we saw him again, but there was never any trouble after that."

Marcail was silent as she digested this new picture of her mother. Their situations were not identical, partly because of the position of respect and admiration her parents always held in the villages, but Marcail did see similarities. She wasn't completely sure she'd have handled it the same way.

True, most of the children had come back within a week, but what if they hadn't? How long would Mother have let the children go without their schooling before trying to find another solution? It was a question only Theresa Donovan could have answered, and she was no longer there to ask.

"I'm not saying that you should do the same thing, Marc." Katie's voice cut into her thoughts. "Please don't think that. You have to follow your heart. At least you're able to talk with Sydney and reason with him. Unless I miss my guess, you see him as a mission field."

She smiled at how easily Katie could read her. Marcail did see Sydney as a freshly plowed field, just waiting for planting, and she prayed every day that God would help her sow the seeds of truth. He was a little boy much in need of a personal relationship with Christ Jesus, and Marcail's constant prayer was to be used of God to that end.

Donovan cried then, and Katie went to check on him. Once alone, Marcail's mind wandered to her last day of school and the lovely lace handkerchief Sydney had given her. Most of the children had brought her something, and she was grateful for every gift. But none of the children had sported Sydney's look, a look that begged her to find him as special as his gift.

Well, he was special, and Marcail took time right then to pray for him as the new year approached. She also prayed that she would return, renewed in spirit and body for the remainder of the year. She didn't know what tomorrow would bring, but she believed it was in God's hands.

# *fourteen*

The weeks Marcail spent at home for Christmas were some of the best that year. She loved Willits and Visalia, but Santa Rosa had been home for such a long time that it was hard to think of it in any other way.

Free from the cares of the classroom and lessons, Marcail felt like a schoolgirl once again. Her father, thinking she would be in Santa Rosa more often, had brought most of her dresses from Visalia when he came for his Christmas visit. Marcail dressed in her best to go out with friends on drives and to dinner, enjoying the time of her life.

Christmas was like old times, even though everyone was sorry that Sean and Charlotte weren't able to leave the mission in the Hawaiian Islands to be with them.

The girls loved the dolls their Aunt Marcail had brought, and she was thrilled with their reaction. Marcail herself said she made out like a bandit, with more lovely gifts than she'd ever received before.

It was great fun to sit around and catch up on all the latest news, the most wonderful of which was Rigg's brother Gilbert's decision to go into the pastorate. With his gentle manner and love for God's Word, it was no surprise to Marcail. His mother, May, also told her he'd already met someone special, and it looked like her last son would soon be leaving the nest.

Mr. Parker and his son, Joey, special friends of the family, also filled a part of her time at home. Joey had been in Katie's class when she first taught in Santa Rosa. He and Marcail were the same age, but the difference between them had been marked. Joey's father had been drunk whenever the coins in his pocket had allowed, and Joey had been one of the most neglected children Kaitlin had ever encountered.

Kaitlin's heart had been instantly softened toward this boy and his father. With the help of Rigg's family, they were brought into the circle of their fellowship.

Joey had come to Christ in a very short time, and the family had watched with awe and praise as he grew stronger in the Lord with each passing month.

Mr. Parker had only recently made a decision for Christ, but their ten years of friendship, years when the family helped him overcome painful obstacles such as illiteracy and alcoholism, had given them a bond that transcended most other relationships.

Joey was a foreman at the feed mill, and Mr. Parker worked part-time for Bill Taylor at the shipping office. They had a comfortable house in town, and Mr. Parker was seeing a lovely widow he'd met at the church. Marcail met her one Sunday and thought she was very special.

It was wonderful just to be back under the solid Bible teaching of Pastor Keller. Marcail couldn't help but feel saddened when she thought of her Pastor Zimler in Willits and his complacent attitude toward the Word of God.

As difficult as it was to go back to what seemed a spiritual wasteland, Marcail found as the days passed that she could hardly sit still for the thought of returning. She missed her students and her little house so much that she dreamed of them the night before she left. She knew she would miss her family once again, but strangely she found herself thinking of Dr. Montgomery as she boarded the train for Willits.

# *fifteen*

Marcail couldn't believe how good it felt to step off the train in Willits. The scenery on the ride north was a little more familiar this time. As the train lumbered its way through the mountains and valleys en route to her home, Marcail reveled in the beauty from the window.

There was a slight pang of loneliness when no one was at the train station to meet her, but then she hadn't been able to tell Allie exactly when she was scheduled to arrive.

Mentally thanking Rigg and Katie for the new coat she wore, Marcail started her walk home. She felt snug and warm as she pulled the high collar around the back of her head. Her new boots, a gift from her father, were a little stiff at first, but they were already feeling better by the time her house came into view.

Marcail breathed in the crisp, cold air as she walked, and not until she drew near her front porch did she recognize the sound of someone chopping wood. She peeked around the corner of the house to find Alex in shirtsleeves and swinging an ax.

He had come into her thoughts at odd times while in Santa Rosa, and each time Marcail had prayed very specifically about her feelings. If she was very honest with herself—and she usually tried to be—he still made her uncomfortable. But she was also fascinated.

Lost in her thoughts, Marcail stood long enough that Alex eventually noticed her. Marcail watched as he set the ax down, drew a handkerchief from his rear pocket, and came toward her.

"Welcome home," he said as he wiped the back of his neck. He stopped before her and couldn't hold the smile that stretched over his face at the very sight of her.

"Thank you. It's nice to be back."

Alex's smile deepened over the sincerity he saw in her eyes. When she had boarded the train to Santa Rosa he had wondered if he would ever see her again. The thought had given him no peace of mind. When she still hadn't returned on Saturday and school was scheduled to resume on Monday, he became concerned. He purposely left her wood until Sunday in hopes that he would be there when she returned.

"Did you have a nice Christmas?" Marcail's voice was tentative, telling Alex how hard it was for her to make simple conversation with him.

"Yes, I did, thank you. How about yourself?"

"It was very nice."

"Did you get a new coat?"

"Oh, yes, I did." Marcail's voice told of her surprise that he had noticed. She didn't realize he noticed most everything about her. She touched the lapel on the long, single-breasted navy coat.

"Thank you for chopping the wood," Marcail blurted suddenly, just remembering she hadn't done so.

"You're welcome."

The silence between them deepened, and after a few moments Alex rescued Marcail by going back to work. Once in the house, Marcail listened to the sounds from outside. Her mind ran in numerous veins, and unfortunately she stood daydreaming even after the chopping stopped and all grew quiet.

It was then that Marcail noticed that Alex had lit a fire in her stove. Her heavy coat must have kept her from noticing the heat when she first walked in. Marcail moved swiftly to her front door, opened it, and looked out. But she was too late. Alex, astride his horse, was almost back to his own house and much too far to hear her voice.

❑ ❑ ❑

Nearly a week had passed since Marcail had returned to work, and it was now Saturday, her day to bake and shop in town. She was just about to walk into the dry goods store when Mrs. Duckworth's stringent tone sounded in the cold January air. The sound of her voice could be heard from down the block.

"Don't tell me I don't have the right! I own this building, and if I request to see your books, then I expect to see them!"

Marcail did not hear the hotel owner's reply, but she did spot Sydney sitting in his grandmother's carriage out front. She approached with a smile.

"Hi, Sydney."

"Hello, Miss Donovan." Sydney smiled with genuine pleasure at the sight of her. It was obviously one of his good days.

Marcail nearly shook her head in wonder. She'd never met a more cordial child when he determined to be so. His manners were perfection itself. Get on his wrong side on a bad day, however, and look out! Anything could happen.

"It's getting colder all the time, isn't it?"

"Yes, it is," the boy replied. "My grandmother says that because last year was so mild we'll have a heavy snowfall this year."

"Well, she is the person to listen to, since she's lived here so many years."

As if sensing she was the topic of discussion, Mrs. Duckworth suddenly appeared at Marcail's side.

"How do you do, Mrs. Duckworth?"

"I am well, Miss Donovan. I understand you went to Santa Rosa for Christmas." This last statement sounded like a rebuke.

"Yes, I did. It was nice to see my family." Marcail's voice was friendly, but she struggled with the feeling that she'd done something wrong by not checking with Mrs. Duckworth before leaving. The feeling increased when she noticed Mrs. Duckworth's scrutiny of her new coat and boots.

Marcail's chin rose slightly as Mrs. Duckworth's gaze met her own. The younger woman's eyes were calm, and there was no sign of the groveling this tyrannical woman was usually afforded from the Willits townspeople.

Mrs. Duckworth found herself wondering how she could have admired the girl's spunk on their first meeting. At the moment she found Marcail's confidence quite rude. Were it not for Sydney's admiration of her, she'd be tempted to give her the sack for such impertinence.

"I won't keep you," Marcail said after a moment. "I'll see you on Monday, Sydney. Good day, Mrs. Duckworth."

Marcail waved and went on her way. She wasn't long in town that day, and once she got home and began her laundry she found her mind straying back to Mrs. Duckworth. No one should have the godlike power that Mrs. Duckworth wielded. Of course, that was the problem— no one was bold enough to tell her so.

Marcail realized with a start that *she* was bold enough, but knowing the people of Willits would suffer for her words stopped her in her tracks.

Marcail spent the day thinking about why, beyond her teaching position, God might have brought her to Willits. Often she was tempted to quit, but God always detained her with a gentle reminder that her example to the townspeople, her students, and especially Sydney might bring them to a saving knowledge of Jesus Christ.

# *sixteen*

Marcail's hand went to the back of her neck to rub at a sore spot. It was a cloudy Friday afternoon, and the children had been gone for about 15 minutes. From her place at the desk, Marcail glanced outside and stared for a moment.

It took some seconds to realize it was snowing. A few inches had already accumulated on the ground from the two different nights it had snowed, and for an instant Marcail thought her eyes were playing tricks on her.

Finally convinced that snow was falling, Marcail rose quickly from her desk and hurried toward the door. She pulled the school door shut behind her and stood for a moment, her face lifted toward the sky.

Marcail Donovan had never seen it snow. Having grown up in the tropics and then living in Santa Rosa, where it had snowed only twice and at night when they were all asleep, left her more than a little curious and excited about actually watching it snow.

In a near trance she walked down the steps with her hands spread wide to catch the white particles falling to the ground. Her tongue came out as she tried to taste a snowflake.

She had not taken time to grab her coat and was surprised at how warm it felt outside with only her sweater. Marcail began walking toward the trees that lined the road in the distance, loving the way the snow looked against the backdrop they formed. She entered a small copse of oaks and spent the next 20 minutes alternating between standing under their shelter and dashing out into the snow to make new tracks and feel the cold flakes on her face.

Marcail became aware of the cold about ten minutes too late. She wrapped her sweater a little more tightly about her and scolded herself for not taking her coat. The clouds had thickened and the wind had picked up suddenly, and as Marcail came back onto the road she realized that having the snow blowing in her face was no longer fun.

She squinted against the sting in her eyes and wondered how she could have been so foolish as to come this far from the school. She decided to make a run for it, and ran a good 30 yards before realizing she was going in the wrong direction. She turned back, but the wind caught her breath so suddenly that she decided to take refuge once again under the trees.

At what she assumed to be the edge of the road, Marcail tripped. She fell hard onto her face, her dress suddenly feeling very wet. Marcail began to shiver so severely she could hardly stand up. When she finally pushed off the ground, she was certain she was heading toward safety, but only a few steps told her she was guessing.

She pressed on, praying for help. Suddenly a dark object loomed before her. For an instant Marcail thought she had found the schoolhouse, but by then she didn't really care. Her only concern was to escape the freezing wind and somehow warm her icy limbs.

The exterior of the building was rough under her hands as Marcail felt her way around a corner. She nearly missed the odd latch on the wall before her. She fumbled for just a moment before the door slid open and the wind nearly blew her inside. Marcail gasped for every breath as she slid the door shut. She turned and leaned against the wall and then blinked in confusion. Dr. Montgomery was headed toward her with a lantern held high.

"I got caught in the snow," Marcail's voice shook as the doctor approached in disbelief.

"Where is your coat?" Alex asked, as he moved to the single window by the door and peered through the glass.

Marcail couldn't answer. Every part of her body was beginning to go numb, and all she could do was shake her head.

"Let's get you to the house," Alex said, more to himself than anyone else. As he moved to hang the lantern, he heard Marcail's softly spoken "No."

Alex turned back and stared at her.

"I'll just stay here until I get warmer," the young schoolteacher stuttered as she rubbed furiously at her arms.

Knowing that now was not the time for discussion, Alex did not hesitate for a moment. He hung the lantern, blew it out, and moved toward Marcail. She couldn't see him approach, so she jumped as a hand touched her in the darkness.

"Put this on," Alex was saying, and Marcail felt a coat surround her.

Before Marcail even had time to enjoy the warmth of the coat, the barn door was thrown open. She let out a small scream when she was suddenly tossed over the doctor's shoulder. Marcail had no time to comment on her position, since Alex was already moving swiftly through the blizzard toward the house.

□ □ □

"No" was the emphatic reply. "I'll be dry in a little while."

Staring at the tiny woman before him who was shivering from head to toe, Alex pulled to the fore what was certain to be the last of his patience.

"You can't stay in that dress," Alex said for the fifth time. "It's wet and you're *freezing*. Now please go and change into the nightgown I've laid out for you, because if you don't take yourself out of those wet things, Miss Donovan, I'll do it for you."

"You can't treat me this way. I'm a grown woman."

"Then act like one," Alex snapped.

Marcail stood mute with embarrassment. Alex's jaw tensed, and a moment later he had his guest by the arm and was leading her to the bedroom. Once inside, he pulled her sweater off before she had time to think. He then spun her around and unbuttoned the back of her dress. Marcail gasped in surprise, but was given no time to respond before she was spun once again, this time to face the doctor, her eyes so big they nearly swallowed her face.

"You will remove *everything* you are wearing," Alex held Marcail's shoulders, his head bent close to her face, his voice unrelenting, "and put on the nightgown. You will then come back out to the kitchen and sit by the fire. It's the only way you're going to get warm."

Alex's face and manner softened slightly as he felt her tremble under his hands, but he exited the bedroom and shut the door before she had time to notice.

Marcail stood alone in the bedroom, so angry and humiliated that she wanted to weep. She told herself that he was overbearing and rude. She also told herself that he was right; she was freezing.

Shame nearly overwhelmed her as she pulled the

bodice of her dress down and remembered his unbuttoning the back. It took some minutes, but eventually Marcail had a pile of damp clothes on the floor and a white flannel nightgown in her hands. She was trembling so violently that she could barely lift it over her head. Once she did, she found herself enveloped in cloth. The nightgown was huge on her slight frame.

"Miss Donovan," Alex's voice called through the door.

"Yes?"

"Are you dressed?"

Marcail's answer was to open the door. Alex barely glanced at her attire before he placed a hand on her back and led her to the large upholstered chair that he'd drawn up in front of the stove. Before he gave Marcail a small push into the chair he wrapped her in a thick quilt.

In her frozen misery, Marcail was unaware of the way Alex retrieved her clothing, hung it to dry, and then fetched a mug and the pot from the stove.

"We have to get you warm, Miss Donovan" was all she heard before Alex bent over her with a steaming cup. He placed it against her mouth with one order.

"Drink."

Marcail did so, only to bury her face in the quilt a moment later in an attempt to evade the cup, as well as breathe past the acrid taste in her throat. He had given her the strongest coffee she'd ever tasted.

Alex tried to get her to drink more of the thick liquid, knowing how quickly it would warm her, but the sound of her small, choked voice begging him to stop was too much for him. He put the cup aside.

After Alex reached to put the mug on the table, he then shifted Marcail in the chair, moving her as though she were a doll so he would be certain every part of her was warm. He made sure her arms and shoulders were tucked into the quilt and then tugged one corner of the quilt up over her head until only her face showed. He pulled another chair close, sat down to face her, placed her feet in his lap, and wrapped yet another quilt around them.

Marcail looked at him through eyes that were beginning to blur, wishing he would go away. Her last thought before her body began to warm and sleep came to claim her was that this couldn't really be happening to her.

# *seventeen*

Alex wouldn't have believed that anyone could be sleeping as soundly as Marcail. She had fallen asleep over an hour ago and not moved a muscle, not even when he carried her to his bed and tucked her in. He assumed she would awaken before he was ready to go to bed himself, but she never stirred, not even when he banged around in the kitchen fixing some supper. He found himself checking her often to assure himself she was okay, but her breathing was regular and her pulse normal, so he had to assume that she was exhausted.

The snow was still falling steadily as Alex tried to make himself comfortable on the sofa in the living room. This was no easy task since the sofa was nearly a foot shorter than his 5' 10" frame.

He was covered with a warm quilt as he turned the lantern low and settled back to think on the events of the evening. Alex wondered if he would ever forget the way Marcail looked when she defied him about changing her clothes, or how small she had felt under his hands as he'd tucked the quilt about her.

A sudden feeling of dread overcame him. Alex wondered if Marcail would have any idea how a situation like this would be viewed by the town of Willits. He began to pray that God would uphold them both in the days to come, and that the townspeople, specifically Mrs. Duckworth, would be reasonable.

❏ ❏ ❏

Marcail woke up and stretched luxuriously in the large bed. The smell of coffee assailed her senses, and for just an instant she smiled. A second later she sat up with a start and stared through the dim light at the strange dresser across the room from her and then at the bed in which she slept. Marcail's heart began to beat so hard she felt breathless. The bedroom door was open, and, moving very slowly, she walked to that door and looked at the man sitting at the kitchen table.

Alex, fully dressed for the day, looked up from his Bible to find his houseguest standing in the bedroom doorway, clutching the front of her nightgown.

"What time is it?"

"About 6:30."

*"In the morning?"* Marcail whispered.

Alex looked at her with tender compassion and rose to retrieve her clothing. "These were by the stove all night, so they're dry now."

Marcail took her clothes and thanked him, her voice stilted.

"I'll fix some breakfast whenever you're ready."

Again Marcail thanked him and stood staring at nothing, trying to come to grips with the fact that she'd spent the night at the doctor's house.

"Why didn't you wake me?"

"First of all you were so exhausted and sleeping so hard, I'm not sure I could have awakened you. And second, it was still snowing, so I didn't see any point."

Marcail didn't look to the window until he mentioned

the snow. Alex watched as she moved slowly toward the window by the door and looked out. A white blanket stretched for as far as her eyes could see, and snow was still coming down. Strangely enough, the sight gave her comfort. The doctor had been given no choice, and Marcail's fear of her situation, if not the doctor, lessened to some degree.

She turned from the window, thanked Alex for drying her clothes, went into the bedroom, and shut the door. Her voice told him she was coming to accept the situation. Alex stood for a few moments outside the door, thinking as he did that Marcail didn't have an inkling of how the folks in town would react if they ever found out what had happened.

❑ ❑ ❑

"What will you do if someone needs you in town?" Marcail asked from her place in front of the dishpan, relieved over having something to do.

Alex picked up a plate and started to dry. "If the bell rings, I'll try to get through."

"The bell?"

"Yes. Since I don't live in town, I have a bell outside of my office so people can call me here at home."

Light suddenly dawned for Marcail. "I've heard that bell at times and wondered what it was."

Alex didn't answer. He was too busy smiling over how long she was taking to wash a few dishes. She'd been extremely nervous at breakfast and had hardly eaten a bite. This surprised him because he knew she'd missed supper. He remembered then how wary she was of him, and found himself wishing he'd get called into town so he could leave her in peace.

"Will you take me home if you get called into town?"

The question seemed to come out of nowhere, but Alex had an answer. "I really doubt I'll be called."

"But if you are?" Marcail pressed him.

Alex didn't even hesitate. "No, it's too risky."

Marcail began to gnaw on her lower lip. Alex had seen her do this several times at the breakfast table when the silence between them had lengthened.

When Marcail was finished with the dishes, she turned to Alex with her hands clasped nervously in front of her. "All done," she said, stating the obvious.

"Thank you for your help."

"You're welcome. Is there anything else I can do?"

"Sure," Alex began, and Marcail missed the sparkle in his eyes. "I have several shirts that need to be mended and washed, and the bedroom needs dusting."

Once again, Marcail caught her lower lip between her teeth and nodded her head, taking in the orders with wide-eyed agreement. Alex's heart melted just a little at the sight of her.

"I'm teasing you," Alex said softly, and watched as she visibly relaxed and even laughed quietly. He also noticed that her cheeks were just a bit flushed.

"How about a game of checkers?"

Marcail agreed and looked as though Alex had thrown her a lifeline. He set up the checkerboard on the kitchen table, poured fresh cups of coffee, and settled down to play.

# *eighteen*

The talk across the checkerboard was light for the most part, and Alex noticed that Marcail was relaxed around him until the conversation led to her calling him Dr. Montgomery, a name she nearly stumbled over.

Marcail noticed that Alex was an easygoing host who seemed to be a genuinely kind individual, but like all doctors she had encountered, he seemed just a bit too sure of himself. She wouldn't have called his demeanor outright arrogant, but it wasn't far off.

As they played, Alex coaxed Marcail into talking about her class, and when she was relaying something that Daisy Austin had said, he interrupted her.

"Since we're going to be spending the day together, why don't you call me Alex?"

Marcail hesitated, and Alex allowed her a few moments to think it over. "All right," she finally said and fell silent.

"You missed your turn."

Marcail stared at him in confusion. He'd just watched her move one of her checkers.

"It's your turn to tell me your name is Margaret, and that I can call you by your first name," Alex explained.

Again Marcail hesitated. "What if my name isn't Margaret?"

Alex blinked in surprise. "Didn't I hear your brother-in-law calling you Marg?"

"No. You heard Rigg call me Mar*c*." She emphasized the hard *c*. "My family's nickname for Marcail."

"Marcail." Alex tested the name on his tongue and spoke sincerely. "That's a beautiful name. It fits you."

Marcail smiled at the compliment. The smile gave Alex courage.

"And may I call you Marcail?"

As he watched her with eyes that were a beautiful sapphire blue, he didn't seem quite so arrogant to Marcail. She found herself liking him just a little.

"That would be fine," Marcail told him, and then watched as he concentrated on his next move on the board. Alex took a little extra time, and Marcail's attention began to roam. A glance out the window told her it was still snowing steadily. Her gaze wandered around the room, and she noticed what a meticulous housekeeper Willits' doctor seemed to be.

There were wooden pegs by the back door, and his coat, her sweater, and some scarves were all hung neatly in line. Not a dish was out of place in the kitchen. There were high shelves along the wall, which led Marcail to believe his wife must have been a tall woman. All the cups, bowls, and plates were stacked in tidy rows, and beyond them sat Alex's black medical bag.

Until now, Marcail had taken little more than a glance at the living room, which sat in the long part of his L-shaped house. It was as neat as the kitchen, with a small sofa and chair, two tables, and a bookshelf.

Marcail's gaze moved to the bedroom door, where she remembered an orderly setting with two wardrobes, a dresser, and the bed. Her eyes slid back to the table where Alex's Bible was placed before one of the chairs.

Looking at his Bible made Marcail wish she had her own copy on hand. Realizing she couldn't remember where Alex's checkers had been, she glanced at the board suddenly and then at the man himself. She found him sitting back in his chair, one hand resting on the table, the other laying casually in his lap. He was studying her intently.

Marcail sat mute under his inspection, not able, for some reason, to take her eyes from his.

"Is there someone special back home, someone who tells you on a regular basis how beautiful you are?"

Marcail could only give a negative shake of her head.

"Since you don't hear it that often, I'll tell you. You're very beautiful."

Alex watched as she caught her lower lip under her teeth. His voice was filled with laughter when he spoke this time. "You're beautiful even when you're trying to chew off your lower lip."

Marcail's hand came up as though she'd never realized it was habit. Her action made Alex's eyes sparkle all the more. Not wanting to make her suffer overly long, Alex stood in one fluid motion.

"I need to go out to the barn to check on Kelsey." He threw these words over his shoulder as he headed for his coat and boots.

Marcail stood also. "Will you be all right?"

"I'll be fine. The wind has died down some, and I've strung a rope from the edge of the house to the barn. I use it as my guide. That's why I carried you over my shoulder last night; I needed one hand free."

Marcail blushed over the reminder, but Alex pretended not to notice. His hand was on the door when she called his name.

"Alex?"

He turned back, his brows raised expectantly.

"Thank you for bringing me out of the cold last night."

"You're welcome," he told her softly, before opening the door and disappearing into a flurry of snow.

❑ ❑ ❑

"I can't think why this has happened, Lord," Marcail prayed in the empty house. "But I want to keep my eyes on You. Alex has been so nice, and he's not as scary as I first thought, but this feels very strange—this being snowed in with a stranger.

"It was silly of me to come out without my coat," Marcail continued to share with God from her heart, "but somehow I don't think it would have made any difference."

Marcail hovered at the window and continued to pray until Alex came back. She was unaware of the fact that Alex was lingering in the barn and doing a little praying himself.

❑ ❑ ❑

"Please bless Marcail, Lord, and ease her anxiety over doctors. Help me to be gentle with her, and give her no reason to fear me. I'm so drawn to her, but I fear if I'm not careful, I'm going to scare her away forever."

Alex continued to pray and think of ways to make Marcail feel at home. Having many books in the house, he hoped she would feel free to sit down and become absorbed in one before he returned.

In an attempt to give Marcail some privacy, Alex didn't rush back to the house. He eventually slid the barn door back and made his way through 15 inches of wet snow. The wind was still blowing, but not as hard, and Alex thought he might be able to get Marcail home.

*But then, why risk it*, he reasoned to himself. *The damage is already done.*

# nineteen

"Are you all right?"

"I'm fine, Marcail. Why wouldn't I be?"

"You were gone so long, I thought you might have become lost."

Alex shook his head. "The wind has died down, and I could see the house as I moved from the barn."

"If it's that clear maybe I should head home. I mean, you've been very kind, but I really hate to take advantage of your hospitality or wear out my welcome."

Alex was tempted to tell her she could stay for the next 50 years and not wear out her welcome, but he kept this thought to himself.

"Even though the wind has died down and it's stopped snowing, the sky looks like it could dump again at any moment. I'm sure you have things to do at home, but we had both better stay put for the time being," Alex told her reasonably.

Marcail nodded and then glanced around uncomfortably for something else to say. It was still a little unbelievable to her that she was snowed in with this man. Since it was still early, it was also hard for Marcail to face the fact that they were going to be together for the remainder of the day. She was wondering what they would find to talk about when Alex spoke.

"By the way, what were you doing out in the snow, and where is your coat?"

"My coat is at the schoolhouse. I was working after the children left when I noticed the snow coming down. I'd never seen it snow before, and I—"

"You'd never seen it snow before?" Alex interrupted her.

"No, and I never meant to wander so far from the school—"

"But I thought it snowed in Santa Rosa once in a while."

"It does, but I've only lived there since I was nine. The two times it did snow, it was in the middle of the night and had stopped before I got up." Determined not to let Alex interrupt her again, Marcail quickly finished her explanation. She then fell silent.

Too busy thinking about how terrified she must have been, Alex wasn't about to break in again. He pictured her wonder and delight over the snow, and then without warning, her terror in finding herself blinded by the wind and stinging flakes, lost and freezing. A thought suddenly occurred to him.

"Were you hurt yesterday in any way?"

"No, I'm fine."

"You didn't fall or anything?"

"I did fall once, but I'm not hurt."

Alex eyed her speculatively, wanting to believe her but afraid her fear was overruling her good sense. "I think you might find that, as a doctor, I'm really not so bad," he told her quietly.

Alex watched as Marcail's face heated. It made the skin on her cheeks look as soft as rose petals, and even though

Alex told himself he was embarrassing her, he could not drag his eyes away.

"Could I have another cup of coffee?" Marcail finally said in a small voice, all the while telling herself not to bite her lip.

"Sure." The question was enough to tell Alex that even if she was hurt, he was not going to know about it. He turned toward the stove, and Marcail once again sat at the kitchen table.

"If you like to read, I have a shelf full of books in the living room." Alex said as he filled her mug. "I need to do a little baking, so please, make yourself at home."

"Can I help with anything?"

"I don't think so, but I'll let you know."

Marcail wandered into the living room then, and even though the light was dim, she could see the titles. She selected a fat volume from the lower shelf and went back to the kitchen table.

Alex had to quell the impulse to turn and begin talking to her once again. She fascinated him, and he found that he couldn't hear enough of her voice, or watch too many of the expressions on her face when she talked. Alex worked in silence for about 20 minutes, mixing dough for bread, before Marcail spoke.

"Where is the ulna?

Alex turned to her with a wide-eyed expression, but Marcail didn't notice. She was bent over one of his medical textbooks, studying it intently.

"In your arm," he told her simply.

"Where?" Marcail finally looked at him.

Alex raised his right forearm, pinky side toward his curious houseguest, and then drew the fingers of his left hand down the outside of his forearm from wrist to elbow.

"It's the bone right here on the little finger side of the forearm." Alex watched as Marcail inspected her own forearm and then went back to her reading.

Alex returned to his mixing bowl with a smile on his face. He found himself selfishly hoping it would continue to snow for days—anything to keep this precious girl close to him.

❑ ❑ ❑

The sun broke through the clouds at about 2:30 that afternoon. The day had been spent in various pursuits, some idle, some intense, but all enjoyable. Marcail was becoming less tense as the day wore on, and Alex, as he offered to take her home, hoped that she would be a little more receptive to his suit in the very near future.

Even as the thought occurred to him, another thought, much more painful and dark, crowded into his mind. It came to fruition as he and Marcail approached her house and found several men from town, including Rowie Kilmer, in her front yard.

"Miss Donovan," Mr. Flynn called to her as Alex held her under the arms and lowered her to the bottom step of her porch. "We were just about to organize a search for you."

"Oh, Mr. Flynn, I'm sorry you were worried."

"Well, we're just glad that Dr. Montgomery found you," he assured her warmly. "You must have gone out early this morning, since the fire is out in your stove."

"Actually," Marcail explained with an embarrassed smile, "I got caught out yesterday."

Marcail failed to notice the change on Mr. Flynn's face or how still the other men had become. Alex, on the other hand, did not miss a single expression.

"Are you saying that Dr. Montgomery is just now bringing you home?" Mr. Flynn questioned her softly.

"Well, yes," Marcail continued, still unsuspectingly. "I got caught in the white-out yesterday, and as you know, the sky didn't clear until just a short time ago."

Since she was moving up the steps toward the door, Marcail again missed the men's faces. She called over her shoulder that the men could come inside out of the cold, but she didn't immediately notice when they failed to follow her or respond.

Once she was out of earshot, Alex spoke to Mr. Flynn, whose eyes were leveled on the younger man.

"You know better than to think what you're thinking, Stan."

"I realize that, Alex," he answered, his voice measured. "But have you given any thought as to how this is going to be received?"

"I've given it plenty of thought, but there wasn't much I could do. Maybe the board would feel better if you had found Miss Donovan's body frozen somewhere here in the woods, instead of healthy and completely innocent about what is going through your minds."

Mr. Flynn nodded, his expression pained, and Alex let his gaze wander to the other men. Most were very worried. One wore a smirk that Alex wanted to wipe off, and Rowie was clearly furious.

Marcail came back to her front door. When she could see that no one was going to come in, she thanked the men, closed the door, and restarted the fire in the stove. It briefly crossed her mind that the men were acting strangely, but within minutes her thoughts were on the late hour of the afternoon and how much she wanted to get done before bedtime.

# *twenty*

Alex had to turn his face away from the pain and confusion he saw in Marcail's eyes. He had not approached her at church for fear of making a bad situation worse, but the desire to sit next to her, put his arm around her, and tell her everything was going to be fine was overwhelming.

But telling her such a thing would be a lie. Everything was not going to be fine, at least not for a while. Alex knew with a dreaded certainty that in order to make things "right," Marcail was going to have to make some painful decisions. He missed every word of the sermon while he prayed for Willits' young schoolteacher.

❑ ❑ ❑

Marcail was cut to the quick when Allie Warren walked past her without a word. She knew her friend had seen her, but Marcail watched as Allie kept her face averted, even when she called a greeting to her.

It had taken half the morning, but the innocent Miss Donovan finally understood that this sudden, cold treatment from the people at church had to do with her spending a night at Dr. Montgomery's home. Her first reaction was shock, and then outrage at what they must have been thinking.

It didn't seem to matter that she'd have frozen to death if Alex hadn't rescued her. In the eyes of the towns-people, she had acted outside the bounds of propriety, and that was not to be tolerated. Feeling lonely and rejected, Marcail walked home from church alone. It was the first week she hadn't been asked to join one of the town's families for Sunday dinner.

She spent the day praying, overcoming her hurt, and working on her lessons for the following week. It was almost a relief to realize that she wouldn't have to see anyone but her students until the following Sunday. Marcail, who still did not grasp the severity of the situa-tion, hoped that everyone would be over their upset by then.

◻◻◻

Marcail looked into the uncertain faces of the six chil-dren in her class and wanted to cry. She had hovered around the door for an hour after she rang the bell, finally accepting the fact that most of the town's families were not going to send their children to school.

The Austins, Vespermans, and Whites had sent their children, and after Marcail directed them to read silently in their readers, she sat at her desk and decided what course of action to take.

First of all, she knew that the children who *had* come to school deserved her undivided attention as well as all the instruction she could offer them. Second, she would dismiss a little early and pay a visit to Mr. Flynn. Marcail, after coming to these conclusions, settled down to the teaching at hand.

◻◻◻

"Mr. Flynn, I would be happy to stand before Mrs. Duckworth and the entire school board and attest to the fact that Dr. Montgomery was the soul of propriety while I was in his home."

"I have no doubt that he was, Miss Donovan, but you've watched Mrs. Duckworth; you've seen the way she runs things in this town. You know that the hands of all the people whose buildings and businesses are owned by her are tied."

"In other words," Marcail spoke with a sinking feeling of dread as his words finally became clear to her, "you want my resignation?"

"I'm afraid I do." He spoke with visible regret. "I was coming to see you about it this afternoon."

"And if I refuse?" Marcail asked, telling herself not to cry.

"Then the majority of your class will not be receiving an education, because they will be kept out of school as they were today."

Marcail had thought the way Mr. Flynn's hands were tied concerning Sydney was awful, but this was atrocious. Her voice said as much when she spoke.

"And if I went to Mrs. Duckworth myself?"

"As before with Sydney, it would only make matters worse."

Marcail sat in silence for a moment. Mr. Flynn could only watch her. At length she stood.

"The word 'quit' has never been a part of my vocabulary, Mr. Flynn, and I don't care to add it now. I'm going to continue to teach at the Willits school whether there is one child in my class or 30. Maybe when the people in this town grow tired of having their lives dictated by one woman, they'll send their children to be taught. It's my hope that if enough of you take a stand, you can make a difference."

# *twenty-one*

Marcail's emotions were in tatters by the end of the week. She'd had only six children to teach and was beginning to regret everything she'd said to Mr. Flynn.

For the first time in her life she was honestly thinking of quitting. In fact, this idea pressed upon her so strongly she walked to the train station to check the schedule for southbound trains.

It was late Saturday afternoon, and even though she was low on flour, sugar, and coffee, she had not come into town for any other reason that day. She felt curious eyes on her as she walked, and nearly turned back home before reaching her destination.

The train station was very quiet at that time of the day. Feeling like a coward, Marcail walked toward the far side of the train office, knowing it would be even more deserted. She slipped around to the front of the office just long enough to read the departure times, and then quickly back to the far side of the building—and into the arms of Rowie Kilmer.

Marcail gasped in surprise and would have taken a step backward, but Rowie had a hold of her arm and drew her up close to the side of the small structure.

"It was all a lie, wasn't it?"

"What was?" Marcail's voice was breathless with fear and a little bit of pain.

"All your talk about teaching. All your denials about wanting to get married. They were all lies."

"No, Jethro, they weren't. I'd have frozen if Dr. Montgomery hadn't taken me in."

As usual, Rowie wasn't listening. "Wasn't I good enough for you? Didn't you think I could take care of you like he could?" His hand tightened on Marcail's arm, and she flinched. "You didn't do nothing but lie, telling me no and then giving favors to the doc in front of the whole town."

If Marcail could have moved she would have slapped him. She began to struggle, but he was so much stronger it did no good. A feeling of panic began to overtake her. She would have cried out, but again he tightened his hold and her cry turned into another gasp.

Marcail watched Rowie looking around as if he planned to drag her somewhere. With his attention momentarily diverted, she threw back her head to yell, but a voice stopped her.

"I might be mistaken, Rowie, but I believe you're hurting Miss Donovan."

Marcail and Rowie's heads turned sharply with surprise, and Marcail could have wept at the sight of Alex Montgomery. This time when Marcail pulled her arm, Rowie freed her. She walked on trembling legs toward the doctor.

"So that's the way it is between you two?" Rowie said with a shake of his head. "Well, you haven't let anyone know, so you can't blame a guy for thinking she's up for grabs."

Alex saw no point in arguing with him, even though he was sickened by Rowie's words about Marcail. It was hard to stay silent, but it helped to have Rowie leave as soon as he'd had his say. Alex looked at Marcail as the other man backed out of sight. She looked devastated. He felt her trembling as he took her arm and led her from the train station.

Marcail didn't speak as Alex led her to the livery. He claimed Kelsey and began the walk toward Marcail's house, leading the horse. When Marcail still hadn't spoken at the edge of town, Alex began to question her.

"Are you all right?"

"Yes." Marcail wasn't, but she didn't know how to begin telling him how much she hurt inside. And besides, he was a doctor of the body, not the heart.

Alex knew she was far from "all right," but he had no idea how to question her. She didn't thank him or even look at him as he opened her door and waited for her to go inside. He stepped in behind her.

"Will you be okay now?"

"Yes, thank-you" was the wooden reply.

Alex felt concerned over her lack of response. He reached out and touched her shoulder.

"Marcail, I'm going to come by in the morning. We need to talk."

"In the morning?"

"Yes, but right now I think you should get some rest."

She was finally looking at him.

"Did you hear me?"

Marcail nodded slightly.

"I'll be by in the morning before church."

Again she nodded, and Alex felt there was nothing more he could do. With a heavy heart he turned toward the door, praying that Marcail would get a good night's sleep.

# *twenty-two*

Alex was at Marcail's front door nearly three hours before church was scheduled to begin. She was up and dressed, her hair in place, but looking so pale Alex feared she might be ill. She greeted him soberly, and Alex thought she might be working hard at fighting the fear over why he was there.

"Would you like some coffee?" Marcail offered while Alex removed his coat.

He accepted the offer, taking a place at the kitchen table. He thought to kill some time before he asked Marcail something that was sure to upset her. But while he still had coffee in his mouth, Marcail spoke.

"I'm not really sure why you've come by this morning, Dr. Montgomery."

*So we're back to Dr. Montgomery*, Alex thought before he answered her question.

"I think we need to talk about what's happened in the last week," he told her quietly. "In fact, I have a question to ask you, maybe two." He paused until he was sure he had Marcail's full attention.

"Marcail, are you going to leave the teaching position here in Willits?"

Marcail did not understand immediately. She sat for long moments in quiet thought. When she did speak, her voice was soft and sure.

"No, I'm not. I've thought about nothing else all week, and I just can't leave these children. I might be sorry, and I might change my mind later, but right now I'm going to stay here and teach."

"Then I'll ask my second question." Alex cleared his throat. "Will you marry me?"

Marcail stared at him, completely nonplussed. Alex could see that he'd shocked her speechless, but he'd given this idea much thought and prayer in the last week, and he honestly believed it was the best course of action. He began to explain his position before Marcail could voice her thoughts.

"I'm not going to tell you that your decision to stay here is wrong, but I can tell you that it's not safe for you to remain single. I think Rowie proved that yesterday. And if you do stay single, you'll not have any children to teach."

Marcail looked crushed. "I thought that if I could only tough it out, that they would all send—"

Marcail stopped speaking as Alex slowly shook his head.

"Marcail," Alex implored her. "Try to understand Cordelia Duckworth. She has an impossibly strict code of morality; it's like a sickness with her. In her eyes you've sinned, and our marriage would make an honest woman of you."

"You can't really be telling me that my class is going to come back if I marry you?" Marcail's head was beginning to clear, and a myriad of questions buzzed through her mind.

"That is exactly what I'm telling you. I've lived in this town for seven years, and I know the way these people think. By little choice of their own, most of their lives revolve around Cordelia Duckworth. If she disapproves of you, you're finished."

Marcail came to her feet. Alex watched as she paced the small area in front of her stove.

"I've prayed so fervently that I would be a light to this town, and now my testimony here is ruined. In fact, by marrying you, I'm really saying that I do have something to be ashamed of."

"I'm sure some will see it that way, but they'll have the same opinion if you leave."

Marcail wished she could wake up from this nightmare. "I just want to teach school," she finally said, her hands spread wide in what might have been supplication.

"I realize that," Alex's voice was compassionate. "And you could do that in another town. But unless you're willing to be married, you're not going to teach in Willits."

Marcail began to pace again and then stepped to the window and looked out. *It would be so easy to run away*, she told herself. *I could pack my bag and go to Santa Rosa or Visalia; everyone in the family would understand. But I've always done that. I've always run to them for help, and this time I want to stand on my own. I want to show them that I've really grown up.*

*He makes it sound so simple. Just marry him and I can teach school. Marry him! I didn't think I'd be married for years. And he's a* doctor! *I'd be married to a doctor!*

Such were Marcail's thoughts for a good ten minutes as she stood before the window. Knowing how upsetting his offer had been, Alex remained silent.

Alex, on the other hand, found the idea of being married to Marcail nothing short of splendid. He knew that it wouldn't be easy at first, but Alex recognized that she wasn't a quitter, and neither was he. He truly believed they could make a go of it.

He was beginning to wonder how long he would have to wait for an answer when she suddenly turned and asked him when he'd come to know the Lord. He didn't really need to answer, because Marcail could tell by his very life that he was set apart. Many people in town attended church, but only a few, Alex included, were obviously sold out for God.

He answered her briefly, and since she shared her own testimony as soon as he was finished, she must have been satisfied. Marcail fell silent and again Alex waited, knowing that she was going to say yes, but obviously still struggling to accept it all.

"When were you thinking we would do this?" Marcail asked softly, as the immensity of the situation began to weigh upon her.

"This afternoon." Alex could see he had shocked her once again.

"This afternoon?"

"Yes. I thought we should go to church together and talk to Pastor Zimler right after the sermon. Word will be out by this evening, and your classroom will be full in the morning."

❑ ❑ ❑

*Your classroom will be full in the morning* had been Alex's exact words. Marcail couldn't help but wonder if he didn't feel a little used. She was standing in Dean and Kay Austin's bedroom collecting herself to become Mrs. Alexander Montgomery.

The morning had fairly flown by. She and Alex had attended church together, drawing speculative glances from every corner of the building. After the service they immediately approached Pastor Zimler about marrying them. He had seemed quite honored by the request and agreed immediately.

Marcail knew her father, before agreeing to anything, would have questioned them at length, as he did all couples seeking to be wed, but Pastor Zimler didn't seem to have a single reservation. Marcail wondered if he wasn't a little oblivious to all that was happening in his own town.

Dean and Kay Austin must have sensed something was afoot; they stayed at the rear of the church until Alex and Marcail were through with the minister. When Alex saw them and explained their decision, the Austins offered their home for the nuptials.

*It's not too late, Marcail*, she told herself. *If you want, you can walk out there and tell Alex that it won't work.* But as soon as the thought of never seeing Alex again formulated, Marcail felt something akin to grief.

*He's giving you a chance to repair the damage that's been done. And you know he must care for you to some degree or he would never have offered. You could leave, but it's time to grow up and face this problem!* Marcail's thoughts continued to run in all directions until someone knocked on the door.

"Come in," she called, and watched as Alex slipped into the room and shut the door. He came and stood directly in front of her.

"Change your mind?" he asked softly.

"I don't know," she answered honestly. "The situation is terribly overwhelming, Alex, but I'm terribly afraid that I could be making the biggest mistake of my life."

Alex reached with a gentle hand and smoothed the hair over Marcail's ear. His eyes were loving, as was his voice, when he spoke.

"I don't believe this will be a mistake, Marcail. It's true that we don't know each other, but I've prayed for a long time about another wife. And now you need to either leave town or take a husband. If you choose the latter, I'm more than willing to be that man."

It was one of the most precious things Marcail had ever had said to her. A peace settled over her as she looked into the kind eyes of this gentle stranger. Her expression was serene when she nodded her head. Alex took her hand within his own and led her out to stand before the preacher.

# *twenty-three*

Marcail Montgomery stood in the kitchen of the little house next to the school and knew that she would not be back, at least not to live. After leaving Austins, Alex had dropped her off so she could collect her things. Now she was ready and feeling just a bit bewildered over the events of the day. One hour ago she had married a near stranger.

Her mind moved abruptly to her brother, Sean, who had been forced into a marriage with his wife, Charlotte. When Marcail had first heard their story and seen the love that had grown between them, she thought it was the most romantic thing on earth. But in truth, this business of being married to a stranger was rather frightening.

A knock at the door interrupted Marcail's tempestuous thoughts. She hadn't heard Alex's horse, and not wanting to see anyone from town, she opened the door tentatively. Allie stood on the porch, her face a mask of pain. Marcail swung the door wide and as soon as it closed, the friends embraced.

"I'm sorry, Marcail. I'm so sorry." Allie was openly sobbing. "I feel just awful about last week, but Mama insisted I stay away." Allie sniffed, calmed somewhat, and then went on quietly.

"I told her you weren't guilty of anything, but she just kept saying I wasn't to have anything to do with you. We had a big fight just now, and I stormed out and came over here. My only regret is that I didn't do it a week ago."

"Oh, Allie—"

"Don't say it, Marcail," Allie cut her off. "Mama is in the wrong. If we've had a fight, it's our own fault not yours."

Marcail felt terrible, but stayed quiet. She watched as Allie suddenly noticed the table where her one bag sat, filled once again with her belongings. The shopping basket that Mr. Vesperman had given her, filled with the few food items she'd had on hand, was also on the table.

"Where are you going?" Allie asked, her eyes begging Marcail not to leave.

"Dr. Montgomery and I were married an hour ago. When he saw how impossible it was for me here, he offered his hand. He'll be here any minute to take me . . ." Marcail hesitated, "home."

Allie burst into tears all over again, and nothing Marcail could say would comfort her.

"This isn't what you want, Marcail," Allie wailed. "That old hag on the hill has forced you into this, and I know you'll just be miserable."

"I'm all right, Allie, really," Marcail tried to assure her. After a few moments the older girl calmed down enough to listen.

"Alex has been very kind, Allie, and I *agreed* to marry him. No one is forcing me. I'm sure it's going to be a little strange at first, but I'm trusting God to take care of me and the marriage."

Allie nodded, the misery on her face receding. Although she didn't agree with Marcail's belief that Jesus

Christ was God, she admired her for her faith and stamina. The young women continued to talk for a few minutes, and when Allie saw that Marcail was really all right, she said she had to be going. They planned to talk again soon, and the new Mrs. Montgomery saw her friend to the door.

Marcail, thinking Allie was alone, was surprised to find Seth Porter outside in the cold, waiting in a small buggy. He didn't seem put out; his warm smile and wave were genuine. He jumped easily to the ground to assist Allie with tender care into the small seat. As they drove away, Seth's arm around Allie, Marcail couldn't help but envy the obvious love between them.

❑ ❑ ❑

Alex walked out of the barn with Kelsey, wishing, not for the first time, that he owned a buggy. He had a feeling that Marcail would never complain, but he certainly wished he didn't have to take his bride home on the front of his horse.

As it turned out, Alex found himself wishing Marcail would complain, or at least say *something*. She was totally silent on the ride to the house. He hadn't expected her to share her life story the first evening, but her silence concerned him.

The reason didn't really occur to him until he saw her into the house. Then he noticed that she looked everywhere but the bedroom. He thought to bring up the subject of their sleeping arrangements after supper, but since his wife was obviously scared to death, he knew he'd have to mention it as soon as he got in from the barn.

❑ ❑ ❑

Marcail's view of Alex's house was vastly different this time—she knew it was now her home. Standing in the opening between the kitchen area and the living room, she looked her fill. Nothing had changed except herself.

At last Marcail forced herself to look toward the bedroom door. Her lower lip went unconsciously between her teeth. This was her wedding night, and she was terrified. Marcail and Kaitlin had talked on several occasions, and her older sister had assured her with complete confidence that there was nothing whatsoever to be afraid of when a husband and wife loved each other. It was glaringly evident at the moment, however, that Katie had never mentioned the possibility of the couple *not* loving each other.

Alexander returned to the house to find Marcail's face completely drained of color, and his bride biting on her lower lip as though she no longer had need of it.

"Marcail," Alex spoke her name and watched as she turned to him with wide, terrified eyes. That she'd been working herself into a fine state of panic was obvious.

"Marcail," he started again. "I don't feel there is any reason to rush anything. I mean, we both need some time to feel a little more comfortable with each other."

Marcail looked very surprised at this announcement. What she couldn't know was that the fear Alex saw on her face was enough to stop him in his tracks. The last thing he wanted was to scare her, and since she'd already been doing a fine job of that herself, he knew that his next words, although difficult, were necessary.

"I want you to take the bedroom, and I'll sleep out here on the sofa."

"Do you mean that?"

Alex nodded, seeing that he'd instantly freed her from a load of fear. He moved toward the bedroom, intending to clear some dresser drawers for her, but spun back on her softly spoken "No."

"I mean," Marcail explained to Alex's shocked countenance, "that you should stay in the bedroom and I'll take the sofa."

"No, I think—" Alex began to protest, but Marcail forestalled him.

"It's silly for you to be on a sofa that's obviously too small for you. I would fit very nicely, and I won't put you out of your bed."

Alex was shaking his head, and Marcail asked him a question that settled the entire argument.

"How well did you sleep on the sofa the night I was here?"

Alex opened his mouth and then shut it again. She was right, but he wanted to make her feel comfortable and at home, and he knew she would have less privacy in the living room.

Marcail could see she had won, and with a decisive nod of her head took her bag into the living room and set it next to the sofa.

# twenty-four

Marcail was up, dressed, and out of the house Monday morning before Alex stirred. It felt odd for her to wake up in his home, and Marcail, not knowing Alex's schedule, had been careful not to wake him. She skipped breakfast in order to be quiet, but she had packed some bread and two cookies for lunch.

As she moved toward the schoolhouse, Marcail skirted the sloppy areas of the road where the snow had melted into giant puddles. She prayed that her class would arrive as Alex predicted. Questions ran through her mind about what she would do if the children didn't show, but she prayed and gave her worry to God every time it reared its ugly head.

The stove was a bit stubborn, but Marcail was determined to ward off the chill in the air. The logs had finally lit when Alex walked in and joined her by the stove. Marcail felt herself blushing, although she didn't know why.

"Good morning." Alex's voice had that distinct early morning growl.

"Good morning."

"Do you always come to school this early?" he asked his new wife.

"Only on Mondays. The stove hasn't been lit all weekend, and I usually need a little more time."

"It didn't look as though you had any breakfast or even coffee. Were you afraid of waking me?"

Marcail looked uncomfortable. "I'll be all right, and I have some bread for lunch."

"Maybe we should sit down tonight and compare schedules. I like to get up early, and I never intended for you to walk all this way in the mud."

"Please don't feel like you need to give me a ride, Alex. I really didn't mind the walk."

Alex didn't reply right away. "I'll see you this afternoon. Have a good time with the kids today."

With that, Alex cupped Marcail's jaw in his long-fingered hand and placed a kiss on the tiny mole that sat at the corner of her mouth. He had kissed her the same way moments after they'd been pronounced husband and wife.

Alex didn't look back as he left or he'd have found his wife watching him, her lower lip tucked neatly between her teeth, and her finger on the spot he'd just kissed.

❑ ❑ ❑

It took most of the day for Marcail to really believe that her marriage had brought her students back to school. Her classroom was full, and other than a slight change in Sydney's disposition, things were as usual.

She told the children her new name and wrote it on the blackboard. Except for Sydney, very few children made mistakes with her new name as the day progressed. Marcail knew he wasn't even trying to call her by her married name.

It had never occurred to Marcail that the 11-year-old's infatuation with her would cause him to experience such violent jealousy, but it became suddenly evident with the way he grew angry when she gave special attention to any of the other boys. Now that she had married, he was becoming impossible.

Marcail was filled with compassion for the way he felt, but she knew she had to redevelop the respect they'd shared in weeks past. She decided to give him a few more days before she took him aside to insist that he call her Mrs. Montgomery.

The day flew by as Marcail knew it would, and just as she was dismissing the children, Alex came in the door. Most of her students greeted him cordially and by name. Marcail was amazed at how accepting they all seemed of the situation.

"I came by to give you a ride home," Alex offered. He knew he was staring, but Marcail appeared as fresh to him as she had been that morning, and he knew she'd just taught 19 children for seven hours.

"I appreciate the offer, but I was planning to walk into town. There are a number of things I—that is, *we*— need." It felt a little funny to be discussing this with Alex, but Marcail knew she was going to have to get used to it, and he didn't seem to notice her slip.

"All right," Alex agreed. "I'll walk with you, but then I need to return to the office. When you are finished, come by."

Marcail agreed and after gathering her things, preceded Alex out the door. They didn't talk much on the way into town, and Alex touched her arm by way of farewell when he left her at the door of the bank.

Marcail had to stand in line at the teller's window. She couldn't see around the tall man in front of her, but as soon as he moved, she was surprised to see that no one was there to help her. She waited only a moment before Mr. Flynn himself came from the rear of the bank.

"How are you, Mrs. Montgomery?" He hesitated over the name, but his eyes sought hers, begging her to understand his position.

"I'm doing very well, Mr. Flynn," Marcail told him graciously, even though she disagreed with the way he had handled things. She could see that her words lifted a burden of guilt from his shoulders, and he told her he would handle her transaction himself.

"I need three dollars from my account," Marcail explained. "And then I'd like you to close my account and move my money into Dr. Montgomery's account. I haven't checked with Alex, but is it all right to add my name to his account?"

"It's fine." Mr. Flynn's voice was hoarse, but Marcail didn't notice. For some reason, Marcail's request to join her funds to her husband's touched him deeply. His wife had told him she thought Miss Donovan was a very special young woman who deserved to be treated better than she was. Now he was convinced of it himself.

Marcail's next stop was Vesperman's General Store. She shopped carefully, thinking that she didn't really know Alex's tastes. Figuring she couldn't go wrong with the essentials, Marcail opted for flour, sugar, salt, soda, coffee, rice, and yeast. Her last item was a tin of salted peanuts. She knew it was an extravagance, but Marcail was in the mood to bake and knew these would be good in cookies.

The street was quite slushy, but Marcail took a long route to Alex's office and avoided most of the mud. She wasn't thrilled about being there, but with her hand on the door, she took a deep breath and went inside.

# *twenty-five*

Marcail stood very still and looked around the small waiting room without really seeing anything. Her heart thundered in her chest, and even though she told herself to calm down, fear gripped her. She tried to examine the reason for her anxiety, but as in the past, the only thing that came to mind was her mother's face.

It wasn't at all logical, but for so many years it seemed to Marcail that it was the doctor's fault her mother had died. They had been a happy, settled family. Then, when Marcail was nine, the doctor had come to see Mother. He hadn't caused her illness, but he had diagnosed it, and Marcail had struggled for years to believe that none of her mother's rapid decline had been his fault. To this day she was terrified of doctors and everything relating to them.

Maybe her sister hadn't handled the situation very well; maybe Kaitlin should have insisted that Marcail see a doctor when she was sick. But because the mere mention of a visit from this dreaded man was enough to make any condition Marcail had worse, Katie had never insisted she go. Instead Katie herself talked with the doctor to find out how to treat her. Thankfully, there had never been anything more serious than a bee sting or a spring cold.

Now she found herself not only standing in the Willits' doctor's office, but actually married to the doctor himself.

"Hi."

Marcail jumped at the sound of Alex's voice and wondered from where he had materialized.

"You looked lost in thought just then."

"I guess I was," Marcail answered as her gaze roamed the room. "I'm still getting used to the idea of being married to a doctor." Marcail didn't realize how that might have sounded until it was out of her mouth. Her gaze flew to Alex, but he was smiling.

"You're not easily offended, are you?" Marcail asked softly, more to herself than anyone else.

"No, I'm not," Alex answered, having heard her clearly. "As I said before, I like your honesty. Come, I'll take you home."

❏ ❏ ❏

As with the few times she had ridden with Alex, Marcail tried to make herself as comfortable as possible without leaning on her new husband. Alex, however, had clearly tired of her trying to put space between them. His chest and arms surrounded her as he held the reins in an easy hold. Marcail wasn't sure how she felt about this, but the ride was brief, and she wasn't forced to examine her feelings too closely.

Alex tied Kelsey at the door and walked his wife inside. Marcail put her basket on the table and was removing her coat when she noticed that the furniture had been rearranged.

The kitchen table was closer to the bedroom door than

it had been, and Marcail could not see the living room sofa from where she stood. She stepped into the living room and her eyes widened with surprise.

The small sofa was on another wall, giving Marcail's "bed" almost complete privacy from the kitchen area. One of the wardrobes had been moved from the bedroom along with a small chest of drawers. Alex had done a nice job of fitting in the added pieces to go with the tables, chair, and bookshelf. In short, he had given Marcail a very private area for sleeping and dressing.

"I put your blanket and pillow in the bottom of the wardrobe. That little dresser was in the barn, so you might want to wipe it out."

Marcail turned to the man who spoke softly behind her. "Thank you, Alex."

"You're welcome. I have to get back to the office, but I'll be home around 5:00."

He left then, and Marcail stood for a long time at the window watching him go. He was nothing whatever like she had imagined. What kind of man stepped in to rescue a woman in need and then rearranged his home to suit her when she was little more than a stranger?

No answers came to mind. Marcail knew that she could stand there all day and speculate, but that would accomplish nothing. With a determined stride she attacked her basket of groceries, putting everything away. She started supper, and then moved to the living room to settle her clothing in the dresser drawers and wardrobe.

The now-familiar headache was beginning, and Marcail had to stop herself from ripping the pins from her hair. Both she and Alex were swiftly losing all privacy, and Marcail couldn't dispel the feeling that she would be further embarrassed in front of Alex if he came home and her hair was down.

No one in Willits, save Allie and her mother, had ever seen her hair down, but Marcail knew that at least part of the reason for her maintaining the severe style lay elsewhere. She looked very young without the piles of thick hair atop her head.

But headache or no, there was work to be done, and Marcail set about her tasks. By the time Alex came in the door, supper was ready and Marcail's personal effects were all put away. They ate in companionable silence. After Alex helped with the dishes, he asked Marcail to come back to the table so they could discuss their schedules.

"Do you feel all right?" were the first words from Alex.

"Yes, I'm fine," Marcail answered him without thought.

What she didn't realize was that her pain showed on her face. Her forehead was slightly furrowed, and her eyes told Alex that she was tired, worried, or in some type of pain. He knew he couldn't push her, but he honestly wished she would tell him what was wrong.

Indeed, it was a good thing that Alex didn't push her, because Marcail wouldn't have known what he was talking about. Since she couldn't always take her hair down when she liked, her headaches had become a way of life with her. Had Alex pressed her, she'd have lost some of the ease she was beginning to feel around him.

"Now, about our schedules," Alex began, and they sat for over an hour comparing times and preferences for the weeks to come.

Alex's schedule was much more flexible, so he told Marcail he would be taking her to school and bringing her home each day, at least until the roads dried out.

They found that they both liked to go to bed at the same time and, with the exception of Saturday morning, got up within a half hour of each other. Marcail brought up the problem of disturbing Alex if she moved about in the kitchen. His response was a broad smile.

"If your banging around means that I get to wake up to a hot cup of coffee, you can bang all you want. At least I don't have to worry about waking you."

Marcail looked uncomfortable. "You know about that, do you?"

"Um hm. In fact, you scared me a little the night of the snowstorm. I kept checking your breathing to see if you were still with me."

"I sleep very soundly," Marcail explained unnecessarily.

"That, my sweet Marcail," Alex told her with a chuckle, "is a gross understatement."

Marcail couldn't help but smile in return. "My brother loves telling people how soundly Katie and I sleep. His favorite story is about the time he held me by my feet one night, my head nearly brushing the floor, and I slept through the whole thing."

"I can believe it. When I carried you to bed that night, I thought you would wake the moment I placed you against those cool sheets, but you only curled into a ball and slept the night away."

A faint blush began to cover Marcail's cheeks, and Alex's eyes sparkled impishly. "I have a sister who blushes as easily as you do, and I think I'd better warn you, my brothers and I tease the life out of her just to see it happen."

Alex shouted with laughter when Marcail's face became even redder. He watched as she bit her lip and sobered instantly.

"What does that worried look mean?"

"I've just never thought about meeting your family. I mean, I didn't realize you had a family." Marcail realized how silly that sounded as soon as she said it, but as she was coming to expect, Alex was amused.

"You must think that doctors crawl out from beneath rocks."

His words brought such a hysterical image to mind that a small laugh escaped Marcail before she could muffle it.

"So you think that's funny?" Alex tried to look indignant.

Marcail shook her head, but her eyes were brimming with laughter, and Alex would have been a fool to believe her.

"Well, you can laugh now, but I can tell you they'll show no mercy the first time they see those rosy cheeks."

Alex watched as Marcail suddenly grew very serious. It was on the tip of his tongue to ask what he'd said wrong when she spoke.

"Will they like me, Alex? I mean, your family. Will they be disappointed that you've married someone they don't know?"

"No." Alex's voice was now as serious as hers. "They'll love you the first time you meet. It's true that they're all a big bunch of jokers, but their hearts are warm and caring. You'll be taken into their hearts and lives as though you'd been there all along."

Marcail nodded, wanting so much to believe him, but still feeling uncertain. "How big is your family?"

"I'm the youngest of five. I have two brothers and two sisters. They're all married with children. My oldest sister and I are the only ones who live away from our hometown."

"And your folks—are they still living?"

"Yes, my father has been a doctor in Fort Bragg for years."

"Fort Bragg? That's out on the coast, isn't it?"

"Right. I think you'll like it when we get there. We have to take the logging train when we go, but once there, it's a great little place."

"Are we going soon?" Marcail asked tentatively, thinking it sounded like they were leaving in the morning.

"About ten days," Alex said with a wide-eyed look, realizing how presumptuous he'd been. "I always go home the weekend before my birthday. I just assumed you would go with me. I'm sorry I didn't check with you."

"Don't apologize. I'd like to meet your family; that is, if they really won't mind our being married and—"

Alex shook his head, and Marcail stopped.

"It's a long ride on the train, Marcail. I was wondering if you would have a problem with my asking Stan Flynn if you could have two days off?"

Marcail looked surprised, but didn't deny his request.

"I thought we would leave first thing Friday morning. That puts us in Fort Bragg in the afternoon, and I thought we'd come home on Monday."

"I don't have a problem with it. It would be a nice break, but I don't know how Mr. Flynn will feel." Marcail sounded as dubious as she felt.

"I'll talk to him. He knows he can be honest with me. Since I know he feels partly responsible for our being married, I somehow doubt he would deny us a little time away."

Marcail agreed, and they continued to talk for a while longer. She found out Alex's exact birthday and that he was going to be 31. With her birthday coming in March, it wasn't hard to figure that he was almost exactly 11 years older than she was. Marcail wasn't sure how she felt about that.

A half hour later it was heavenly for Marcail to finally take her hair down and crawl onto the sofa for the night.

As she fell asleep with a dull headache, Marcail wondered if she should try to explain to Alex about her hair. As she pictured herself trying to do just that, the image caused her to blush all over again. Marcail told herself she was going to have to suffer through the headaches.

# *twenty-six*

The next day Marcail sent a note home with Erin Vesperman in regard to Alex's birthday present. Marcail prayed that there would be enough time to order the new black leather satchel she'd spotted in one of Rigg's catalogs when she was home for Christmas. Why she'd been looking at the medical supplies, she wasn't sure, but she knew what she wanted and could only hope that Mr. Vesperman dealt with some of the same suppliers as Rigg.

Alex was a little late in claiming Marcail, but she had some work to do at the schoolhouse and didn't miss him. Their evening was much like the previous, with a quiet supper and talk across the table. Again, Marcail went to bed with a dull ache around her forehead, but as always, she slept soundly and woke up refreshed and ready to take on the day.

Alex had made the coffee that morning, and when Marcail was enjoying her second cup, he surprised her with a question.

"I don't want to put you on the spot, Marcail, but I was wondering—how do you feel about Dean and Kay Austin?"

"I think they're very nice." Marcail was a little taken aback by such a question.

Alex nodded. "The three of us have been meeting for Bible study on Wednesday nights for a long time, and I was wondering if you'd be interested."

"Alex," Marcail thought she understood, "you don't have to ask me. I know you have things you want to do that don't include me."

"That's just it—I *want* to include you. I want you to join us, but I don't want you to feel like you should."

"How do the Austins feel about my joining you?"

"Kay was in yesterday, making sure I planned on bringing you."

Marcail warmed with his words. It had seemed the majority of the town was against her. Then both Mary Vesperman and Cindy White had talked to her in the bank, telling her how much they appreciated her stand. And now knowing that the Austins wanted to include her in their Bible study meant more than Marcail could say.

"So you'll come?" Alex had seen the look of pleasure in her eyes.

"Yes, I'd love to."

"Great," Alex too was feeling very pleased himself. His Wednesday night study was important to him, both spiritually and emotionally, and he'd have definitely felt the void if Marcail had stayed home.

When Alex picked her up from school that afternoon, he surprised her with the news that Kay had asked them to supper that evening. He told Marcail when he would be back for her, and she took advantage of the time to do a little baking.

By the time Alex returned, Marcail was flushed from her baking efforts, but the cookie tin was full. Marcail also had a basket to go to the Austins.

"You've been busy," Alex commented with pleasure as his nose tested the air. "What is that I smell?"

"Probably the peanuts. I like cookies with peanuts in them."

Marcail held one out to her spouse and waited for the verdict. Her smile was triumphant at the look of rapture on his face.

"I take it you like them?"

Alex quickly schooled his features into a blasé mask. "They're pretty good, but it's hard to tell after just one. I'd better try another."

He started toward the basket, but Marcail neatly scooped it up with one hand and held it behind her back.

Alex's brows rose, along with the corners of his mouth, at her impertinence, and he came to stand very close to his wife. When Alex leaned very close and put his arms around her, Marcail began to wonder if she should have hidden the basket. He seemed to take an inordinate amount of time stealing a second cookie, and Marcail's face was a dull red by the time he finished.

Alex never took his eyes from his wife's face as he reached around her slight form and retrieved the cookie without ever touching her. As she watched him, Marcail had the sudden impression that Alex was not all that interested in the baked goods. The idea scared her a little and caused another emotion, one she could not define.

Alex kept his place by Marcail as he ate the second cookie, and did nothing this time to hide his pleasure.

"These are really excellent, did you know that?"

"I'm glad you came to that decision after only two; one more and you wouldn't want any supper."

"Now you sound like a teacher," Alex told her as he wiped the crumbs from his hands.

The smile Marcail gave him was brilliant. "I do, don't I?"

Alex only laughed, shook his head, and escorted his wife out the door.

❏ ❏ ❏

Kay Austin said little to the new Mrs. Montgomery when she first walked in the door. Not until they were in the kitchen, and alone, did Kay give any hint as to what was on her mind.

"Are you all right?" Kay asked the question while looking directly into Marcail's eyes, and Marcail suddenly felt tears stinging her own.

Marcail nodded a little. "Why do you ask?" she whispered.

Kay hugged her before answering. "Because there was not one bit of color in your face when you were here on Sunday to marry Alex. I know Alex well enough to know that he's a very gentle and compassionate person, but this can't have been easy for you. So tell me, are you really okay?"

"It doesn't seem real yet," Marcail admitted softly. "And you're right, Alex couldn't be more kind, but he's still—" Marcail hesitated.

"A stranger," Kay finished for her. Marcail nodded. The older woman reached out and gently squeezed Marcail's arm.

"You can talk to him about anything," Kay told her. "He's very understanding, and he's also a man who really strives to obey God every day of his life. I know he prayed about marrying you and believed it to be the best thing, or he never would have asked.

"Maybe you think I'm being too optimistic, but years ago my older sister Addie was widowed suddenly while she had four children under the age of five. So her children could eat, she married a near stranger three months later. She and Hank have had a wonderful life together. In fact, Hank is a lot like Alex, with his gentle ways and quiet humor. As hard as it must be for you to believe this, I really think that the two of you will make a go of it."

Her words did much for Marcail's spirits, and the evening proved to be both relaxing and refreshing. After supper, Marla and Daisy went off to bed, and the adults gathered around the kitchen table for the Bible study. As they studied in the book of James, Marcail found out in a hurry that Alex, Dean, and Kay were serious about knowing God better and dedicating their lives to His glory.

# twenty-seven

Alex had been in his office for two hours on Saturday morning before Marcail stirred from her sofa-bed. Sleeping in seemed almost decadent, but as tired as she'd been on Friday night, Marcail needed the extra rest.

There was cleaning to be done, clothes to be washed, and baking to be tackled. Alex had told Marcail he would not return until midafternoon, and Marcail took advantage of the privacy to bathe and wash her hair. She luxuriated in the water a little longer than she should have, but it felt so soothing that after scrubbing every inch of herself, she just wanted to relax.

Fifteen minutes later, Marcail was dressed in her undergarments and looking over her dresses. They all needed to be washed, but she wouldn't have anything to wear if she got all three of her dresses wet. She wished she'd brought a couple of work dresses from Kaitlin's until she suddenly remembered the several dresses hanging on the far end of her wardrobe. Marcail opened the second door, something she hadn't needed to do as yet.

Marcail had given little thought to the previous Mrs. Montgomery, but now as her hand went to the fabric of the dresses, her mind began to wander. What had she been like, and how much did Alex miss her? How long had she been gone? Did Alex know where she was spending eternity? And many more questions.

There were five print dresses and two solids. Marcail looked with some envy at the bright calico and gingham cloth, and then noticed the sleeve of the blue gingham was torn. Marcail pulled this dress out and saw in an instant that it was different from the rest. It was faded and the top button was missing. Marcail knew by looking at the other gowns that this one was a wash-day dress.

Without giving herself much time to think, Marcail pulled the dress over her head. It had barely settled on her shoulders before one of Marcail's questions regarding Alex's first wife was answered—the dress was huge on her. Marcail suddenly remembered the nightgown Alex had given her the night they'd been snowed in, and wondered how she could have forgotten.

"Well, Marcail, what are you going to do?" the small brunette asked herself as she looked down at the way the dress hung on her frame. She knew she was wasting valuable time thinking about how she looked when her only plans were to wash and clean. Marcail swiftly buttoned the front that bagged enough to hold another person, and rolled up the sleeves that hung past her fingertips.

Her hair was still very wet, so after pulling the heavy tresses away from her face with a comb, she let the back hang free and went to work.

❑ ❑ ❑

Alex was glad to leave the office for the day. He knew the bell could ring at any time, but he was looking forward to seeing Marcail and was anxious to discover how she had spent her day. It was incredible how often she was on his mind. After stabling Kelsey, Alex's step was swift to the front door.

Marcail had just taken two loaves of bread from the oven when the door opened. Thinking she'd heard Kelsey's hooves, she wasn't at all surprised when Alex walked in the door.

"Hello," Alex spoke as he hung his coat. Still wearing the workdress, Marcail was standing near the stove, bending over a pan of cookies. She missed the way he turned with a ready smile that died abruptly on his lips.

"Hi." Marcail spoke without turning. "I'm just about to put these cookies in so you'll have some dessert to eat after your lunch. You must be hungry, since you—"

Marcail didn't finish the sentence. She'd finally turned to find Alex staring at her, his face holding an expression she'd never seen before. They stood in silence for a moment, and then Marcail watched his gaze slide over her dress. A sinking feeling settled around her heart.

"I'm sorry about the dress, Alex," she said softly. "I wanted to wash all my dresses and just acted without thought. I should have checked with you before wearing one of your wife's dresses. Please forgive me. I won't do it again." Marcail could tell she was babbling, but he seemed so pensive.

"I never thought of Linette as being big," Alex finally said, "but that dress swallows you."

"I'll change just as soon as something is dry."

Alex shook his head and smiled. "There's no need. You should wear them if you can. As you said, they are my wife's dresses, and you're my wife."

Marcail nodded, but because he was still watching her, she was not convinced.

"I wouldn't have believed that you were hiding so much hair in that bun you wear." Alex's eyes took in the way her hair, so black it was almost blue, hung to her hips, each strand falling in a glossy wave and curling of its own accord at the end.

"I'll put it up," Marcail spoke, unable to keep the disappointment from her voice. It was the first time in days she didn't have a headache. She turned to find her box of pins.

"Don't pin it up on my account. I like your hair down."

Marcail turned back, afraid to believe what she'd heard. "You don't mind my wearing it down?"

"Not at all." Alex's voice was matter-of-fact.

"And you don't think I look 16?"

Alex smiled. "Sixteen," Alex let out a slow whistle. "That would make you roughly half my age, and that scares me a little. Right at the moment, you look like a girl playing house in her mother's dress, but no, Marcail, you do not look 16 with your hair down."

Marcail's relief was so obvious that Alex smiled again and wondered for an instant why she wore it up if she didn't want to. When she continued to smile, he wondered if she would still be smiling if she knew how much he wanted to hold her, letting her fill his arms the way she already filled his heart, or if she knew how badly he wanted a real marriage, and not just a marriage of convenience to salvage her testimony before the townspeople.

As he constantly did these days, Alex prayed for patience. He believed that if he could just give this woman time, court her, and tenderly care for her, they would someday have a marriage in every sense of the word.

That Marcail was unaware of his thoughts was obvious in the way she went about her business in the kitchen as though they'd been married for years. Alex silently congratulated himself for keeping the emotions he felt from showing on his face.

"How did things go at your office today?" Marcail asked as she poured Alex a second cup of coffee.

Alex was so surprised by the question that he didn't answer for a moment. He realized then that no one in Willits ever asked him that question. Linette had been burdened with a weak stomach and never wanted to talk about his work. His parents checked with him on a regular basis and nearly picked his brain dry when he went home, but that was only a few times a year. Alex suddenly recognized that he'd been lonely before Marcail, and that he'd missed someone taking a personal interest in his work.

"Things were fine. Saturday mornings are usually pretty hectic, but today was quiet. I was able to restock my bag, so if I'm called out, I'll be all set. Oh," Alex said abruptly, "I made some lotion for one of my patients who suffers with dry skin. I added some fragrance after filling her bottle and brought you some."

Alex went to where his coat hung by the door and returned to hand Marcail a glass bottle filled with a thick yellow fluid. Marcail pulled the cork and inhaled the fragrance. It smelled like summer flowers, and she smiled as she held the bottle beneath her nose.

Alex watched as she rubbed a small amount on her arm. That she was more than pleased with the gift gave him tremendous satisfaction. Acting as though he'd given her a diamond instead of a small bottle of perfumed lotion, Marcail thanked him in her soft voice.

In that instant Alex wondered what type of home she'd grown up in, where she had obtained such an appreciation for small things. His thoughts made him realize, not for the first time, how little he knew about his wife.

# twenty-eight

The rest of Saturday flew by in a buzz of activities. Alex was not called away, so he chopped wood and worked in the barn. Marcail finished the baking and worked on her school lessons for the following week. At one point Alex came in to find Marcail standing on a chair, putting dishes away.

Before she could take another breath, he was taking the dishes back down, and telling her he was going to lower the shelf. Marcail tried to explain that she didn't mind using the chair, but he had become a man with a mission and didn't even answer her. When she saw how determined he was, she worked with him for a time, but as he began to pull the shelf from the wall, nails creaking and dust flying, she moved into the living room to get out of his way.

By the time Marcail was ready to start supper preparation, the shelf and dishes were back in place, and she went to work on the evening meal. Alex washed up and helped her. In no time at all, they had put a filling meal on the table.

As the evening progressed, Alex noticed that Marcail was more animated than he'd ever seen her. He wondered how stressful it was for her to teach. On the other evenings they'd spent together, she'd been communicative but not enthusiastic. He then pondered if her bubbly mood had anything to do with the lotion he'd brought. He told himself with an inner smile that if this was the effect he could expect, he'd bring her a different bottle every night.

Alex took a bath in his bedroom after supper. Marcail helped him heat the water, and then to give him as much privacy as she could she took herself off to the living room to a book she was reading. An hour later, when Alex was still behind closed doors, Marcail decided to get ready for bed, telling herself she could use the extra sleep.

❑ ❑ ❑

Alex took an unusually long time with his bath that night, but not because he was overly dusty or wanted to put space between him and Marcail. Once away from Marcail, he found his mind trying to work through the puzzle of the change in her that night. His mind lingered on the fact that she hadn't taught school that day, but then he put that idea aside. Marcail never seemed beaten down or tired when he picked her up in the afternoon.

Alex dried off and sat on the edge of the bed. He let his mind see her as she'd been when he'd come home from work—bent over the stove, looking adorable in that huge dress, her hair falling in thick waves down her back.

Her hair! Alex realized with a start. He jumped up, pulled on his pants, and opened the door as he slipped into his shirt.

"Marcail," he called before rounding the corner into the living room.

"Yes?"

"May I come into the living room? I need to ask you something."

"Sure," Marcail answered from her place on the sofa. She was already in her nightgown and robe, but was sitting on the sofa with her Bible. She watched as Alex came in and sat beside her, even though the sofa was already made up for the night.

Alex had not carried his lantern from the bedroom, and Marcail's was turned rather low. Alex reached and increased the flame before he spoke.

"I need to ask you about your hair," Alex began, watching her face closely in the lamplight.

"My hair?"

"Yes. Does it give you a headache to put your hair up?" Alex came straight to the point, and Marcail blinked at him.

"Yes it does, but how did you know that?"

"Because every other evening you've seemed to be upset about something or in some type of pain. And tonight you weren't, so I figured either your job is very stressful or you get headaches from putting all of this on top of your head."

Alex's hand came out and brushed back the locks that had fallen over her left shoulder. "Marcail," Alex continued, "why do you wear your hair up if it hurts you?"

Marcail was surprised he didn't know the answer. "It's part of my contract with the school," Marcail explained softly. "I must wear my hair up at all times."

Alex was stunned. *What a bizarre rule*, he thought incredulously. The next instant he realized why she always wore such dark clothing.

"Your dresses, I should say the *dark color* of your dresses— are they a part of the contract too?"

Marcail nodded, and Alex could only look at her. He asked himself just how badly he wanted to take on the Willits school board.

"If you're thinking of going to Mr. Flynn, please don't." Marcail had accurately read his mind. "I've learned to live with the situation, and I knew the terms of the contract before I signed it."

"So before you taught here, you would normally wear your hair up, and just live with the pain?" Alex just barely managed to keep the speculation from his voice.

"No, not exactly. I seldom had occasion to wear my hair up, and when I *would* get a headache, I didn't relate it to my hairstyle. Such a thing never occurred to me until I moved here."

"So you didn't actually know it would be a problem?"

"No, I guess I didn't."

"Before we were married, did you go home each day and take your hair down?"

"Most days, yes. As long as I knew I was home for the day."

"Did that help?"

"Yes. I mean, I would still get a headache, but it would be gone before bed."

It occurred to Alex that they could cut her hair, but the thought made him cringe, and he mentally shook his head no.

"You need to come home each day and take your hair down. Lie down if that will help. If you find that still doesn't alleviate the pain, then we'll have to think of another solution."

Marcail didn't reply. She was again thinking how different he was from her original view of him, and that most of the time she didn't even remember his title of "doctor."

"You're looking rather pensive," Alex commented softly. "Want to share?"

Marcail gave a small shrug. "You're just different than I first thought."

"Good different, or bad different?"

"Good."

Alex nodded, feeling satisfied and thinking absently how lovely she looked in the lantern light. "Have you started to *feel* married yet?"

"Not yet. I mean, I wrote my family and all, but even after seeing it on paper it's still pretty unreal in my heart."

"Would it help if I kissed you good night, or would that scare you?"

Marcail hesitated.

"You can be honest," Alex encouraged her.

"I think right now it would scare me, but I'm afraid if I say no, you'll never offer again." Marcail could hardly believe she'd been so open with her feelings.

Alex was thrilled with her answer and chuckled softly as he left his place on the sofa and stood before his wife. The sound of his laugh, as well as the way he stood looking at her, sent a chill down Marcail's spine.

"Make no mistake, Marcail, I *will* offer again—I will *definitely* offer again."

Marcail sat very still as he turned and moved on bare feet out of the room. She had wanted to get some extra sleep, but as it was, it took some time before she found her rest.

# *twenty-nine*

Marcail, usually a morning person, exercised great effort to haul herself from the sofa the next morning. Her nose lifted toward the smell of coffee coming from the direction of the kitchen, and almost of their own volition her feet moved to the table. She sat in a kitchen chair, yawning and looking very fuzzy around the edges.

Alex, having been up for nearly an hour, placed a mug of hot coffee in front of her, took a chair opposite, and worked at not laughing. He'd never seen Marcail this way—without her robe, her hair a disaster, and struggling to focus on the cup before her. Alex realized then that he'd never seen her anything but cheerful in the morning. He wondered which Marcail he liked best.

"Good morning," Alex finally spoke when she looked a little more lucid.

"Good morning." Marcail attempted a sleepy smile. "I can't seem to wake up this morning." Alex watched as she took another sip of coffee, propped her elbow on the table, and leaned her chin into her palm.

"Did you sleep well?"

"Once I got to sleep, yes."

Alex was tempted to ask if his question and their

discussion the night before had upset her, but he kept his thoughts to himself.

"How did you sleep?" Marcail said without blinking as she stared at some spot over his right shoulder. Alex wondered if she was headed back to sleep.

"Fine." This time he could not keep the laughter from his voice. Marcail, even in her sleepy state, noticed.

"You're laughing at me."

"You're right," Alex chuckled.

"If you keep it up, I'm going to go back to bed."

"If you do that, we'll be late for church."

Marcail sat up straight, sobering instantly. "I'd completely forgotten it was Sunday." Marcail, who never gave up or hid from any task, was tempted for the first time to tell Alex she was not up to going.

"This first Sunday will be the hardest." Alex accurately guessed her thoughts. "And don't forget that families like the Austins, Vespermans, and Whites will be there. You'll also see Allie, who has shown you her loyalty."

Marcail nodded, trying to convince herself of his words. "Are you not at all bothered about going this morning?" For some reason she had to know.

"Not for myself," Alex told her simply.

His real thoughts, thoughts of protecting her no matter what, stayed quiet within him. He knew that if anyone so much as looked at her cross-eyed, he'd champion her like a mother with a hurting child.

Alex rose from the table to start breakfast, all the time wondering if anyone in town knew what a sacrifice she'd made. She had been threatened, humiliated, frightened, rejected, and nearly forced into marriage so she could stay in town, teach the children, and possibly tell someone of Christ's love.

Alex didn't for one instant fault her motives or feel used. In fact, he agreed with her and praised God that she consented to marry him. But part of him wanted people to praise her, to understand her commitment and love for the children, and to put her on a pedestal because of it.

Then Alex's thoughts went to Jesus Christ and His life on earth. No man was more misunderstood, no man had suffered more humiliation and rejection than He had. The "pedestal" He was put upon was a cross, to die for sins He could not possibly have committed.

Alex glanced back at the table to where Marcail still sat. She'd retrieved her Bible and sat reading quietly. He might be able to share his thoughts with her someday, but for now, he prayed. He knew God would show her in His special way that she'd done the right thing, and that He was going to honor her obedience.

❑ ❑ ❑

By the time church was over, Marcail was convinced that rejection would have been easier to take than everyone's self-satisfied looks over their belief that she was no longer a "fallen woman." It was enough to make Marcail's blood boil, and she tried hard to keep her emotions in check.

They were eating lunch at Austins when Kay noticed Marcail was about to explode. Intending to give Marcail and Alex some time alone, she sent the girls on an errand after the meal.

"Talk to me, Marcail," Alex said as soon as he'd shut the parlor door.

"Two women I don't even know actually offered to have the party at their house when our baby is born!"

Alex was not at all surprised. He'd tried to keep her at

his side as much as possible, but it seemed the people at church were determined to separate them.

"Honestly!" Marcail continued. "It was almost easier to take the cold shoulders I received last week than those ridiculous, speculative glances on the faces of certain people."

He was silent as he watched her flushed face. Marcail stood shaking in the middle of the room, her arms crossed over her chest and one small-booted foot tapping an angry tattoo on the rug.

A few minutes of silence followed, and then Alex watched as Marcail's shoulders slumped. She moved to the sofa and sat down heavily. Her body was still now, her hands limp in her lap, her foot motionless. Alex joined her on the sofa. She turned her head slightly away from him, but not before he'd seen the tears gathering in her eyes. He waited for her to bury her face in her hands and sob loudly, as his first wife had done so many times, but it was not to happen.

Alex watched her profile in fascination as silent tears streamed down her cheek. Marcail turned back to look at him, the tears still flowing. Not even when she spoke did she sound like she was crying, just slightly out of breath. It was the most heartbreaking thing Alex had ever witnessed.

"I know it's my pride, Alex; that's all it is. But I feel so hurt, so wounded that everyone believes the worst of me."

Alex put his arms around her, and Marcail allowed herself to be pulled against his chest. An occasional shudder ran over her frame, but other than the hot tears seeping through the fabric of his shirt, he'd have never known she was crying.

"Can you hear me?" he said softly after some minutes.

Marcial nodded against his chest, but did not lift her head.

"It's going to take some time, but everyone will soon be used to our being married, and no one will think any more of it. I'm sure some of the older women in town think this is all very romantic. In their own clumsy way, they're trying to show you support."

Marcail raised her head to look at him. Alex, still one arm around her, gently wiped the tears from her face with his free hand. The action made Marcail feel cherished. He looked down at her with tender eyes, and Marcail found herself wanting to cling to him.

"You're not embarrassed about our marriage, are you, Alex?" The thought had just occurred to her, and her voice held a hint of wonder.

"What a silly question," Alex spoke softly and pressed a kiss to her forehead.

*I like you, Alex*, Marcail thought to herself. *I like you a lot.*

"Are you going to be all right?" Alex spoke into her thoughts, his voice warm and caring.

"Yes," Marcail answered, thinking his arms felt wonderful. "Thanks to you, I think I'm going to be fine."

Her words gave Alex a very satisfied feeling, although neither one spoke again for some time. The girls eventually came back, and the Montgomery family was joined by Dean, Kay, and the girls. The remainder of the afternoon was spent in good fellowship and fun.

# *thirty*

Marcail stood across the kitchen from her husband, her entire being radiating frustration. It was Friday morning, and they were leaving for Fort Bragg in just an hour. They were also having their first verbal disagreement.

It had started ten minutes earlier while they were still getting ready to go. Alex noticed Marcail was putting up her hair. He questioned her, and the argument ensued.

"Marcail, I don't think you should put your hair up for the train ride."

"I admit it would be more comfortable down, but I don't really have a choice."

"I disagree. If you just put your coat on, and keep your hair inside, it will never be noticed."

Marcail stared at him in amazement.

"Or," he continued, "you could put your hair up now and take it down as soon as the train leaves town."

"I will not take my hair down on the train." Marcail's voice was adamant.

Alex figured as much, but at this point he was willing to try anything to save her from a headache, including the risk of angering her.

"Well, I will not have you suffering with a headache all

day," Alex told her without force. "Now I could ask you, and then leave the choice to you, but I'm not going to do that. I *do not* want you to wear your hair up today."

Marcail opened her mouth and closed it again. He had not raised his voice an octave or made her feel at all threatened, but she suddenly knew that every one of Dr. Montgomery's patients took their medicine when they were told. Still, everything inside of Marcail balked at the idea. Her chin rose a notch.

"And if I put my hair up anyway?"

"I'll take the pins out on the ride into town," Alex stated quietly, feeling pain for having to argue with her.

"Marcail." Alex's voice had not changed, but this time his words got through to her. "I have no desire to start our trip with an argument, nor do I wish to deceive anyone in town, but your headaches concern me. We *are* leaving town, so no one will be offended."

Alex had thought to have this discussion with her on Wednesday before Bible study. He knew she would want to keep her hair up even though they would be going to and from the Austins after dark. But Alex had been called out, and Marcail had stayed home.

"Did you figure I'd wear my hair down the entire weekend in Fort Bragg?"

"Yes, I did. I rather thought you'd enjoy the change."

*I would enjoy the change*, Marcail thought. *I'm just being stubborn because I don't like being ordered around.*

Marcail was on the verge of telling Alex her thoughts when he disappeared into the bedroom, giving her time alone. She stood for a moment in indecision, and then continued with her packing, leaving the pins behind. She figured she would have hours on the train to apologize and explain.

❑ ❑ ❑

The scene from the train window on the way to Fort Bragg provided one surprise after another. The tracks wound their way west through hills and valleys, forests and plains. Alex and Marcail rode for the first hour in silence, just content to take in the scenery.

"Still mad at me?" Alex was the first to break the silence, and Marcail turned from the panorama to face him.

"I don't know if I was actually mad, but I was frustrated. There are times I don't like to be ordered around."

"I'm afraid I didn't handle it very well. Maybe it comes from being a doctor, but I can't stand to see suffering. We both know how miserable you'd be at the end of the line if your hair was up."

"I don't need to be so obstinate," Marcail admitted and then suddenly smiled, "but up to now, I believed that all the dictators were in other countries."

*"Dictator?"* Alex tried to sound outraged, but there was laughter in his voice.

Marcail laughed with him, and then watched his face turn serious. "I know this will seem like an abrupt change of subject, but there's been no opportunity for me to talk to you about my folks."

"Your folks?"

"Right. Their situation is a bit unusual, and I want to prepare you as much as I can." Alex searched his wife's face and then began his story. "My mother is completely bedridden. She has been since I was little more than a baby. I was too young to remember what happened, but they tell me she fell from a small ladder and injured her spine. My father found her almost immediately, but even though several specialists came to see her, they said nothing could be done. She has no use of her legs at all, and at times her arms grow numb and she can't move them."

"Does she ever get out of bed?" Marcail's face mirrored her compassion.

"No. She's propped against the headboard of the bed for most of the day, but she never gets up."

Alex fell silent for a moment, and Marcail's mind ran with images of a woman being bedridden for 30 years. "How does she do it?" Marcail finally whispered.

Alex smiled before answering. "She lets God use her right where she is. In fact, you won't be able to spend more than 30 minutes with her before she praises Him for her condition. She writes about ten letters a day, and she knows if she wasn't in that bed, she would never have been a letter writer."

"Letters to whom?"

"People all over the world who have heard about her or come to the house to meet her. She never talks about herself, but writes Scripture and words of encouragement to those who hurt or have not yet found the Lord."

"She sounds wonderful. How does your father handle all of this?"

"He tells people she's the light of his life," Alex told her with a tender gleam in his eye. "He teases her about never going dancing with him, but when we get there you'll see how well they manage. Their bedroom is on the first floor and set up with all the conveniences. Dad takes all his meals with Mother, and they sleep in the same bed every night."

"Is there someone who comes in to be with her during the day?"

"Yes, her name is Ida, and she's been coming for years. She cleans and prepares supper every afternoon."

"What about mornings?"

"Well, mother usually sleeps late, and she has Danny."

"One of your brothers?"

Alex chuckled at the thought. "No, Danny is a dog—a big dog. You'll meet him as soon as we get to the house. He's huge, but there isn't a vicious bone in his body, so don't let him scare you."

Alex fell silent once again and let Marcail have her thoughts. Alex's parents did indeed sound wonderful. It suddenly became clear why he was a thoughtful, caring person—he'd learned from godly people. Marcail's mind moved to his siblings.

"Tell me about the rest of your family."

"I think I told you I'm the youngest of five." Marcail nodded and Alex went on, "the oldest is my sister Dorothy, she's 39 and doesn't live in Fort Bragg. She's married to a man named Stan Crandall, and they live in Eureka with their four kids.

"My brother Skip is 37, and is actually named after my father, Samuel. He has three children, Amber, Jess, and Cole, and his wife is Judith."

"Do they live in Fort Bragg?"

"Yes, he shares the medical practice with my father."

Nodding, Marcail understood for the first time how her sister-in-law, Charlotte Donovan, felt when she was new to the family and trying to place everyone.

"Susan is in the middle at 36. Her husband is Jeremy Grey. They have four kids, Price, Nellie, Madeline, and Stuart. Jeremy's family owns and operates the bank, so he and Sue live right in town. My folks' house, which is also my dad's office, is at the edge of town."

"Who's next?" Marcail asked, hoping she could keep it all straight.

"Quinn, who just turned 34. His wife is Hannah, and their kids are Cindy and Derek."

"What does Quinn do for a living?"

"He's a logger."

"You didn't tell me the names of Dorothy's children."

"No, I didn't. You won't meet them this trip, and I figured you'd have enough to keep straight."

"That's true. What do I call your folks?"

"Well, they'd love to hear Mother and Dad, but something tells me you wouldn't be comfortable with that. Don't hesitate to call them Samuel and Helen; Judith always does."

"Is she the one who blushes?"

"No, that's my sister Sue." Alex chuckled at the thought.

"I can tell I'm going to spend the entire weekend lit up like a candle," Marcail commented without humor. Alex laughed, his eyes lit mischievously as he watched her.

In fact, he was still smiling impishly when Marcail reached into her bag for the lunch she'd packed. He sobered up when she threatened to eat his lunch. Marcail knew without a doubt that the weekend would be anything but boring.

# *thirty-one*

Marcail could smell the ocean even before she disembarked from the train. Her nose lifted as her feet hit the platform, and her eyes closed in bliss as she inhaled the smell of her childhood. A cold wind tugged at her coat and hair, but Marcail took no notice.

Alex came from behind and bumped her with the bags. The feel of the bags hitting the back of her legs and Alex's quick apology were enough to break the reverie. She turned to ask him the direction of his home, but she saw that his nose was raised, and he was sporting the same look of pleasure she'd just experienced.

Marcail watched him until he opened his eyes and noticed her scrutiny. He smiled without embarrassment, and Marcail grinned back at him.

"Is it good to be home?" she asked softly.

"Immensely! Come on, Marc," Alex used her nickname for the first time. "I'll take you home to Mother."

❑ ❑ ❑

The Montgomery house was a large structure that appeared to have been added to over the years. The central house was two stories, with wings on three of the four sides.

Alex walked directly in the front door without knocking, and Marcail followed. He moved with purpose through a spacious living room, set their bags by the long sofa, took Marcail's hand, and led her to a door at the end of the room.

Marcail had envisioned someone rather sickly, but the woman waiting in bed to meet her looked the picture of health with her sparkling blue eyes and warm smile.

No words were spoken as Marcail approached the bed. Helen, immediately noticing the hesitant smile of her new daughter-in-law, reached to hug her. Marcail couldn't help but respond to the love she saw there and went willingly into her embrace. When Helen released her, she patted the bed and Marcail sat down. Again the room was silent as Helen looked at the exquisite features of Marcail's face. She then turned to Alex.

"You didn't tell us that she has the face of an angel."

Alex's smile nearly stretched off his face as he saw Marcail blush. He leaned from the far side of the bed to kiss his mother's cheek.

"Hello, Mother."

"Hello, dear. Happy birthday, a few days early."

"Thank you," Alex replied with a twinkle in his eye. "And now if you'll permit me, I'll make the introductions. Mother, this is my wife, Marcail. Marcail, this is my mother, Helen Montgomery."

"Marcail." Helen spoke the name softly. "We've been mispronouncing it."

"With a soft *c?*" Alex wanted to know.

"Yes."

"I think that's the norm, especially if a person sees the name before they hear it."

Alex and his mother went on talking for the next few minutes. Marcail's attention began to wander around the room, and she found it as well equipped as Alex had described. The bed was spacious, with a lovely head-board and footboard. There was a small dining table with four chairs, and a small sofa, much like the one in Alex's living room. The room even boasted its own little pot-bellied stove.

Marcail's gaze moved past the stove and then shot back when she spotted a dog lying next to it. At least she thought it was a dog. It was big enough to be a small horse. Marcail was unaware of the way both Alex and Helen had stopped to watch her. Marcail's eyes were like dinner plates, and her mouth opened but no words came out.

"Come here, Danny," Helen finally spoke.

The enormous dog responded immediately, and as he slowly approached, Marcail moved back on the bed until she was against the footboard. Alex's arms seemed to come out of nowhere, and Marcail relaxed when she felt them.

"He won't hurt you," he said softly in her ear, and Marcail let her head fall back against his shoulder. She couldn't believe how good it felt to have him touch her. It wasn't that his family frightened her, but everything here was new and strange, and the feel of his arms was as secure as the feel of walking in the front door of her own home.

Danny came forward on Alex's command, and Marcail reached out to pet him. His entire back end moved in ecstacy over that attention, and Marcail knew in an instant that Danny was as gentle as Alex declared.

After a few moments Helen sent Danny to get Ida, something he'd been trained as a puppy to do. The housekeeper brought a light snack that was enjoyed by all, including Danny. Time seemed to race by, and Marcail was surprised when Alex said it was after 5:00 and he wanted to take her upstairs to get settled before going to meet his father and brother. Following Alex's lead, Marcail kissed Helen as they left the room. Alex reminded his mother they'd be back soon.

Alex and Marcail didn't see the smile that passed between Ida and Helen on their exit. Both women were thinking the same thought—their precious Alex had found a jewel.

# *thirty-two*

Alex and Marcail had not reached the stairs before his father and oldest brother, Skip, came from their shared office to meet Marcail. Their smiles were warm and their hugs strong as they welcomed this "petite Montgomery," as Skip instantly called her.

Some moments went by before the Montgomery men turned their attention to Alex to congratulate him and wish him an early birthday greeting. Suddenly, and without hint of a noisy arrival, the house was converged upon by Montgomerys. In the space of a few seconds Marcail and Alex were separated, and Marcail was left alone to meet the rest of the family—one more brother, two sisters-in-law, one sister, one brother-in-law, and nine nieces and nephews.

Their welcome of her was exuberant, and Marcail was looking very pleased, if not slightly overwhelmed, when Alex finally made his way back to her side for the next 20 minutes.

All the families had brought food to eat, and a meal was in preparation when Alex led Marcail from the room. He headed her up the stairs, their bags once again in hand. In the hallway at the top of the stairs, Marcail finally spoke.

"I need to go down and help with supper."

Alex continued to usher her along. "They have all the hands they need. You haven't had a moment to yourself since we arrived. I think you should get settled in our room."

Marcail was escorted into a large, immaculate bedroom. The inviting room was tastefully decorated, but Marcail's attention was riveted to the wall opposite the door. The wall displayed the headboard of a solitary, full-sized bed. Marcail walked slowly into the room and stood at the footboard. She heard the door shut behind her, but she stood still, certain she could not face Alex just now.

"Look at me, Marc," Alex commanded softly.

Marcail hesitated before turning to find him in the room's only chair, the bags at his feet.

"If you're thinking this is a setup to get you to do something you're not ready for, you couldn't be more wrong."

Marcail swallowed audibly, but didn't reply.

"There are other beds up here, but I feel our marriage is a private matter. I'd just as soon we stay in the same room." His voice was very reasonable, and Marcail listened attentively. "We have three nights here. If you feel at all threatened after we sleep in the same bed tonight, and I do mean *sleep*, I'll move across the hall."

Marcail stared at her husband and then at the bed. *It's certainly wide enough*, was her first thought. *And he's proven to you repeatedly that he'll not hurt you. Aside from all that, he is your husband.*

"Marcail?"

Alex's soft calling of her name made her remember she hadn't answered him.

"All right, Alex," Marcail agreed, noting that he didn't

seem triumphant or even very pleased, just accepting of her decision.

□ □ □

The family had a bit of a surprise for Alex and Marcail when supper was over. They all gathered in Samuel and Helen's bedroom so each family could present them with a gift for their home. Marcail was so surprised she wasn't sure what to say. Samuel and Helen gave them six tea-cups with hand-painted flowers and matching saucers. A large mixing bowl came from Skip and his family. Jeremy and Susan presented them with embroidered pillow slips. Quinn and Hannah gave them ornate candle-sticks and tall, tapered candles.

After the gifts were opened Marcail and Alex thanked everyone with grateful warmth. Marcail did so because the family had made her feel so accepted, and Alex because he'd so wanted his wife to see his family for the warm, generous people they were.

The celebration over, the children were served dessert and then stayed in Grandma's room for a story. The adults, all but Helen and Samuel, headed toward the large dining room table for pie and coffee.

As the family became acquainted with Marcail, and she with them, the dialogue took many twists and turns. Marcail was on her second cup of coffee when the con-versation turned to a family, new to the area, that Quinn and Hannah were counseling. Alex asked how things were going, and Marcail had the distinct impression that the marriage was in trouble.

"How many kids do they have, Quinn?" Sue wanted to know.

"Four. All under the age of six."

"I spend a lot of time praying for those kids," Hannah

interjected, "since their folks fight whenever the two of them are in the same room."

"It seems they don't even like each other," Quinn's voice was sad on this note.

Marcail, having just taken a sip of coffee, spoke without thought. "They must like each other a little if they have four kids."

The table grew abruptly quiet. Marcail, eyes still on her clean pie plate, became very still. She raised her head slowly to find every adult at the table grinning at her.

Marcail felt the blush begin on her chest and work its way upward to her throat and face. The smiles around the table grew wider, and before Marcail could guess what was about to happen, Skip grabbed the lantern and held it close to her face.

"Would you look at that face," he nearly whispered. "Lit up like a house-afire."

Marcail's face was so hot she thought it would flame. Turning her gaze to Alex, she found his look to be compassionate, but it also told her there was nothing he could do.

"Well, if there were any doubts in our minds about *why* Alex married Marcail, and there weren't," Quinn spoke now, "they're all put to rest. Montgomery men love a girl who blushes."

There was laughter around the table, and some of the attention was turned from Marcail. She was able to relax to a degree, but Alex had been right; they did tease her from time to time just to see her face flush.

Her deepest blush came when everyone decided it was bedtime, and they all left to go home for the night. What no one knew was that her blush this time had nothing whatsoever to do with her in-laws.

❏ ❏ ❏

Marcail stood across the bedroom from Alex, not fully believing she'd agreed to share this room and bed. They'd just come in together, and Marcail watched as Alex sat on the bed and pulled off his shoes. His back was to her, but she told herself she'd sleep in her dress before she'd take her clothes off right then.

Marcail's thoughts were beginning to turn tortuous when Alex stood, went to the commode, and lifted the pitcher from the bowl.

"I'll go down and get some water for the morning," he said, as though he was simply mentioning the weather. Whereupon he strolled casually out the door.

Marcail stood frozen to her spot for a few seconds before, in her haste, she nearly tore the buttons from her dress. She didn't know how long she had, but she planned to be in her nightgown, under the covers, and sound asleep before her spouse returned.

# *thirty-three*

Alex made his way slowly downstairs, and as he expected, found his father in the living room reading a newspaper. The elder Montgomery laid the news aside and smiled as Alex took a chair across from him.

"Is Marcail settled in?"

"I think so. She's getting ready for bed."

Something in his son's voice alerted Samuel. He was very close to all of his children, but Alex was the most like him. There was something on his mind, and Samuel knew if he stayed quiet, Alex would share.

"She's not like Linette," Alex commented softly.

"Yes, I'd noticed. Does that bother you?"

"Only for Linette's sake."

This remark might have confused someone else, but Samuel knew his son to be extremely loyal. He had loved his first wife and always wished she could have been happier.

"You were both very young when you started out, Al," his father reminded him. "And Linette never liked surprises, not even as a child."

"That's true, but I never should have assumed that she knew we wouldn't be in Fort Bragg forever. I mean, with you and Skippy already set up here, it just seemed so logical." Alex gave a helpless shrug. It seemed that all this should have been said years ago, but the truth was, they had never talked about it. He let his mind run, and in an instant all the pain returned.

He and Linette had grown up together. They had been nearly inseparable from the time they could walk, and as they grew older it just seemed a natural turn of events to be married. Within a year of their wedding Alex had gone away to medical school, and to keep things simple, Linette had moved back with her parents.

Alex came home as often as he was able, and at the time his absence didn't seem to affect their relationship. Near the end of his schooling, however, when Alex came home to say he'd found a nearby town that needed him, Linette changed instantaneously to a person he'd never known.

She raged at him over leaving Fort Bragg for Willits and threatened to stay behind. He told her that if she was so against their move they wouldn't go, but she began hiding her feelings at that point. They'd been living in Willits for nearly a year before Linette's true feelings came to the fore again.

Alex could do nothing right in Linette's eyes. He would be treated to days of silence for sins he couldn't remember committing. It didn't take long for Alex to see that Linette depended on him for her every happiness.

The marriage as a whole was not miserable, but Alex found himself starved for the sight of his wife's smile and a true helpmate to fill his days.

Linette was as much work, if not more, than many of his patients. Nevertheless, he loved her, and as he weathered each new storm he grew in the Lord. As head of the family, he tried to involve Linette in his study of the Word, but unless it made her happy, she would have nothing to do with it.

Alex had decided that they would have to return to Fort Bragg, but the very day he decided to give his wife her wish, she had the accident.

"I've lost you."

Alex came abruptly back to the present. "I guess you did. I was thinking about the changes in my life. First with Linette, then without her, and now with Marcail." It was obvious Alex had more to say, but he hesitated.

"It's all right to admit that Linette was not an easy woman to live with, Al," his father told him gently. "And it's also okay to tell me how much you love your new wife."

"I do love her, Dad, only I can't tell her."

Samuel was silent for a full ten seconds. Considering the fact that Alex had only mentioned the new schoolteacher one time in a letter last fall, his words were no surprise. Then a week ago he'd written to say he was bringing his wife home for his birthday.

"Then you'll just have to show her," the older man finally said.

Alex nodded slowly and felt relief over his father's approval. Not that he doubted receiving it, but knowing that his father was in his corner did wonders for Alex's outlook.

Father and son sat up for the next two hours while Alex shared how he'd met Marcail and why they were married. Again, Alex felt no condemnation from his father. He listened carefully when Samuel told him how important it was that he get to know Marcail's family as soon as possible. Alex hadn't thought of it, but agreed wholeheartedly.

They parted company sometime before midnight, and as Alex expected, Marcail never stirred when he slipped beneath the covers beside her.

# *thirty-four*

Marcail woke to an empty bed. Stretching contentedly, she remembered where she was and quickly turned her head to see if someone was on the other pillow. Someone *had* been there, that much was obvious, but the sheets were cold and Marcail wondered what time it was.

She lay there a moment, feeling lazy, and had just decided to get out of bed when the door opened a crack. Alex's head came in next, and he looked toward the bed with raised brows.

"Good morning," Marcail called, and Alex took it as an invitation to enter.

"Good morning. How about a little coffee?"

"Ohhh, thank you." Marcail spoke with surprised pleasure and pushed herself against the headboard to receive the offered cup. Alex took the end of the bed, leaning against the footboard with his own cup.

"How did you sleep?" he asked solicitously after Marcail had taken a few sips.

"Like I always do, but I suspect you already know that."

"Meaning?"

"Meaning, I never heard you come or go, so I assume I slept as usual."

"You do sleep hard," Alex commented softly, his eyes on her disheveled appearance.

Marcail told herself she was not going to blush. She concentrated on her coffee cup in the silence that followed.

"How would you like to have breakfast at the beach?"

The cup paused halfway to Marcail's mouth.

"Who's going?"

"Just the two of us."

"What about your folks?"

"Dad's at the office, and I think I told you, Mother sleeps late. I'm sure my family will be around for the rest of the day, so I thought this might be my only time to show you Fort Bragg. Unless you're starved, I thought we'd take a basket and eat at the beach."

"I'd like that," Marcail said sincerely, seeing how much Alex wanted to leave the decision to her, but also how much he wanted to take her.

Alex stood and moved toward the door. Marcail noticed for the first time that he was dressed and ready for the day.

"I'll be ready anytime you get downstairs."

"All right. By the way, Alex, what time is it?"

"Almost 10:00."

Alex grinned at the shocked look on his wife's face before slipping out and shutting the door.

❏ ❏ ❏

"This was my grandparent's house," Alex said as he pointed to a simple green house. "Quinn and Hannah live there now."

"What did you say Quinn did for a living?"

"He's a logger."

"Oh, that's right, and their kids are Amber, Jess, and Cole."

"No. Amber, Jess, and Cole belong to Skip and Judith. Quinn's kids are Cindy and Derek."

Marcail nodded but stayed silent. She hadn't needed more than a few days to know the name of every student in her class, but Alex's family was still beyond her.

Mentally placing everyone she'd met, Marcail realized that Alex had turned the horse and small buggy down the road toward the ocean. They moved closer to the view Marcail had seen from the Montgomery house, and in a matter of minutes they were pulling to a stop beside what appeared to be a private beach. Marcail sat transfixed as she watched and listened to the ocean beat on the shore. The sound was like music in her heart.

Alex, assuming it was her first view of such a majestic sight, stayed silent and let her look her fill. The quiet moment was broken when Marcail suddenly scrambled from the carriage. Alex watched in amazement as she sat in the sand, stripped off her shoes and stockings, and dug her toes in the sand. A moment passed before he heard her laugh with delight.

Alex stepped down from the buggy and went to sit on the sand beside his wife. She was still smiling, but there were tears standing in her eyes. He watched her, a questioning look on his face. Finally she noticed him.

A faint blush stained her cheeks before she spoke. "Don't mind me, Alex. It's just been so long."

"What has?"

"Since I've seen the ocean and felt the sand under my feet."

Again his look was questioning, almost baffled, and for the first time Marcail stopped to think how little he knew about her. After all they'd only been married for 13 days.

"I was born in Hawaii," Marcail told her husband softly.

*"The Hawaiian Islands?"*

Marcail smiled at his tone. "Right. I lived there until I was nearly nine. My parents were missionaries."

Alex could only stare, first at Marcail, and then out to sea. He had of course realized how little they knew of each other, but this! This was so surprising that Alex hardly knew what to say.

He turned his head back to look at Marcail and found her watching him. Seeing her sitting there with her hair down her back and her bare toes peeking out from beneath the hem of her dress made it easy to envision her as a girl running on the beach.

"Do you miss it?" he asked suddenly.

"Not anymore. When I was nine, I thought I would die of homesickness, but it's been 11 years, and I love my life here. I do miss my brother, Sean, and his family. He's one of four pastors at the mission there, working with the village families."

Again Alex just stared at her.

"What are you thinking?" Marcail had to ask.

"That you're an awful lot of surprises for such a small package."

Marcail wasn't offended. She smiled and looked back out to sea. "Does my being small bother you?"

"No, should it?"

Marcail shrugged and then admitted, "I was never going to marry anyone who towered over me as much as you do."

"Why?"

The question brought Marcail's head around. "Because I didn't want my husband to view me as a child."

"Is that what you think, Marcail?" Alex's voice was suddenly intense. "That I think of you as a child?"

Marcail shrugged, realizing the conversation had taken an unexpected turn. She wasn't sure what to say next.

Alex didn't care for the shrug, but he was at a loss as to how to tell Marcail what he really felt. To divulge that he found her lovely and desirable at this moment, while they were having to share a bedroom, could do irreparable damage. Frustration rose within him, but he prayed for calm.

They sat in silence for a few moments, and Alex knew his first premonition was right—he was going to have to let the subject drop. As he moved to the buggy to retrieve the basket and quilt, he told himself that someday his wife would know exactly how he viewed her.

# *thirty-five*

By the time they returned from the beach, some of Alex's family were at the house. Alex and Marcail were taken into the group without the slightest hesitation.

"Did you show Aunt Marcail where we live?" six-year-old Derek wanted to know when he found out they'd been on a drive.

"Yes, we went by your house."

"Then where did you go?" Jess, who was 11, piped up.

"To the beach."

"Wasn't it a little cold?" This came from Amber, who at 14 was taller than her new aunt.

Alex, who couldn't remember feeling cold at all, smilingly shook his head and glanced at Marcail's feet. Her shoes and stockings were back in place now, but he clearly remembered the way one foot had stuck out from under her dress while they were eating.

A single stroke of his finger had told him that his wife's feet were very ticklish. A fiendish glint over this newfound knowledge had entered Alex's eyes. Seeing that threat, Marcail had scurried for the far end of the quilt and tucked her feet protectively beneath her. She informed him, in her best teacher's voice, that he was *not* to tickle her feet. Alex continued to tease, but after some convincing arguments, she rung a promise out of him that he would not touch her feet while she was trying to eat.

Now, back in the living room, Alex raised his head to see that Marcail had been watching him. She knew the exact direction of his thoughts. Her look turned stern all over again, but all Alex could do was grin.

An hour or so after lunch, with nearly everyone present, news came that there had been a small fire at the hotel. The Montgomery doctors didn't hesitate a moment before going to assist. Alex gave Marcail his usual kiss on the corner of her mouth and went out with the others. Quinn also went along to help.

Susan took her four children home so that Stuart, her youngest, could get a nap. All were coming back for supper, so the children and women settled in various parts of the house for play or talk.

For the next two hours Marcail was in Helen's bedroom with Judith, Amber, and Hannah. Marcail loved the way they included her and would have sat all day, but Jess and Cole began to argue in the living room. When Judith arose, Marcail asked if she could go instead. Judith was more than happy to allow her, and within minutes Marcail had solved the argument by taking both boys outside for a game of catch.

Marcail held her own very nicely with her nephews. Jess had a good arm, and Marcail's hands stung on some of his harder throws. Jess was putting his all into one throw when Cole said something to Marcail and distracted her. The ball, hard as a rock, hit her on the side of the head.

Marcail's hand came to her temple and both boys froze. Marcail's eyes slid shut, knowing that any second her head would begin to throb. A few seconds passed, and Marcail opened her eyes. The boys had come up without her hearing, and Marcail tried to smile.

"I'm sorry," Jess said softly.

"Me too," Cole added.

She reached and hugged the boys, not wanting them to know how much her head hurt.

"Let's sit on the porch and talk awhile, shall we?"

Both boys nodded with relief, thinking their aunt was fine. It was wonderful to sit down, and Marcail was able to keep her pain private. Not knowing whether she was hurt badly or not, Marcail saw no need in alarming the family and upsetting these sweet little boys.

The three were still on the front porch when the men came back from town. Marcail, feeling a little disoriented, didn't notice them until the boys became very still.

Quinn and Samuel went into the house after saying hello, but both Skip and Alex stopped to talk with the three on the porch. Skip immediately noticed the guilty looks on his son's faces. Alex wondered at Marcail's strained smile, but thought he'd have to wait until they were alone to find out the cause.

"What's up, boys?" Skip spoke gently to his young sons.

"It was my fault," Cole began.

"But I was the one who hit her," Jess finished for him.

Skip said nothing for a moment. "You hit Aunt Marcail with the ball?" he guessed, since the offending object was still in Jess's hand. Alex's and Skip's eyes swung to Marcail simultaneously.

"I'm fine," Marcail nearly stuttered. "It was an accident." She hated the way they were looking at her, and when Skip suggested they step into the infirmary, Marcail came to her feet so fast she felt dizzy.

"There's no need really," she began to babble, her eyes wide with apparent panic. "I mean, accidents do happen and—"

Alex instantly measured up the situation and came to the rescue. He stepped forward and pulled her into his arms, effectively cutting off her flow of words. Skip saw immediately that he and the boys were not needed, so he ushered his family into the house.

Marcail, still not believing they were going to leave her alone, held herself stiffly in her husband's arms. His hands held her gently against his chest, but Marcail was not comforted. Alex, working at keeping the emotion from his voice, began to question Marcail.

"Where did the ball hit you?"

"In the head," Marcail answered after only a slight hesitation.

Alarm slammed through Alex, but again he hid his emotion. He moved gently until he was grasping Marcail by the upper arms in an attempt to look into her eyes.

"How long ago did this happen, Marcail?"

"I don't know," she said softly.

"Was it right after we left?"

"No, not that long."

"Show me where the ball hit."

Marcail reached for the spot above her left ear. Alex's hand followed hers and found a huge knot. His finger probed gently, but careful as he was, Marcail moved from his touch. Alex stood silent a moment, mentally debating his next move. Had this been any of his other loved ones, he would have ordered instead of asked, but with Marcail he chose to tread lightly.

"Are you going to panic if I suggest you lie down for a while?"

The thought sounded heavenly to Marcail, but she was worried about the boys' reaction. "I don't want to frighten Jess or Cole, or make them feel any worse than they already do."

"I'll handle the family." Alex was more relieved than his voice portrayed. "You stay right here, and I'll be back in a few minutes."

Marcail sank down on the porch steps as soon as he left and tried to pray. She'd put such store in this weekend; not just the break from teaching, but also the chance to get to know Alex and his family better.

Marcail's attempt at prayer was interrupted when Alex appeared beside her. He stooped, hooked an arm beneath her knees and one behind her back, and lifted her high against his chest.

"Oh, Alex," Marcail gasped. "That makes me dizzy."

"Just close your eyes," he told her calmly, and surprisingly Marcail complied, letting her head rest against his shoulder.

With her eyes closed, Marcail was unaware of the hands holding the door open for their entrance, or the compassionate, concerned adult eyes that watched as Alex bore his wife through the living room and up the stairs.

Marcail was not able to keep track of their progress as they moved though the house. She knew when Alex sat her on the edge of the bed, and that he was unbuttoning the back of her dress, but when her nightgown dropped over her head, she was taken totally off guard. Even so, that she was too tired to question or fight him.

She watched with eyes that hurt as he hung her dress on the back of the door. His hands were gentle as she was tucked beneath the covers, and the pillow felt as soft as a cloud to her throbbing head. She was going to thank him for something, but at the moment the thought eluded her as sleep swiftly crowded in.

# *thirty-six*

Marcail woke to the calling of her name. Her foggy brain told her someone was being very insistent. Since she didn't like the cold washcloth that was rudely calling her from slumber, she forced her eyes open and focused on Alex, who seemed to be engrossed with her face.

"I thought you were going to let me sleep for a few minutes?" Her voice was husky.

"I did." Alex's voice sounded hushed in the still room. "You've been asleep for nearly two hours."

Marcail was silent as she digested this. She heard sounds from downstairs, and at the same time her nose detected a wonderful smell.

"How does your head feel?"

"I'm hungry," Marcail told him.

"Well, that's a good sign. I'll bring you something."

"No. I'll come down."

Alex nodded after a brief hesitation. "All right." He rose from his place on the edge of the bed and retrieved Marcail's dress from the hook.

Marcail lay still as he placed it over the footboard. "I'll wait for you in the hall. Call if you need me."

Marcail thought it was a little silly of him to stand in the hall and wait for her, but that was before she threw the covers back and swung her legs over the side of the bed. The room took a moment to right itself, and Marcail wondered if her injury was more serious than she realized.

Then a sudden thought occurred to her, and she knew in an instant it was correct. Alex was far more worried than he was letting her know. For *her* sake he was downplaying his reaction. The idea moved her to the brink of tears. She had not expected anyone outside her own family to be so understanding about her fears, and especially not a doctor, but Alex was proving otherwise.

"Marcail?" Alex called from beyond the door, making her realize how much time she was taking.

"I'll be right out."

The door did open soon after that, but Marcail didn't come into the hall. She looked a bit hesitant, and then did something she never expected to do.

"Alex, will you button me?"

To his credit, Alex responded as though the question was as everyday as breathing.

"Oh, sure."

On these simple words he stepped behind her. Within seconds they were headed down the hall. At the top of the stairs, Marcail hesitated.

"I didn't brush my hair or put on my shoes."

"Your hair is lovely," Alex said as he took her hand. "And since we don't stand on ceremony around here, you don't need your shoes unless your feet are cold."

Marcail wondered at the lovely feeling that spiraled through her over his words, and the way his long fingers curled around her own.

❑ ❑ ❑

Supper was another uproarious affair, and even though Marcail's head ached, she loved it. It reminded her of meals with Rigg's family. After the dishes had been cleared, the group converged on Helen's room for a game of Sticks.

Marcail was unfamiliar with the game, but she learned that it was something of a family tradition with the Montgomerys. She also learned the reason it was new to her: Helen had invented Sticks herself. The family had been playing it for years.

The game consisted of bodies draped all around the room, the more the better, a huge stack of cards with questions or commands printed on each, and dozens of small wooden sticks. Marcail was rather lost at first, until someone explained that the person with the most sticks at the end of the game was the winner.

Helen was in her element as she handled the cards. The questions ranged from easy for the children to outrageous for the adults. The cards that resulted in the most fun were those with commands. The players laughed until they cried when Skip had to stand on his head and say the pledge of allegiance, but everyone had to forfeit a stick when he did so without laughing. At times it seemed that Helen made up the rules as she went along, but she was always fair.

As the evening neared an end, Skip, Alex, and Hannah had the majority of the sticks. Marcail, whose head still ached a bit, was beginning to tire when Helen called her name as the next turn.

"All right, Marcail," Helen said with a determined look in her eye, "sing us a song in a foreign language."

"Oh, Mother," and "Oh, Grandma," were the sounds around the room. Marcail looked surprised at everyone's reaction until Susan spoke.

"That's mother's favorite question, Marcail. She's been asking it for years, and no one has ever done it."

Marcail's face was neither mischievous nor triumphant. The look she gave her mother-in-law was tender as she began to sing a Hawaiian lullaby she'd learned in the Islands. Her voice was high and pure and sweet, and the room was utterly still even after she was finished.

The room remained silent as Skip, Alex, and Hannah stood and gave *all* their sticks to the newest member of the family. Marcail's eyes filled with tears over such a lovely display of love and acceptance.

The room's silence was shattered as each family member erupted with questions. Alex found himself thanking God that he'd found out that morning where his wife had been born. He stayed quiet while the family questioned her and learned quite a bit about where she'd grown up. Some 20 minutes later Alex noticed her fatigue but wasn't sure how to get her out of the room without embarrassment. Thankfully his father noticed also.

"I think maybe the rest of these questions can wait until tomorrow at Al's party."

No one argued, since the next day was Sunday and all had yet to bathe their families. After everyone cleared out, Marcail thought how nice it would be to wash her hair, but she decided she was just too tired to make the effort.

"Want me to fix a bath for you?" Alex offered sweetly after they'd bid Samuel and Helen good night.

"It sounds wonderful, but I don't think I have the energy."

Alex nodded with understanding and silent agreement, thinking she could always bathe in the morning. He didn't mention that she could sleep late if she needed to, and probably would if he woke her in the night like he planned to do. It would be nice to see Pastor Cook and introduce her to his church family, but Marcail's health was more important.

As he waited in the hall, he realized his wife had admitted to him that she was tired. For her to admit even that spoke of how far they'd come in a few weeks. The fear was diminishing, and as Alex waited for his wife to ready for bed, he praised God for that.

# *thirty-seven*

"It's dark outside, Alex! What time is it?" Marcail asked with sleepy dismay when her eyes finally adjusted to the light of the lantern.

"A little after midnight, I think."

"Why did you wake me?"

"Because I don't take chances with head injuries," he said as he pulled her into a sitting position on the side of the bed. It had been a chore to wake her from her nap the day before, but he found it nearly impossible in the middle of the night. Then he remembered the cool washcloth he'd used on her face earlier. It did the trick.

"I still don't understand why you woke me," Marcail scowled, swaying just a bit on the edge of the bed.

Alex put a hand out to steady her and explained, "People who get hit in the head as hard as you did have a tendency to go to sleep and not wake up. And since I'd like to do everything I can to have you around as long as the Lord wills, I woke you."

Marcail's brow lowered, and her tone was grumpy, "If I'd known what kind of a noisy roommate you were going to be, I'd have sent you across the hall on the first night!"

Alex smiled with amusement, but also relief. If she was feisty, she was going to be all right.

"I suppose," Marcail went on, her voice just as cross, "that you want to know my mother's maiden name or something equally as silly to see if I really know who I am. Well, I know exactly who I am! I'm a woman who's considering leaving her husband if he doesn't let her go back to sleep!"

Alex laughed outright at this, but he was also wise enough to listen to her. Within minutes she was tucked securely back beneath the covers and on her way to sleep.

Alex took a little longer to find his own rest. His mind dwelt on this unusual marriage in which he found himself. How did a man who'd been married for several years, widowed, and then married again, keep from touching his new wife? How did a man share a bed with his wife and manage to keep his distance, even though he found her desirable?

It had to be the Lord, Alex concluded. He knew himself to be a man like any other, with God-given desires. But God had also given him a wife who needed special nurturing at this time, and for that God's sustaining strength was proving to be more than sufficient.

As though the Lord spoke to him, Alex suddenly remembered Joseph from the New Testament, a man who'd married the woman he loved when she was carrying the Son of God. The angel had not told Joseph he could not touch Mary, but he chose to keep her a virgin until after the baby was born.

Alex was not trying to be blasphemous by comparing himself and Marcail to Joseph and Mary, but thinking of Joseph was an encouragement to him. Of course Joseph had known that the pregnancy would come to an end, whereas Alex had no such guarantee. Still, Joseph had been God's man for the job, and God had blessed him.

Alex rolled onto his side to see the woman lying next to him. The moonlight came through the window and illumined just a part of her face, but Alex didn't need the light to know how lovely she was.

"I love you, Marcail," he whispered, knowing she would not hear. "And I pray that someday you'll love me too." Alex slept then, but not before he asked God to let that day be soon.

❏ ❏ ❏

When Alex woke again it was light outside. He'd intended to wake Marcail one more time before morning, but his body must have had other ideas.

Alex padded downstairs, barefoot and without a shirt, to find his father having breakfast in the kitchen. He knew his mother would still be sleeping. His father was ready for church, but had time before he needed to leave. Alex joined him.

"Good morning," Samuel greeted his youngest son.

"Morning," Alex returned as he poured himself a cup of coffee.

"Did I hear you up last night?"

"That you did. Sorry we disturbed you."

"No problem. I take it you woke Marcail to see if she was all right?"

"Right. She got hit pretty hard, and I wanted to be sure."

"How is she?"

"If feisty is any indication, she's in perfect health."

Samuel looked confused. "Marcail doesn't strike me as the feisty type."

"You've never woken her from a sound sleep. She all

but told me if I didn't leave her alone, I could sleep across the hall."

Samuel laughed. "With as hard as you tell me she sleeps, I'm surprised you could rouse her."

"It wasn't easy, but at least it gave me peace of mind. I was going to wake her again before morning, but I slept through."

"I'm sure she's all right. She was pretty chipper last night until the end of the game, and then through the family's interrogation."

Alex smiled. "Have you noticed that when she's comfortable with you, she shows every emotion on her face?"

"Your mother and I find her as guileless as a child," Samuel commented.

"That she is."

"You know, Al," Samuel went on, "everytime we've talked this weekend, it's been about Marcail. Your mother and I both wonder how *you* are doing."

"I'm doing just fine," Alex assured his father. "Physically I'm in good shape, spiritually I'm learning to trust God in a brand new way, and emotionally, well, let's just say I'm getting there."

Samuel, who'd risen to retrieve the coffeepot, patted his son on the shoulder and thanked him for his assurance. "If you don't get a chance to talk with your mother alone before you go tomorrow, I'll tell her you're doing well. It will put her mind at ease."

"Have the two of you really been worried?"

Samuel smiled and then chuckled. "Not worried exactly, but try to realize, Al, that we've never seen you this way before. You and Linette were like brother and sister, and you didn't really have a courtship, just a wedding. But now, well now you have this look of delight on your face most of the time. If Marcail is in the room, you can't keep your eyes off her."

Samuel laughed at the dumbfounded look on his son's face. "I've got to get to church early today. If Marcail sleeps late enough, the two of you can breakfast with Mother."

Alex silently watched his dad leave. He realized that if his family could see his love for Marcail, then quite possibly it would be just a matter of time before Marcail could see it herself.

# *thirty-eight*

"I can see you're feeling much better," Helen told her daughter-in-law as they breakfasted in her room.

"Yes," Marcail said with relief. "I feel like I'm back to my old self." It was 10:30, and Marcail had just had her bath. She was now having breakfast with Alex and his mother.

"Well, that's wonderful. I'm sorry you'll miss church, but your health is more important."

"If your pastor is anything like ours, I haven't missed a thing," Marcail said as she set her coffee cup down. Instantly she regretted her words. "I'm sorry," Marcail apologized. "That was completely uncalled for."

"That's all right, dear," Helen assured her. "Alex has talked with us about your church situation."

Wishing that Alex had talked with her, Marcail remained silent. The state of their church concerned her deeply, but she hadn't as yet been comfortable enough with anyone to bring up the matter.

"I take it you're accustomed to solid Bible teaching," Helen mused, beginning the conversation again.

"I guess I've been spoiled no matter where I've lived. In Santa Rosa, Pastor Keller never minced words over the fact that Jesus Christ is the Son of God and the Bible is the

Word of God. Then in Visalia, my father was my pastor. He never leaves doubt in anyone's mind that Jesus alone can save us from our sins and give us a fulfilled life on this earth.

"Pastor Zimler doesn't even mention any of those truths. I fear for him, since the Bible speaks about how seriously God takes positions of leadership. He leads an entire church of people down a rosy path of lies week in and week out. He stands in the pulpit and tells us that if we try hard and do good, God will remember our good works when we die.

"Well, heaven is God's home," Marcail said, really in her element now. She sounded just like a teacher. "And He alone dictates how you come to that home—through His Son. Woe be to the man who preaches otherwise."

Alex and Helen couldn't have agreed with her more. They continued to discuss the Willits church for some time, until Alex made a comment that nearly brought Marcail out of her chair.

Alex stated sadly, "That's the way it is when the pastor of the only church in town sits in the pocket of the richest woman in residence."

"What did you say?" Marcail asked in shock.

Alex repeated himself, and Marcail gawked at him. Of course! It was all so clear now. The pastor was just preaching what he was told to preach!

"Alex," Marcail's voice was pained, "such a thing never occurred to me."

Alex's look was compassionate. "It's not very pretty, is it? But Marcail, we're going to keep praying, praying that more than three or four men will come forward and say they've had enough. I'd rather we go without a preacher than go on as we are now."

"Alex," Marcail suddenly wondered aloud, "how did

the different families in town come to Christ in the first place?"

"Pastor Zimler has only been there for about three years," Alex explained. "Dick Peik, the man in the pulpit before him, was a man of God. Both on Sunday and Wednesday nights, he taught us how to know God and glorify Him in our lives. He was only in Willits for 18 months, but his effect can still be felt."

"That encourages me, Alex," Marcail said, soft determination in her voice. "God has not turned His back on Willits. Since I believe He's put me there and given me a love for the people, I also believe He will use me to further the news that His Son is the Light in this world."

Both Alex and Helen were so moved by Marcail's obvious burden that no one spoke for a time. Breakfast was finished in silence, each wrapped momentarily in his own thoughts.

❑ ❑ ❑

"You mean, you don't include your mother in your birthday lunch?"

"It was her idea that we go to the beach," Alex defended himself. "She will be included in the gift-opening, which is always in her room. Honestly, Marcail, she doesn't feel excluded."

Marcail's fierce look softened. She'd quite simply fallen in love with her mother-in-law, and the emotions she felt were making her very protective.

The day was unseasonably warm, and Marcail had to admit that it was perfect for the beach. The cool temperatures from the day before had not kept her from enjoying herself when she went with Alex, but it was going to be nice to leave her coat behind.

Everyone brought quilts to sit on and food to eat. It

looked like a feast to Marcail. Meat sandwiches, bread and butter, apples and cheese were passed to all waiting hands. Cups of water were dispersed to quench everyone's thirst.

After Jeremy said grace the talk was light and fun, and for some reason, Alex's family was bent on teasing him. It went on for some time before Skip accused Alex of killing off more patients than he cured. There were a few teaspoons of water left in Alex's cup, and without warning he tossed the contents at his oldest brother.

Skip ducked, and Marcail got it right in the face. There were cries of outrage from the women and laughter from the men, including Alex.

"I'm sorry, Marcail," he chuckled. "I was aiming for Skip."

Marcail was silent as Alex passed her his handkerchief. She wiped her face and then without taking her eyes from her husband, she sat swirling the water in her own cup, one that had just been filled.

"Now, Marcail," Alex began placatingly, immediately seeing her intent. "You have to admit it was an accident. I meant it for Skip, and it was only a few drops."

When all she did was grin mischievously, Alex resorted to a threat.

"I'll get you back if you do it, Marc."

"What will you do?"

"I just might throw you in the Pacific," Alex said, knowing he'd never do such a thing.

"You'd have to catch me first," Marcail said with sweet confidence, and the entire family erupted with laughter and catcalls.

When the noise died down, Alex's look was nothing short of condescending. "I don't think that would be a problem."

The narrowing of Marcail's eyes told him in an instant that he'd said the wrong thing, but his brain told him to move a moment too late. Before he could take a breath, Marcail had thrown the entire contents of the cup in his face. Staying on the blanket just long enough to enjoy the stunned look on his face, Marcail jumped to her feet and ran down the beach.

The shouts from the family told Marcail that Alex was after her, but she didn't look back as she made fast tracks away from her wet husband.

"Go, Marcail, go," came a woman's voice.

"She's not very submissive, Alex. You'd better do something about that when you catch her." This time it was Skip.

"Use every trick in the book, Marcail. Don't hesitate to bite him," Susan shouted as Marcail ran on.

The sounds of the family faded, and Marcail's feet pounded the sand. Alex, who was just beginning to wind, wondered why it wasn't a requirement that a man know all about his wife before he married her. Why were the vows said *before* he knew that she could sing in a foreign language or run like the wind down a sandy beach?

Marcail spotted a huge fallen tree and darted around the far side of it. She paused, ready to go again if Alex was still bent on pursuit, but as she hoped, he came up on the other side and stood, breathing hard and staring at her. A bit winded herself, Marcail knew she had more in her if needed.

"Where," Alex said on a gasp, "did you learn to run like that?"

"I'm not approaching the advanced age of 31, like a certain elderly husband I know."

Alex's eyes narrowed. "You're already in hot water, and now you're pushing your luck." Alex dropped to the sand and leaned his back against the huge log. Marcail stared for a moment at the back of his head before deciding the danger was over. She rounded the log and dropped to her knees beside her husband.

Her legs had no more hit the sand when Alex hauled her across his lap. Marcail's eyes showed her shock, but Alex only smiled triumphantly. He bent his head and wiped his wet cheek against her own.

"Oh, stop it, Alex!" Marcail laughingly wailed. "You're getting me all wet."

"That's the point." He-spoke with amusement as he covered both sides of her face with the moisture from his own.

As swiftly as the laughter had come, it subsided. Marcail found Alex's mouth so close to her own she could feel his warm breath on her cheek. Alex hesitated a mere heartbeat before his lips touched down on her's.

It was the first time he'd kissed her squarely on the mouth, and it wasn't a brief kiss. In fact, Alex held Marcail tenderly and kissed her for several minutes. But he also succeeded in holding his emotions in check, causing her to feel cherished, not frightened.

Back at the quilts, both Jess and Cole asked if they could go find Uncle Alex and Aunt Marcail. Their father said no, and when asked why, he told them that someday they would understand.

# *thirty-nine*

After the gifts were opened and the cake eaten, Alex's family hugged Alex and Marcail goodbye, telling them to come again soon. The day had been a wonderful celebration, but Marcail found it lovely to have a quiet supper with just Samuel and Helen. Since they would see only Samuel in the morning, they said their goodbyes to Helen before bed.

Marcail and Helen both felt as though they were losing a newfound friend.

"I'll write you," Helen assured her.

"And I'll write back."

"In His time, the Lord will bring us together again," the older woman assured her softly.

Marcail nodded, her throat closing with emotion. She knew she must be tired. It felt wonderful to climb into bed some minutes later. For the first time, Marcail wished that Alex had come to bed at the same time. She fell asleep thinking about the way his arms had felt as they held her close.

❑ ❑ ❑

The next morning Samuel drove Alex and Marcail to

the train station in his small buggy. He lingered while the train pulled away, and Marcail waved until the train rounded a curve and took them out of sight. She settled back in her seat for the long ride and felt Alex's eyes on her.

"Your family is wonderful," she said with sincerity.

"I think so. They were quite taken with you."

"The feeling is mutual."

"I'd like to get to know your family someday soon," Alex said, thinking of his father's words.

"I've thought about that. Maybe we could go to Santa Rosa when school lets out."

Alex nodded, wishing he could think of some way for it to be sooner, but no ideas came to mind. "We'll plan on it," he promised her.

They were fairly quiet on the way back to Willits, both thinking of the work awaiting them. Alex's mind wandered to two patients who were expecting, and Marcail's mind dwelt on Sydney. She prayed that he would come to understand how important he was to God, knowing that only God could change him.

◻ ◻ ◻

Alex and Marcail fell back into their routine on Tuesday as though they'd never been away. There were letters waiting for Marcail when she checked her mail after school, but she could tell that they'd been written before her family received the news of her marriage.

After school on Tuesday, she told Alex she would see herself home. She wanted to go directly to Vesperman's and check to see if Alex's gift had arrived. It had, and she went away with a huge smile on her face and plans for the next day.

Marcail was up early on Wednesday morning. She moved quietly as she made fresh biscuits, scrambled eggs, and fried some of the bacon Alex had received from a patient just the day before. It didn't take long for the aromas from the kitchen to draw Alex from his bed. When the door opened, Marcail was standing by his chair, guarding a lumpy, wrapped parcel which sat next to his plate. She looked hesitant, and when she spoke she twisted her hands nervously before her.

"Happy birthday, Alex," Marcail said in a rush. "We have a tradition in the Donovan household of putting our birthday gifts next to our plates at supper. I realize I'm a few meals early, but I was rather excited about your gift and wanted you to have it now."

Marcail was thrilled over her plan when Alex's face broke into a broad smile. She stood back so he could sit down and then sat herself, watching with spellbound attention as he unwrapped his gift.

Alex was so surprised over the satchel he was speechless. It was the finest he'd ever seen. It was on the tip of his tongue to ask Marcail how she could have afforded such a gift on the little he brought home when he remembered she was a paid teacher.

Suddenly Alex realized how well they had been eating since Marcail moved in; not just her cooking, but the food itself. Cookies with peanuts in them, more meat than usual, and muffins and other baked goods were just the start. Alex also realized in that instant that he'd never even mentioned their finances or offered her a dime of money.

"If you're not pleased, Alex, we can order something else." Marcail's soft, unsure voice cut into his thoughts, and Alex realized she'd misunderstood his silence. He immediately rose and came to stand next to her. He bent low, kissed her cheek, and then hunkered down before her.

"It's a wonderful bag, and I wouldn't trade it for any other. But I have to admit, I'd forgotten about your salary."

Marcail looked very confused, and then her face cleared. "Well, I did have to take some money from our savings account, but Mr. Flynn increased my salary because I'm not living in the house by the school. I wanted this to be special, and I know it will last you for years to come, and—"

Marcail rattled on, but all Alex heard was "our savings account." She must have combined their accounts and not mentioned it. It would be easy for his pride to rear its ugly head at this moment, resentful of the fact that his wife probably made more money than he did. In truth he was so touched by her actions that he wasn't the least bit upset. He silently thanked God for the generous wife he'd been given. When she was finished explaining, he kissed her again, thanked her, and then proceeded to load the supplies from his old bag into the new one.

Marcail watched him with tremendous satisfaction. He'd looked so hesitant for a moment that she thought he was going to refuse the gift. The gift and good breakfast were a fine start to the day, and when Alex finally left Marcail at the schoolhouse, she had the feeling that the entire day might be very special.

Her thoughts, however, were drastically altered long before noon. Sydney was at his worst, and Marcail had no choice but to keep him inside during the morning recess. He sat at his desk looking miserable, and after Marcail checked on the children outside, she sat down in the seat in front of him.

"What's wrong, Sydney? Aren't you glad I came back?"

"I guess so, but I still don't like you having to be married."

He'd said this to her in the past. She knew it was nothing personal against Alex, but since it was partially his grandmother's responsibility that she *was* married, she never knew how to answer him. Sydney spoke before she could reply.

"I hate my grandmother; I just hate her."

This statement was a first.

"Oh, Sydney," Marcail said softly. "You might be angry, but I don't think you hate her."

"I do. It's all her fault you had to get married and then go see the doctor's family."

Marcail hadn't realized Sydney understood Cordelia's part in the whole affair. "Why do you hate her because I went to Fort Bragg?"

"Because you're going to love them now and probably move away."

"I'm not going anywhere, Sydney." Marcail reached out and held his chin in her hand. "Don't you know that a teacher's love is like a mother's love. It doesn't divide, it multiplies."

Sydney stared at her, and Marcail wondered, not for the first time, what Sydney's parents were like.

"If a mother has more than one child, her love is not equally divided between the two, so it's 50-50. She loves each one, 100 percent. It's true that God has given me a distinct love for Dr. Montgomery's family, but the special love I feel for you hasn't changed in the least."

It took a moment for Sydney to nod. His face softened.

"*Now* Sydney, we've got to talk about why you're in here and not out playing with your friends." Again the boy nodded, and Marcail went on. "No matter what you're feeling, you *do not* have the right to pull the hair of the person in front of you or to kick the desks of those around you. Do I make myself clear?"

"Yes, Mrs. Montgomery. It won't happen again."

It was, of course, what he said every time. When, she asked herself on the way back to her desk, was he going to see that changes made on his own were never going to be anything but temporary? The thought plagued her until after lunch, but then something happened that made Marcail nearly forget about her class.

At about 2:00 Marcail was sitting at her desk and listening to the primary form read. Her profile was to the door, but she noticed that someone appeared to be moving around at the back of the schoolhouse. She wanted to give the offending student a chance to sit down without a reprimand, but whoever it was, he was causing the other students to become restless.

Marcail looked resignedly at Sydney's desk, but she was surprised to find him sitting quietly. Her gaze flew to the rear of the room and locked with the loving, concerned eyes of Patrick Donovan.

# *forty*

═══════════════

"Please take your seats, Erin and Kathy," Marcail said to the two little girls at the front of the room. "You may join the rest of the class in silent reading at your desks."

After making this announcement, Marcail walked swiftly to the back. She turned at the doorway of the cloakroom for one more check on the children, and then stepped over the threshold straight into her father's arms. The feel of those strong limbs surrounding her caused tears to threaten.

"Hello, honey," Patrick whispered.

"Oh, Father, I'm so glad to see you."

"Well, you didn't have to make up a story about being married to get me to come." His tone was light, but his eyes begged her to tell him it had all been a tale.

"I'm sorry there was no warning."

Patrick felt as if his worst nightmares had come true. He'd missed so much of Marcail's life, and since he'd returned to the states, she'd become his last chance to share in the joys of courtship and marriage for at least one of his children. Patrick suddenly brought his thoughts up short; now was not the time to go into it. Marcail must have realized this also, since she was the first to speak.

"I dismiss the children in about an hour. I'd like to introduce you just before they go. Would you mind having a seat in the back?"

"Not at all," he answered, thinking that after all those hours on the train, it would feel good to sit on a chair that didn't vibrate or rock.

Patrick sat in a small wooden chair at the rear, and Marcail returned to the front.

"All eyes forward, please," she commanded softly. The children were swift to obey.

"You may put your readers away until tomorrow. Right now we're going to take a little time to look at our map of California." Marcail spread the map on her desk. "You may leave your desks quietly and come forward to gather around my desk."

The children complied, and in a moment they were having a discussion about various locations in the state. Marcail asked how many children had lived outside of Willits. Several raised their hands and were given a chance to show the class where they had lived. It was half past two when Marcail showed them the town of Visalia and told them she'd moved from there when she took the teaching job in Willits. They had all forgotten the stranger at the back of the room until Marcail instructed them to take their seats.

"We have a very special guest with us today. I'd like you to all be on your best behavior when you meet my father." The children looked surprised, and Marcail waited until her father had reached the front of the room.

"Children, this is my father, the Reverend Patrick Donovan."

The children greeted him cordially. Marcail let her father have the floor. The children were allowed to ask questions until they were released. Patrick fielded queries about where he lived, how long he was staying, his occupation, his family, and the train ride from Visalia to Willits.

Patrick was appropriately impressed with his daughter's class and the skillful, competent way she handled them. He was also impressed with the way the class responded to him. He loved their open expressions and genuine interest in their teacher's father. The half hour flew by, and Patrick walked with Marcail to the door to see the children off.

A moment of silence followed. Marcail wondered where to begin. Patrick sat down in the front when she returned to her desk and waited.

"I don't have any reservations about telling you the whole story, but Alex will be here in a few minutes to take me home, and I think we'll be more comfortable talking there."

"I didn't come here to wring some sort of confession out of you. Your letter covered a lot, but it didn't say if you were all right, and *that's* why I'm here."

Marcail nodded. "I'm glad you came. I am all right, but I want to tell you how it came about and have you meet Alex. We could just start walking home, but then Alex won't know where I am."

"I don't mind waiting," Patrick told her with a smile and then his eyes grew misty. "You're an excellent teacher, Marcail, just like your mother was. In fact, you look so much like her I—" Patrick stopped, not wanting to make her cry, but Marcail couldn't stop the teardrops that escaped her eyes.

"There isn't anything you could say to me that would mean more."

Alex chose that moment to enter the schoolhouse. He found a strange man sitting with his wife and the evidence of tears on her face. He wasted no time in coming to her side.

"Marc?" he questioned softly, his arm going around her as he knelt by her chair. When Marcail took a breath and didn't answer immediately, Alex rose and turned a speculative look at the stranger in the room.

Alex would never know that his protective manner with Marcail, as well as the use of her nickname, went a long way toward reassuring the older man that his daughter was in safe hands. He wasn't thrilled with the situation, but neither was he almost sick with worry as he had been a few times. In fact, as Patrick also came to his feet, his hand outstretched to shake Alex's, the thought occurred to him that he'd already seen all he needed to see.

❏ ❏ ❏

Patrick's mind was not as easy some ten minutes later, when he was finally in his daughter's home and saw the very obvious evidence that Marcail slept apart from her husband. His eyes closed in prayer.

*Oh, Father, it hurts me,* he prayed silently, *to know that two of my children have not married for love. You in Your grace worked a miracle in Sean's and Charlotte's lives, but it's happened again with Marcail. All I can ask is that here too, You will intercede. Bring love to this home so Marcail and Alex can know the joy of children and have a loving earthly partner to see them through the years.*

Patrick would have prayed on but Marcail came in from saying goodbye to Alex, and he turned to greet her. He stepped forward swiftly when he saw her arms were loaded with wood.

"Oh, honey, why didn't you call me to help you?"

"I'm all right," she laughed. "Besides, you're our guest, and I don't want you to work."

Marcail stacked the wood by the stove. She dusted her hands together and looked at Patrick.

"You didn't really answer the children earlier, so tell me, how long can you stay?"

"As long as you need me."

Marcail smiled, but told him seriously, "I am really doing fine."

They were sitting across the kitchen table now, coffee brewing on the stove. Patrick looked at his daughter and marveled for the hundredth time at what a lovely young woman she'd become. It was far more than physical beauty; she was lovely on the inside as well.

"You were never really mad at me for going back to the mission field alone, I mean, like Katie and Sean, were you?" he asked suddenly.

Marcail thought for just a moment. "I don't think anger is the right word for what I felt—confusion maybe, but not anger. I was pretty young, and Katie, who's always been like a second mother anyway, was so constant for me. I just naturally clung to her."

Marcail had no idea of the pain her words caused Patrick. To think of his little nine-year-old daughter, confused and hurting as she watched him leave, was almost more than he could take.

"That was all a long time ago, Father," Marcail commented, seeing more than Patrick thought. "It was hard, but I watched Katie trust in God, and I learned to do the same thing. Believe me, I've used that knowledge more than once since I arrived here."

Marcail let a few moments of silence pass and then began to recount to her father the entire story. She spared few details. Patrick was as shocked as Marcail had been over the power Mrs. Duckworth wielded in town. She finished her story by telling him all about her weekend with Alex's family. He was thrilled at the loving way they had obviously welcomed her.

Marcail talked all through supper preparations, and with only a question here and there, Patrick listened. Alex was on time, and Marcail was very pleased at how easily the men conversed.

Marcail began to feel very selfish over talking nonstop about herself, so as the three sat down to supper, she asked Patrick about the people in Visalia. Marcail missed it, but Alex noticed the tender light in Patrick's eyes upon his daughter's question.

# *forty-one*

"Everything in Visalia is great. The folks who knew I was coming send you their love."

Marcail smiled as she thought of the people there who loved her. "How are Duncan and Lora?"

"Great."

"And Sadie?"

"Sadie is doing fine." Patrick said softly, but Marcail had turned to Alex to explain who all of these people were and missed her father's expression.

"My brother, Sean, met and married his wife, Charlotte, in Visalia. They lived there almost up to the time they went to minister in Hawaii. Their pastor was a bit older, and when he decided to leave the pulpit, God called Father to fill it. Duncan is the sheriff and his wife is Lora. They both attend Father's church. Sadie is Charlotte's aunt. She comes on Sunday morning, which is a tremendous answer to prayer, but we're still praying for her salvation."

"We don't need to pray for her salvation anymore." Patrick spoke softly, and Marcail turned to look at him. The look of utter serenity that crossed his features caused Marcail to jump to her feet and throw her arms around his neck.

"When?" Marcail laughed with delight. "When did this happen?"

"About a week ago. She's been coming to our midweek services off and on for several weeks. Last week she stayed late and talked with Lora. Lora told me the sound of longing she heard in Sadie's voice was heartbreaking. By the time they had finished talking, though, Sadie told Lora that all her fears were gone.

"Then Sadie and I talked the day before I received your letter. She told me that for the first time since her husband passed away, she is not afraid of death. She wakes up knowing that if today is her last day on earth, it will be her first day in heaven."

"Oh, Father," Marcail breathed, not needing to say more. Alex, too, was deeply moved. They continued to share, each about his own work and the people in their lives. When Alex mentioned Dean and Kay Austin, Marcail told her husband she'd completely forgotten about Bible study.

"I stopped to see Dean on my way home," Alex explained, putting her mind at ease. "I told him they might not see us."

"Please don't cancel your plans on my account," Patrick was swift to say. "If I can't accompany you, I'll find something—"

"Of course you can go with us," Marcail cut in. "The Austins would love it."

And thus it was settled. The dishes were done in record time, and the three set out for town. Marcail took the cake she'd baked for Alex, and they had a small celebration before the girls went to bed. As it turned out, they did not get to their Bible study.

Because Patrick had been a minister for many years and was a good deal older than the rest of the adults,

Alex, Dean, and Kay went into detail about the situation with their present pastor and asked what they should do.

Patrick's first suggestion was to continue on in prayer, but for Cordelia Duckworth, and not just their pastor. He was convinced that she was the root of the problem and that was where they needed to concentrate their efforts.

Marcail was silent, but she'd believed that for a long time. She had no desire to see Sydney's grandmother crushed beneath the heels of the community, but someday, someone was going to have to say no to that woman. As always happened when Marcail's thoughts moved in that direction, she got the uncomfortable feeling that she would be that someone.

❑ ❑ ❑

Patrick stayed until Friday morning. The Austins graciously opened their home to him, and he stayed both nights in their spare room. His days, on the other hand, were spent with Alex or Marcail. He joined Alex on his rounds, and even stayed in the examination room when Alex saw a few of his younger patients. He took in more of Marcail's expertise with her class and marveled repeatedly at her ease and ability to teach.

It was not easy to see Patrick go, but both Alex and Marcail were thankful for the brief time they had shared. Alex believed that God had given them these days to assure both himself and his new father-in-law that God's hand had been on their marriage.

They told Patrick of their plans to visit Santa Rosa when school let out. Patrick assured them that when he stopped off in Santa Rosa to see Katie and Rigg, he'd pass along the news.

Patrick left with a peaceful heart, believing that with Alex by her side, Marcail would come to no harm. What

# *forty-two*

"You look a bit sleepy this morning," Alex commented over breakfast as he watched Marcail stare into her cup.

"I guess I am," Marcail said, covering a yawn. "I'm rather glad it's Friday, since Sydney's been weighing on my mind so heavily this week."

*That*, Alex thought to himself, *is an understatement*.

It had been two weeks since Patrick left, and Marcail, after hearing about Sadie's salvation, threw herself into the business of leading Sydney to the Lord. She found it to be exhausting work, and some days she believed they'd made no progress at all. Every night she fell asleep giving Sydney to God, but oftentimes, as the school day went on, she acted as if her efforts alone, and not those of a sovereign God, would save her young student.

Before Marcail knew it, it was time to leave for school. The puddles in the road had long ago dried up, but Alex enjoyed taking his wife to work, so he ignored her every time she suggested walking. She had walked home on a few occasions, but only when Alex could not get away.

The schoolhouse was quiet as Alex took Marcail's books to her desk. As always he kissed her, but after their kiss on the beach in Fort Bragg, his kisses were different. No longer did he hold her jaw and kiss the corner of her mouth, hitting more of her cheek than anything else. She now seemed very willing to accept his embrace and tender kiss, full on the mouth.

He didn't linger this morning as he was always tempted to do, but kissed her twice. His love for her grew daily, and he could never get enough of touching or talking to her. Marcail walked him to the door and smiled with contentment as he rode away.

She was at her desk, writing out a few notes, when she heard movement at the back of the room. It was a bit early for the children to be arriving, but Marcail looked up to see Sydney standing just outside the cloakroom door.

"Why, Sydney," she said with pleasure, "I didn't hear you arrive. How are you today?"

"Fine," the young boy answered, his sullen tone telling Marcail he was anything but. The young school teacher sighed mentally. On the days when Sydney was boisterous and unruly, Marcail knew where she stood. When he was withdrawn and uncommunicative, as he was now, he frightened her.

She knew there was no point questioning him when he behaved like this, so Marcail went back to the paper in front of her, thanking God the week was over and praying the day would be better than she hoped.

The morning progressed fairly smoothly, but Marcail's prayerful heart was never far from the unpredictable Sydney. The other children seemed to take their cue from him; they were quiet as well.

Marcail dropped into her chair at lunch as though she'd worked two days without a rest. She'd just reached for her lunch tin when Alex entered. It was a pleasant surprise. Marcail felt like she was seeing the first friendly face all day.

"Hi," Alex spoke as soon as he sat down. He thought she looked tired, which wasn't like her, and it concerned him. It also made the reason for his visit more difficult.

"Hello," Marcail smiled at him, unaware of the way her fatigue showed.

"I can't stay," he began, "but I wanted to let you know I won't be by after school. I've got to head out to the Castleton place, and I won't be back until evening."

"I don't mind the walk," Marcail told him honestly, thinking it would give her a chance to clear her head and time to pray.

"All right," Alex said, still hating the idea. "I'll see you as soon as I can."

Marcail walked him to the door and then went back to her lunch.

The afternoon was a waste of time. The children went from being obediently quiet to continuously talking out of turn, and Marcail let them go nearly 45 minutes early. It was cool but more than comfortable, and she felt that the students who normally had rides could use the exercise.

Marcail straightened the room and worked at her own desk for over an hour before gathering her books and slipping into her coat. Once outside, she closed the door behind her and moved unsuspectingly toward the steps. Her foot never reached the first step. It caught on a string that had been tightly drawn across the top.

Marcail's books flew through the air. Her hands went out to grasp for the railing and encountered only thin air. In an attempt to right herself, she turned partially with her back to the steps.

Her momentum was too great though, and the change in position didn't help. She ended up falling very hard, most of her weight going onto one side of her back. Marcail gasped for breath after the initial impact. Pain ran from the back of her head to the back of her right thigh. She lay still for long moments, breathing hard with pain and trying to determine if anything was broken.

Marcail didn't realize she was shaking all over until she tried to stand. For the first time since she'd moved to Willits, she wished the schoolhouse was more centrally located. After some effort, Marcail found herself on her hands and knees looking up at the steps above her, and to the thin string tied tautly across the top.

The ache inside of her was more painful than any of her bruises. This had been a deliberate and malicious act. Marcail was absolutely crushed. More from lack of will than from pain, Marcail collected her books with an effort and removed the string, slipping it into the pocket of her coat.

The walk home was accomplished without real thought to where she was going or how fast. She didn't touch the stove or start supper when she arrived, but slipped out of her coat and decided to lie down. She removed her shoes and lowered herself gingerly onto the sofa, careful of her bruises as she pulled a blanket over her.

She told herself she was just going to sleep for a few minutes, but even though her back throbbed, her body had other ideas. Sleep overcame her quickly, blissfully wiping away the steps, the string, and the troubled face of one little boy from her mind.

# forty-three

Marcail woke to a feeling of pressure on her hand. She focused slowly to find Alex kneeling down by the sofa, holding her hand. Her whole body ached like a bad tooth, but she didn't say a word.

"I know you like to sleep in on Saturday mornings," her husband's voice was soft, "but you were out so hard when I came home last night, I thought I should wake you and let you know I'm leaving for work."

"It's Saturday morning?"

"It sure is. You must have stretched out right here after you got home." Alex's voice was compassionate, and his fingers stroked down her cheek and then touched the collar of her dress.

Marcail wanted to sit up, but didn't think she could manage it. "I'm sorry I didn't get you any supper last night," she apologized, not really thinking clearly.

"I didn't wake you to make you feel bad. I'm fine, and I just hope you caught up on some of your rest." Alex stood then. "I'm off to work. I probably won't be home for lunch, but I should be done for the day around 2:00. There's hot coffee on the stove when you get that far."

Marcail said a soft goodbye that Alex attributed to

sleepiness just before he kissed her. He didn't notice that she lay absolutely still as she watched him leave.

"Is it possible to feel worse today?" Marcail asked herself, as the door closed on her spouse. She had never taken a severe fall before and didn't know what to expect. Her skin had always bruised easily, but none of the bruises were ever the result of a serious accident.

As though her skin had turned into dried leather in the night, Marcail gingerly moved into a sitting position. She was careful to keep her back away from the sofa back, but the bruised side of her bottom and thigh were telling her to lie back down.

Marcail fought the urge. She pushed herself off the sofa and stood. It took some minutes to make herself move again, but Marcail knew that waiting any longer would not change a thing. Her first step forward told her it was going to be a long day.

❑ ❑ ❑

Alex was thrilled to see his last patient leave at 1:30. He was tired and ready to go home. He cleaned up the examination area and readied his bag for emergencies. He was ready to leave when the door opened. Alex concealed his disappointment over being kept longer in town and went out to the waiting room. To his surprise he found Sydney Duckworth waiting for him.

"Hello, Sydney," Alex said carefully, looking past him once or twice to see if his grandmother was going to follow him through the door.

"Hello, Dr. Montgomery. Is Mrs. Montgomery here?"

Not until Sydney asked the question did Alex really look at the boy. His eyes were scared, his features even more pinched than usual.

"Is there something I can help you with, Sydney?"

Alex offered kindly, thinking the boy seemed very upset.

"No, no," Sydney spoke as he backed toward the door. "I just thought maybe Mrs. Montgomery had come with you, and I would say hi."

"I'm sorry, Sydney," Alex smiled gently, knowing the boy was half in love with his wife. "I don't believe she planned to come into town today. Maybe you'll have a chance to talk with her at church tomorrow."

The words seemed to put the boy at ease, and Alex stood for a time after he'd left, trying to put his finger on what had been wrong. No answers came, and Alex, always ready to see his wife, put Sydney out of his mind and hurried toward the livery.

❑ ❑ ❑

Wishing she'd gotten more done, Marcail looked despairingly around the house. The laundry was washed and hung out, but no baking had been done and supper wasn't even a thought in her mind. The day had passed in a painful fog, and Marcail had fought going back to bed every minute. She stared in surprise when Alex walked in the door, never dreaming it was that late in the day.

"Hello," he greeted her. "Did I startle you?"

"Not really," she admitted. "I just didn't realize the time." Marcail took a breath and kept talking, believing that she owed Alex an explanation.

"Alex, I'm sorry I didn't get much done today, but the truth is, I took a fall down the schoolhouse stairs yesterday, and it's made me kind of stiff and lazy."

"You fell down the stairs?" Alex's voice showed his concern, but since Marcail was so fearful of doctors, he told himself to move slowly and not press her. "Are you all right, Marcail?"

"I bruise easily, but I'm sure I'll be fine." Marcail's voice was as even as ever, and Alex, truly believing that by now she would be comfortable enough to tell him if she were really hurt, took her at her word. He took in her composed features and nodded with satisfaction. He also decided to put her mind at ease about the household chores, so he got out the bowl to mix bread dough.

"I really should be doing that," Marcail said from behind him.

"Not if you don't feel well," Alex said reasonably. "Anyway, I've always enjoyed baking. Oh, by the way, Sydney stopped in to say hello. I think he wanted to talk with you about something. I told him he'd probably see you tomorrow at church, and he seemed satisfied with that."

Alex had his back to Marcail and completely missed the look of misery that crossed his wife's face. Marcail did help Alex finish the baking, and if her movements were a little slower than normal, he didn't seem to notice.

Alex fixed supper after he'd done some odd jobs outside. They were just finishing when the bell rang, summoning the doctor's services in town. Alex, usually very pragmatic about his work, looked a bit let down. Marcail was secretly pleased because he was usually gone for at least two hours, and she'd been hoping for some privacy for her evening bath. She knew it was going to cost her to prepare the tub, but the soak was going to be worth it.

Ignoring the dishes, Marcail shuffled around preparing her bath the moment Kelsey galloped out of the yard. As Marcail had suspected, it took great effort to drag the tub out and fill it, but as she sank into the water, she had her first relief in 24 hours.

Sparing her right side as much as possible, Marcail soaped up and washed her hair. It was impossible to maneuver the rinse bucket with only one hand, and Marcail moaned as she was forced to lift her right arm above her head, taxing her bruised shoulder to the limits.

The job done, she sat back in the tub and tried to catch her breath. She found she was trembling all over again, but having her hair and body clean had been worth it.

It was a tremendous effort to leave the tub and dry off, but again Marcail moved slowly and got through it. She stood, nightgown in hand for some minutes, knowing that to lift it over her head was going to hurt. Holding the garment in front of her and feeling the cold of the room, she knew how warm she would be if she could just make the effort, but still she stood rooted.

Feeling weary in body and spirit, she would have continued to stand still, but the door opened quietly behind her. Marcail, wrapped in her own little world of pain and disillusionment, never heard the door's movement. As it was, only seconds passed before she heard Alex's horrified call. Forgetting for the moment the pain in her body, she turned to find him coming toward her, looking every inch the doctor she knew him to be.

# *forty-four*

Marcail backed into the living room away from Alex until his hands on her upper arms brought her to a gentle stop. She was holding the nightgown to the front of her, as though it were a suit of armor.

Alex looked into her terrified eyes, knowing he had to do something that would probably destroy all the trust she'd come to have in him.

"Marcail," he spoke softly. "I have to check your back."

Marcail shook her head and opened her mouth, but no sound came out.

"I can tell," he went on in that same gentle voice, "even from across the room, that your bruises are serious. I *have* to check them."

"I told you I've always bruised easily," Marcail finally blurted out, sounding as breathless and terrified as she really was.

Alex's heart broke, but there was no way he was going to ignore the coal-black bruises and scrapes he'd seen on the back of her body.

With gentle insistency, his hands still holding her upper arms, he drew her back toward the kitchen where the lantern burned bright on the table. He turned her carefully toward the light, nearly changing his mind when he felt the violent trembling of her entire body.

Alex did not rush his examination, and had Marcail been capable of thinking clearly, she would have realized that his manner was completely professional. She felt his hand on her shoulder blade, the skin of her bottom, and the back of her thigh. It felt like forever, when in fact only a minute had passed before he was turning her so that her bare back was once again shielded from his eyes.

The light bounced off of the tears standing in her eyes, and Alex turned without leaving the room. He spoke over his shoulder.

"Put on your nightgown, Marcail." His voice sounded sad, but nothing registered with Marcail beyond her pain and humiliation.

She scrambled into the long, warm gown, and without a word, moved stiffly into the dark living room to sit on the sofa. Following with the lantern, Alex found her sitting sideways, protecting her back he was sure. She didn't change position to look at him as he placed the lantern on the table behind Marcail's turned back. He lowered himself to sit next to her.

Looking at his wife's stiff back covered by her still-wet hair, Alex was at a complete loss for words. Helplessly, he glanced around and spotted her hairbrush on the table where he'd set the lantern. He picked it up and began to draw it through her hair.

Moments passed in silence.

"You don't have to do that," Marcail said, her voice as flat and distant as when they'd first met.

"I realize that."

Again silence fell.

"You said you bruise easily." Alex spoke and let the sentence hang.

"Yes."

"Have *you* seen your back?" Alex wanted to know.

"No."

Alex digested these monosyllabic answers for a moment and then knew it was time for some gut-level honesty.

"I'm learning the hard way that I can't assume anything with you, Marcail. So I'm going to ask you some specific questions, and I expect honest answers." Alex paused a moment with her hair, but Marcail didn't reply.

"Does your back hurt?" The question had an obvious answer to his mind, but he needed to start somewhere.

"Yes."

"How much?"

Here Marcail hesitated. "Quite a bit," she finally returned.

"You say it happened at the school—was it on your way home?"

"Yes."

"Down the steps?"

"Yes."

"How did you fall?"

"I can't tell you that."

This answer was the last thing Alex expected, and he stopped brushing again.

"Why can't you tell me?"

"Because I'm too weary to fight you if you overreact."

Alex thought this statement was as cryptic as they came, but after a moment's thought, a horrifying idea came to mind.

"Marcail, did someone push you?"

"Not exactly."

Again Alex felt completely in the dark, and suddenly very discouraged. He'd begun to think that he knew this woman, that they were slowly becoming one, but she was as closed to him right now as she'd been before they wed.

Alex picked up the lantern and took it with him as he moved to the other side of the sofa. There was not as much room there, but Marcail shifted back slightly so Alex could sit in front of her.

The lantern light flickered across her eyes, eyes that had lost hope. Alex had never seen Marcail like this; it frightened him.

"Talk to me, Marcail," he pleaded with her softly. "Let me help you. I won't do anything you don't want me to do, but please don't shut me out when I care so much." Alex reached for one of her hands and held it between his own.

Marcail, in a fog of pain and anger, saw for the first time how difficult this must be for Alex. The look of concern she saw on his face was like a sudden lifeline. Prompted by his gentle touch and tender eyes, Marcail began to speak.

"I've gone over it and over it in my mind, and I can only figure that he saw us kissing."

"Who saw us kissing?"

"Sydney. He was at school so early yesterday morning. I didn't even hear him arrive. He's infatuated with me, you know, and it must have upset him to see you kiss me goodbye. He was quiet all day, and that always scares me, but I never dreamed he would—"

Marcail halted, and Alex urged her to go on. She pointed toward the string she had placed on the sofa table and Alex reached for it. Marcail spoke when it was in her hands.

"This was tied across the top step when I left the schoolhouse yesterday."

Alex could only stare at the heavy string, stunned

beyond belief. He desperately wanted to hold her, but knew it would only give her pain.

"He's been my mission field since I arrived, Alex. I mean, I love the other children, but I felt so strongly that God wanted me to reach out to Sydney and that he needed me."

"Shhh," Alex spoke as he stroked her hand. "Don't try to understand it all now. We'll have plenty of time to pray and figure out what to do when you feel better."

"I don't think I could pray anyway. I want to, but the hurt—it's so bad . . ."

Alex quieted her again and helped her to stand. It didn't seem to register with her that he was taking her into the bedroom. He helped her carefully onto her good side in bed and covered her with the blankets. He'd lit the bedroom lantern and turned it low. Kneeling down, he found her staring sightlessly at his chest.

"I'm sorry, Alex," she said, her voice filled with utter defeat. "It seems that all you do lately is take care of me. What a disappointment I've turned out to be as a wife."

Alex didn't reply. Nothing could be further from the truth, but Marcail was in no shape to hear anything right now. He watched her eyes close and then flutter open again, this time in fear.

"Are you going somewhere, Alex?"

"No, I'll be right here," he assured her.

Marcail's small hand came out of the covers and touched his chest. He felt her grip the fabric of his shirt and say softly as her eyes closed in sleep, "I hope the bell doesn't ring again tonight."

# forty-five

Long after Marcail slept, Alex sat in the kitchen struggling with his anger. The look on Sydney's face earlier that day was now easy to identify—it was guilt. Even at the very obvious evidence of his crime, Alex was not angry at Sydney but at his grandmother, and not just angry—livid.

He tended to be overprotective where Marcail was concerned, but this, this was an outrage! Because of the selfish, blind foolishness of an old woman, a little boy was being raised to think he could do anything that came into his head.

A sudden image from months ago, before he and Marcail were even friends, came to mind. He remembered one of the Austin girls telling him that Miss Donovan had not been feeling well so school had been dismissed early. Alex had stopped to check on her, wondering as he did about the scratch on her face. He now knew exactly who had caused that scratch.

The recollection did not help Alex's mood. He found his anger kindled anew at the very thought. However, just as suddenly as Alex's anger flamed back to life, it died. He sat very still when he realized he was being swept away by his emotions.

Alex reached for his Bible, always present on the kitchen table. He turned to a couple of verses he recalled, James 1:19,20, and read aloud in the still house. "Wherefore, my beloved brethren, let every man be swift to hear, slow to speak, slow to wrath; for the wrath of man worketh not the righteousness of God."

After he read, Alex began to pray. He started by confessing his wrath, and then gave the whole ugly affair to God. He thanked God that the ringing of the bell had been for a minor incident and he'd been able to come right home. As he prayed, Alex realized *he* was not the one who should be offended, but that sins had been committed against God.

He also realized that he was going to need to take his cue from Marcail. She had been afraid of how he would react, so he figured she must have some idea how she wanted things handled. It might take some time before she felt up to it, but as Alex climbed into bed beside his bruised wife, he determined to learn all he could from her concerning Sydney Duckworth.

❑ ❑ ❑

Alex left the house first thing Sunday morning to see Stanley Flynn. He told him briefly that Marcail had suffered a fall and was not feeling well. He also told him not to expect her back at school for at least two days, possibly longer.

As he rode home he realized he might have made her furious with such a move, but unless he missed his guess, she was not going to want to do much of anything for the next 48 hours.

❑ ❑ ❑

Marcail lay motionless in Alex's soft bed. Usually able

to sleep through anything, the closing of the front door, along with the pain in her back, had startled her awake. She found herself silently imploring Alex to be coming in, and not heading out for the day. She rolled, ever so carefully, onto her back. A moment later Alex appeared in the doorway.

Marcail's fingers moved on the covers in a semblance of a wave, and Alex entered. He pulled the curtains back on both windows before retrieving a chair from the kitchen and placing it close to the bed. Not until he was seated and had taken a close look at Marcail's features did he speak.

"I have quite a few questions I'd like to ask you." Alex's mind was so set on the accident that he failed to ask Marcail how she felt.

"About my fall?"

"Not directly. I want to know about Sydney, and how he behaves in class."

Marcail nodded. "I'm still kind of sleepy, but I'll do my best."

"It doesn't have to be right now. I went to see Stan Flynn this morning. I told him you'd fallen, and he wouldn't be seeing you for at least two days."

Marcail's eyes widened at this, but Alex went on.

"I know you care about your class, Marc, but you can barely walk." Alex's voice was extremely reasonable. "You also have to teach for the next three months, and I don't think it's wise to tax yourself when you still have so many weeks before you're through for the summer."

"I may be through teaching long *after* the summer," Marcail said suddenly, and Alex stared at her. "I've decided to talk with Cordelia Duckworth, but I want to wait until school is out and I've had a few weeks off."

Alex could see this had been on her mind and wanted to show his support of her decision. "I'll go with you."

"You don't have to."

Alex's anger flared. Thinking she was still trying to keep him at arm's length, he retorted in a tight voice, "Whether you like it or not, Marcail, we *are* husband and wife."

Marcail blinked in surprise. "I never said I didn't like being your wife," she told him quietly.

"No, you haven't *said* anything, but you still think and *act* like a single woman. I'm sorry, Marcail," Alex rose wearily, thinking how tense all of this was making him. "I shouldn't have said that." He went on before Marcail could reply. "Would you like to sleep some more or have a little something to eat?"

"I'm not very hungry," Marcail told him.

Alex nodded. "I'll leave you to rest then."

Alex did leave her, closing the door on his way out. Marcail was still awake when he checked on her two hours later.

## forty-six

"How about some soup?" Alex asked as soon as he saw that Marcail was awake.

"That sounds good. If you'll give me a few minutes, I'll come to the table."

It was on the tip of Alex's tongue to ask if she needed help, but he knew what her answer would be. He left and shut the door once again.

Marcail had prayed for most of the two hours that had passed, but the strain of her conversation with Alex was still present. She did not know what to do.

*Maybe I do act like I'm single,* she thought to herself defensively. *But it's hard to get close to someone you hardly know.* The moment the thought formed, Marcail saw it for the flimsy excuse that it was. Alex had showed her in countless ways that he wanted a real marriage, but Marcail had been hesitant. What she was waiting for, she didn't even know herself.

*What a mess.* Marcail muttered as she painstakingly climbed out of bed. Once on her feet, she realized she would have to go to the living room to get her robe. A glance at the kitchen table and the aromas filling the air told her Alex had been busy.

Marcail came back to the table feeling modestly covered and actually experiencing hunger pains. Alex prayed before they ate, and the meal progressed in near silence. As Alex cleared the table, Marcail spoke up.

"Did you want to hear about Sydney now?" Her voice was tentative, and Alex turned from his task at the basin.

"I would like to hear, but only if you're up to it."

"What exactly did you want to know?"

Alex rejoined her at the table. "I want to know if this is typical of Sydney. I mean, his behavior in your class—has he tried things before?"

Marcail nodded. "Sydney is unpredictable at best. He has trouble with his temper, not an unusual occurrence in any child, but he turns violent with little or no warning."

"Is this the first time the violence has been directed at you?"

"No. One day, very early in the year, he threw a rock and hit me in the face. I think he scared himself, because for a long time after that things were calm. Beyond that, he's pulled away from me when I have his arm, and shoved past me so strongly that I've had to take a step backward."

"What does he do to the other children?"

"Kicks their desks, pulls hair, that type of thing. I don't consider any of it harmless, and I always punish him. But since I can't go to Mrs. Duckworth, my hands are tied. I have used his love for me to get through to him at times. My telling him that I'm disappointed seems to carry more weight than anything else I say or do. By the way, how did he seem at your office?"

"I didn't recognize it at the time, but he looked guilty. At first I thought he was afraid of something, and then he seemed so relieved when I told him he'd see you at church."

They fell silent for a time, and then Marcail spoke. "At first I was too shocked to feel anything, and then I felt betrayed. Now I'm afraid. I'm afraid of Sydney, and I won't be able to let him out of my sight for the remainder of the year."

"Are you sure you should wait until summer to confront Mrs. Duckworth?" Fearing for her safety and halfway hoping she would lose her job, Alex wished he could order her to quit.

"Yes, of that I'm sure. I don't know why, except that I feel a definite peace about finishing the year. If I go to Mrs. Duckworth now, I'll lose my job as well as all touch with the children.

"Who knows," Marcail went on, her voice expressing a glimmer of hope. "Maybe God will use this accident in a mighty way—a way that would bring Him glory."

Alex didn't reply to this, and Marcail left the table moments later. She made up her bed in the living room, and Alex took that as a sign that she wanted to be left alone.

❑ ❑ ❑

Alex's prediction about Marcail not wanting to work right away proved to be true. It was Tuesday afternoon before she put a dress on and began to even *start* feeling like her old self.

Things had continued on a strained note between husband and wife through this time, but Alex's care of Marcail could not be faulted. He was at home as much as his work allowed, leaving notes at his office to ring the bell for emergencies only. He had Marcail soaking in a warm bath both morning and evening, and even though Marcail hated it, Alex checked her bruises after each evening bath.

After supper Tuesday night, Marcail said she was desperate for some fresh air. Alex, knowing it could only do her good, helped her into her sweater. She planned to walk around the perimeter of the yard until he finished the dishes.

As it was, Alex had barely started the dishes when Marcail came back through the door. She tried to hide it, but Alex saw fear in her eyes.

"What's happened?"

"The Duckworth coach; it's coming up the road."

Alex's brows rose in surprise, but he spoke calmly. "It would seem, Marcail, that this incident is going to come to a head long before summer."

The young schoolteacher could only nod. Alex told her if she wanted to wait in the bedroom he would answer the door and then come for her. Marcail was tempted, but felt the problem was really hers and she should be present.

She took a place at the kitchen table, her hands clenching in her lap when the knock sounded. Alex answered the summons, and both were surprised to see Sydney standing alone on the step.

Marcail's heart broke at the sight of him, and she watched as he looked up at Alex and then peered tentatively past him to get a better view of her. His eyes were huge and questioning in his pale face, and Marcail wasn't sure what he expected to see. A moment later, he covered his face with his hands and burst into tears.

# *forty-seven*

Marcail said nothing as Alex put a hand to Sydney's back and guided him to a kitchen chair. He pressed a clean handkerchief into the boy's hands and then sat down in the chair beside him.

Marcail, watching from her place across the table, was not sure what to say. She knew only that her heart was breaking with love for this little boy. She understood that to reject him right now would be devastating, but neither was she going to accept his standard line about it not happening again.

After some minutes, Sydney began to contain himself and look at the adults at the table.

"Sydney," Marcail spoke, sounding very much like a teacher. "Does your grandmother know you are here?"

"Yes, Mrs. Montgomery," he sniffed.

Marcail nodded. "She's not waiting out in the carriage, is she?"

"No, ma'am."

Again Marcail nodded. "Then why don't you tell us why you came."

This time it was Sydney's turn to nod, and suddenly he looked terrified all over again. His words were halting, but understandable.

"I came—to tell you—I'm sorry—" he stopped as though out of breath, and Marcail spoke.

"I forgive you, Sydney."

Sydney nodded again but didn't look at all relieved. "Can I ask you a question?" He paused, glancing between both adults, whose expressions were open and patient, before settling terrified eyes on his beloved teacher.

"Will I go to hell for what I've done?" he burst out, his face crumbling, tears barely held in check.

"Come here, Sydney," Marcail beckoned compassionately and shifted in her chair so she could take him in her arms. It was too much for the 11-year-old, and his tears came in a torrent. Another five minutes passed before he was able to breathe normally. Both Alex and Marcail took that time to pray silently.

Finally raising a tear-stained face, Sydney asked, "Will I, Mrs. Montgomery? Will I go to hell for what I've done?"

Marcail hugged him close once again. She stroked the hair from his damp little forehead and began to speak softly.

"What you did was very wrong, Sydney. I think you understand that."

Sydney's head came away from his teacher's shoulder. "It was a sin, a big sin?"

"Yes, you did sin. We all sin."

"Not you," Sydney spoke vehemently.

"Yes, I do, Sydney. The Bible says that *all* sin," she told him gently.

"So you're afraid of going to hell too?" Sydney's voice was full of wonder, and Marcail almost smiled.

"No, Sydney, I'm not," she continued with complete assurance. "You see, God has made a way for us to come to Him. Jesus Christ is the way. When we believe Jesus died to save us from sin, He comes to live inside of us.

Then when we die, because of our belief in Him we'll go to heaven and live forever with God.

"So you see, Sydney, even though I sin, God has provided the gift of His Son to save me, and I've accepted that gift." Marcail hesitated, afraid that she might turn him away forever, but her next words had to be said.

"I don't think you've ever accepted God's gift of salvation, Sydney, and I'm afraid that without Jesus Christ, you'll never change. Each time something has happened, you've told me it will never happen again. But it does. God can change you, Sydney. He can help you control your temper and change the way you treat other people."

Marcail fell silent then, allowing her young student to absorb all she'd said. It seemed he wouldn't say anything, but he suddenly turned to Alex.

"I've hated you at times, and that's a sin, isn't it?"

"Yes, it is," Alex told him, his voice noncondemning. "But what Mrs. Montgomery was telling you is true—we all sin." Alex opened his Bible to the book of 1 John.

"You see right here in the first chapter, verse 8, it reads, 'If we say we have no sin, we deceive ourselves, and the truth is not in us.' But then if you turn back to the Gospel of John, chapter 3 verse 36," Alex held the Bible so Sydney could read along with him, "it says, 'He that believeth on the Son hath everlasting life; and he that believeth not the Son shall not see life, but the wrath of God abideth on him.'

"You can believe on the Lord Jesus Christ, and let Him make the needed changes in your life, as Mrs. Montgomery and I have. God is waiting for you to take the gift that He offers. Believe on Christ with your whole heart, and then learn to live God's way."

Alex's voice was kindness itself, and Sydney couldn't help but respond to the tenderness he saw there.

"And you think God would really want to give the gift to me, even though I've hated a lot of people?"

"Hate is a serious thing," Alex told him. "There is a man in the Bible named Saul who hated people so much that he had them killed. Then one day Saul learned that what he was doing was wrong, and he let Jesus Christ come into his heart. God changed his name to Paul and turned his life completely around."

"Would I have to change my name?"

"No," Marcail smiled as she answered. "But if you let Him, God can change your life."

"That's what I want," Sydney said after a moment, "but I'm not really certain—" He hesitated, and Marcail stepped in.

"I accepted God's gift when I was just a little girl. My father prayed with me, and I said something like this, 'Dear Father in heaven, I believe You sent Your Son to die for my sins, and right now I ask You to come into my life—take away my sins and live in me.' My father went on to explain that this didn't mean I would never sin again, but that God would never leave me, and when I did sin, all I needed to do was confess and turn away from those sins to be right with Him."

"Can I pray now?"

"You certainly can. If you want to pray out loud, I can help you, or you can pray silently in your heart."

Sydney opted for silent prayer, and both Marcail and Alex bowed their heads as he prayed. Sydney was done first, having told God he was sorry for his sin and that he wanted Jesus Christ to live in him. He then sat looking at his teacher until she raised her head.

He loved Mrs. Montgomery more than he had ever loved anyone else on the earth. When she'd first started talking about his need to believe in Christ, he thought he'd better do it in order to really prove to her how sorry he was for tripping her.

Then Dr. Montgomery had shown him the verses right out of the Bible, and Sydney had suddenly really wanted to know Christ. The verses he read gave him hope, more hope than he would have believed possible. And with this new hope burgeoning within him, it was very easy to sit quietly and wait for his teacher to open her eyes.

Marcail kept her head bent for some time, praying that Sydney's decision had been real, and not just something done to please her. She honestly saw no other way for him to become a sound, well-adjusted adult. Marcail trusted in God to change him, especially since his home life was so lacking in proper discipline. Sydney needed someone to answer to, and who more perfect than a loving heavenly Father.

Marcail asked God to become very real to Sydney in the weeks to come, so that even though he now had someone to answer to, he would understand that God was the most loving father any boy could want.

When Marcail finally raised her head, she found Sydney smiling at her. Marcail held her arms out once again, and this time there were no words of apology or regret, just genuine love between two of God's children.

# *forty-eight*

In the days and weeks that followed, Marcail saw that
Sydney's conversion had been genuine. She learned in
the first week that her speculation over why he had
tripped her had been correct. But his remorse over the
incident was sincere, and the changes in him proved it.

Marcail was not certain what he said to his grandmother, but nearly every afternoon the Duckworth
carriage was late. He would stay after school to talk, ask
questions about the Bible, or recite the latest verse he was
memorizing.

Life in the classroom was not without its flaws, but
Marcail was thrilled with the new Sydney. In fact, the
entire class responded positively to the changes they
saw in him. Marcail shared privately with the children
she knew were praying for her and for Sydney. They
continued their prayers, only this time they prayed that
Sydney would grow in the Lord.

The weather was improving, and the class was now
able to spend extra time out of doors, working on everything from nature projects to their spelling lessons. The
end of the year was drawing to a close at an alarming
rate. Even though Marcail was very pleased with the
year, a dark shadow lay over her heart. It seemed the

closer she and Sydney became, the further Alex and she moved apart.

He no longer took her home since the weather was so warm. In fact some mornings when Alex had to be out the door very early, she walked to school. This was really not a problem, but the most evident change in their relationship was the fact that he stopped touching her.

As they rode Kelsey, his touch was an impersonal one. He no longer kissed her goodbye or even walked her inside the schoolhouse once they arrived. At one time, Marcail would have said she preferred it this way, but she was discovering with heartrending clarity that she missed her husband's touch.

He was never rude or short-tempered with her, but along with his touch, the fun, light teasing he'd always lavished on her had also left their marriage. Much of the time he was busy at the office, but even when they did spend time together, it was like living with a polite stranger. Marcail would have been surprised to learn that Alex would have described her the same way.

Something had died inside of Alex when he found his wife so severely injured and knew that if it had been up to her she would never have told him. He had really believed they'd come a long way, but it seemed all feelings of love and trust had been on his part.

He tried to understand how shocked and upset she'd been after the fall, but her reserved attitude toward him continued even after Sydney had come to the Lord. At a time when he thought she would be walking on a cloud, she was as aloof and cold to him as when they'd talked months before on the road to the schoolhouse. Both husband and wife needed a good dose of togetherness, with no patient or student interruptions.

❏ ❏ ❏

The last day of school was only two weeks away when Marcail decided she needed to remind Alex that she was going to Santa Rosa. If things had been warmer between them, she would also have reminded him that he had planned to accompany her. Now, however, her pride had come to the fore, and she told herself she wasn't going to beg him to do something he didn't want to do. It never once occurred to her *not* to go, or to wait until he brought the subject up.

They were having a rare evening alone when Marcail finally filled him in on her plans. Alex didn't say much from his place on a living room chair. He nodded quietly as she spoke, until she told him she wouldn't be back until the end of June.

"The *end* of June?"

"That's right." Marcail's chin raised slightly. "I haven't seen my family since Christmas, and with school out, there is really no reason for me to stay here all summer."

If she had slapped Alex in the face, she couldn't have hurt him more. Marcail hadn't meant it the way it sounded, and had it not been for the brief expression of pain she saw in his eyes, she wouldn't have said a word. But she *had* seen Alex's look of hurt, however brief, and decided to remind him that he'd planned to go.

"I thought maybe you'd come with me." Her voice was hesitant.

"I can't be gone an entire month," he told her softly.

"Then maybe you could come for half the time." Marcail wasn't sure why she said that after she'd told herself she wasn't going to beg.

"Are you sure you wouldn't mind my going along?" Alex was feeling too vulnerable to agree straight out-of-hand.

"I know my family wants to meet you." Marcail evaded the question neatly.

*So that's why I'm going—to meet your family*, Alex thought to himself. At the same time he knew someone was going to have to bend in this cold war in which they were now engaged. He was desperate enough at the moment to be that someone.

"All right; I'll stay for two weeks. When did you plan on leaving?"

"Saturday, a week from today. The day after school is out."

Alex nodded again and went back to the book in his lap. Marcail's eyes dropped to her school lesson, but she stared sightlessly at the page. The only thing she could see right then was her room at Kaitlin and Rigg's. It sat at the bottom of the stairs and sported *one* double bed.

# *forty-nine*

It was a very silent couple that boarded the train for Santa Rosa on Saturday, June 4. Kelsey had been delivered to the livery, and Alex had arranged to have the local veterinarian cover for him. It wasn't the same as having a doctor on call, but none of Alex's female patients were expecting, and having the elderly Dr. Crow on hand was better than nothing.

Marcail sat by the window, and Alex took the aisle seat. There was little conversation between them for the first 15 miles, until a sudden shifting of the car caused Marcail to fall into Alex's shoulder.

"I'm sorry," she said as she righted herself in the seat.

"I don't mind. I'm still getting used to the fact that you don't sleep on the train."

"I don't know what you mean."

"Linette never lasted more than two miles."

Marcail looked into his face as he spoke and suddenly realized how much she missed his talking with her.

"You never talk about her; is it very hard for you?"

"It was at first," Alex admitted, not understanding just yet that this was Marcail's way of trying to open the door that had been shut between them for so many weeks. "It's been four years, however, and time does heal."

"You grew up together, didn't you?" Marcail tried again when it seemed Alex would not go on.

"Yes. My folks have told me we were inseparable from the first time we laid eyes on each other. I don't know if we should have been married, but we were." Again Alex hesitated.

"Why do you say that?" Marcail was surprised.

"Oh, I didn't really mean it the way it sounded, but we were such good friends. As kids I'd always been her champion, and we could talk about anything, even argue, and still walk away as friends.

"But then later our friendship made our marriage difficult. I think I must have been more like a big brother to Linette than a husband. She always believed it was my job to make her happy. She came to depend on me so heavily that when she became miserable living in Willits it put quite a strain on our marriage."

"Why didn't she like Willits?" Marcail wasn't certain that any of this was her business, but Alex was really talking to her for the first time since she'd fallen down the schoolhouse steps, and she desperately wanted him to continue.

"It wasn't Willits specifically—that was the problem. Linette never wanted to live away from Fort Bragg. She couldn't seem to grasp that Fort Bragg already had two doctors and I needed to go elsewhere. I was thankful we were able to be as close as we were, but it wasn't good enough for her." Alex paused, his eyes staring out the window at nothing. Some of the pain flooded back to him.

"How did she die?" Marcail couldn't keep from asking.

"The actual cause of death was a head injury when she fell from a chair, but the fall, or rather the weakness that brought her off the chair, was caused by tuberculosis. In the mid to late stages of tuberculosis, patients run fevers in the afternoon and evenings, and Linette was trying to do too much when she wasn't up to it. I think she must have become a bit dizzy while on that chair, or possibly fainted."

Sharing absently about his past without really looking at his wife, Alex now turned to find that Marcail had gone very pale. She also looked tremendously grief-stricken, more grief-stricken than she should have been for a woman she didn't even know.

"What is it, Marcail? What did I say?"

"My mother died of tuberculosis," she admitted softly. "It's amazing what you can block out. I'd completely forgotten how ill she'd been every evening."

"How old were you when she died?"

"Nine."

Alex's heart broke just a little at the thought. A child is so young, and so much in need of a mother, when only nine years old. Alex wanted to say something, but Marcail was ready to talk and there was no need.

"They kept her illness from us until we arrived in San Francisco. I'll never forget the first time I saw my aunt's house. It was huge. I'd never been away from Hawaii, and I didn't know they made houses like that. I was terrified of it. I remember holding onto my mother's hand with all my might as she led me inside. Her hand was so hot I thought she must be scared too.

"We had a few days of rest, but I could tell something was wrong. Katie and Sean were not as fun as they had been, and I thought maybe they were as sad about leaving Hawaii as I was. Then one night when Mother and

Father put me to bed, Mother said the doctor had been to see her.

"I remember the peace I saw on her face even as she told me she was going to heaven very soon. I also remember thinking that the doctor was the most awful man on earth. I figured if he hadn't come, then Mother would still be well. Father tried to tell me otherwise, but my mind was made up. When I saw him at the funeral, I thought he didn't look like such a bad man, but my heart was convinced that he'd caused my mother's death."

"And you've been afraid of doctors ever since," Alex finished for her.

Marcail could only nod. She'd never intended to tell anyone that story, but found that a burden had been lifted from her heart. She also found the touch of Alex's arm as it slipped around her the most comforting thing she'd ever felt. Marcail snuggled unreservedly against his side, loving the clean smell of his shirt. Hope burgeoned within her that he might still care.

Neither one talked after that, which was fine with Marcail. She needed the quiet to gather her thoughts and pray about her family meeting Alex. A week ago there would have been grave doubt in her mind, but the train ride had restored her hope. Knowing that Rigg and Katie were going to love this man she had married left her feeling suddenly lighthearted.

# *fifty*

Marcail's feet had barely touched the platform before Rigg swept her into his arms. She laughed as he released her and turned to hug Kaitlin. After a brief hug Katie surprised Marcail by beginning to chatter in Hawaiian. Marcail, from long habit, answered her sister in kind. Marcail looked thin to Katie, a sure sign that the younger girl had been unhappy. Katie, momentarily forgetting all the wonderful things her father had said about Alex, presumed he was to blame.

Alex stood dumbfounded as Katie spoke swiftly and Marcail answered. He felt like a fool. For months he'd believed his wife knew a simple Hawaiian lullaby because she'd been born in the Islands. Now she stood speaking fluently in a language he had no hope of understanding.

It took a moment to gather his wits and drag his eyes from his wife, and when he did, he looked over to find Rigg grinning at him.

"You're doing better than I did. The first time I heard them go at it, my mouth nearly swung open." Rigg, still smiling, held out his hand to his new brother-in-law. "Welcome to Santa Rosa, Alex."

"Thank you," Alex spoke sincerely, and then glanced again at his wife. "They're not arguing, are they?"

"No," Rigg told him calmly.

"Then you understand them?"

Rigg shouted with laughter. "I don't understand a word of it, but believe me when I tell you, you'll *know* if the conversation turns angry."

Alex could only nod before glancing down beside Rigg and spotting a young girl struggling with a squirming toddler. Rigg noticed at the same time and rescued his daughter Gretchen from the terror of her little brother.

"Alex," Rigg spoke and smiled again, "I'd like you to meet my Gretchen. Gretchen, this is your Uncle Alex."

"Hello, Uncle Alex," Gretchen greeted him politely, and Alex studied the traces of Marcail he saw in her face. He greeted her and gave her his warmest smile.

"And this," Rigg went on, "is Donovan. Donovan, this is your Uncle Alex. Can you say hello?"

Donovan's answer was to shove his thumb a little further into his mouth, but Alex could see the beginnings of a smile. In fact, Donovan must have liked what he saw, because he abandoned his thumb long enough to hold out his arms, inviting Alex to take him. Alex didn't hesitate, and the youngest member of the Riggs family gave his father a cheeky grin as he settled on his new uncle's arm.

Rolling his eyes in amusement, Rigg attempted to draw his other daughter out to be introduced. Gretchen had been a picture of manners and grace. Molly, on the other hand, was not quite so amenable.

"Come on, Molly," Rigg coaxed gently as she hid behind his left leg.

Alex watched as she wrapped her little arms around her father's pant leg and peeked out, ever so carefully, to see him. A huge smile broke over Alex's face; it was like looking at a tiny version of his wife.

Rigg, knowing how Molly was going to appear to Alex, watched the younger man carefully. As he then called Katie over to be introduced, he found himself thinking that although their marriage might have started out as a convenience, without a doubt this man had fallen in love with his wife.

❑ ❑ ❑

An hour later, Marcail and Alex stood across from each other in Marcail's room. Marcail told herself that she was not going to blush, but she had to tell Alex there was an alternative to sharing the bed. She watched as his eyes took in the one bed, the large dresser with mirror, the dressing screen in the corner, and the oak chest at the foot of the bed.

After he'd looked his fill, Alex's eyes settled on his wife. They were not hesitant or questioning, but steady, waiting for her to make the next move. She did not disappoint him.

"My sister is the soul of discretion, Alex, and if you want, I could ask her for a cot. Or," Marcail went on quietly, "we could share the bed like we did in Fort Bragg."

Alex knew this was not an invitation for intimacy, but that was fine with him at this point; he felt the place for such things was in their own home. He also understood that Marcail had no inkling of how tiring it had been for him in Fort Bragg.

"I have no problem sleeping beside you while we're here, Marcail." Alex stated this carefully, so his wife would know he had not missed her meaning. "However, I rose early and came to bed late in Fort Bragg so you would have privacy. I'd like to get a little more rest while I'm here, and that will probably mean less privacy for you. So you see, the choice is really yours."

Marcail nodded after just a moment's hesitation. "I don't think that will be a problem."

Alex, who'd been holding his bag, then placed it beside the bed. He slipped out of his coat and placed it over a chair. Marcail took her cue from him, and reached for her own bag. She put a few things in the top dresser drawer and then went to the closet in the corner.

A moment later she disappeared behind the dressing screen. Alex, more than a little curious about what she was up to, lounged back on the bed and waited. Less than five minutes passed, and Marcail appeared in a lovely white dress with a round neckline and puffy sleeves. Her hair was down, pulled back at her neck with a white ribbon.

Alex thought she looked like a breath of spring air. She also looked a little flustered over the way he stared, so she explained in halting tones why she had changed.

"It's warm here, and my other dresses are heavy, and well, I—"

"Don't explain, Marcail," Alex said smoothly. "I quite approve. It is hot here, and I hope your family won't mind my shirtsleeves."

Marcail shook her head. "I think you'll find we're pretty relaxed."

They continued to talk until they heard a commotion outside the door. It sounded as if Molly was squealing and Rigg was trying to quiet her. Alex's brows rose in question, but Marcail, as much in the dark as he, could only shrug.

Alex swung off the bed and opened the door so Marcail could precede him out of the room. They walked past the stairs and into the living room. When she saw Molly sitting on her brother's shoulders, Marcail halted abruptly. Alex nearly ran into her.

"Sean!" Marcail whispered, her mouth dropping open in a most unfeminine way.

Sean's smile was boyish as he caught sight of his sister. He swung Molly onto the sofa and crossed the room to hug her. Alex, quietly watching this reunion, had only one thought, *she had never planned on marrying anyone even as tall as I am, but all the men in her life are huge. I've never considered myself short, but Rigg and Sean dwarf me.*

"This is Alex," Alex heard Marcail say before Sean's hand took his own.

"Alex, this is my brother, Sean."

"It's good to meet you," Alex began. "I take it that Marcail knew nothing of this?"

"Right. We meant to be at the train station but didn't get away on time. Charlie?" Sean suddenly called over his shoulder. Alex watched as an adorable redhead approached.

"It's short for Charlotte," she said to her surprised brother-in-law.

Introductions were made all around. Alex met Ricky, who was a picture of Sean, and Callie, whose hair was the exact shade of her mother's. The entire family was gathered in the living room, and things were just settling down when Charlie announced that she was expecting once again. There was another round of mayhem as hugs and congratulations were shared. When the room was finally calm, Alex found himself next to Katie. His voice was very quiet and gentle when he spoke privately to her.

"Unless I miss my guess, you have an announcement of your own to make."

Katie could only stare at him for the space of several

heartbeats. "How did you know?" Her voice as soft as his own.

"I'm not sure how I know; I've just always had this knack for sighting such things."

"I haven't even had a chance to tell Rigg."

Alex chuckled at her dry tone. "Then this is decidedly not a good time to reveal your news."

"Is it because you're a doctor?" Katie was still captivated by his perception.

"No, I don't think so. My father and brother are both doctors, but they've never been able to do it. I can't do it unless the woman herself knows, so you must give off some type of signal."

Katie nodded, looking deep in thought.

"I didn't want to intrude," Alex continued, still for Katie's ears alone. "But since you haven't decided whether or not you like me, I'd hoped to do or say something that would put your mind at ease concerning Marcail."

Again Katie could only stare. Had she not been so surprised, she would have blushed to the roots of her hair over being read so easily.

"It must be rather difficult to live with someone who can read your mind," Kaitlin spoke at last. "Poor Marcail, she's never been able to keep a single emotion from her face."

Alex frowned at Katie a moment as he thought of Marcail's reserve in the last weeks.

"You'd be surprised," was all he finally said.

Kaitlin, having had no idea what a sensitive subject this was, was a little taken aback at the look that had passed over Alex's face.

The subject was changed then, but Alex couldn't get his sister-in-law's words out of his head. He wondered if he knew his wife at all.

# *fifty-one*

The next day was Sunday, and Alex began seeing a Marcail he'd never met before. She was not the normally quiet and thoughtful person she seemed to be at home. She talked almost nonstop and laughed with an abandon he didn't know she possessed.

He continued to pray about their relationship, turning his emotions over to God. He was starting to feel desperate to know which Marcail was really his wife. Unfortunately the events of the morning church service would only cause that desperate feeling to intensify.

Alex met all of Rigg's family, and that was no small group. They were a cheerful, warm bunch, and Alex was grateful for their welcome. He also met many of Marcail's church family. Marcail had told him that Pastor Keller was an excellent Bible teacher, and Alex found himself looking forward to the sermon.

But before it began, Marcail, Kaitlin, and Sean all rose from their seats and moved to the front. Alex saw in an instant that they were going to sing. He knew Marcail had a nice voice, but he also knew how soft it was and wondered if they would even hear her at the back of the church.

They started with a Hawaiian hymn. It was beautiful, and the room was utterly still when Sean soloed. He was a perfect tenor, and Alex couldn't decide which he liked more, Sean's solo or the three voices blended together in perfect harmony. But this was before their second song, an English hymn, during which Alex heard his wife's true solo voice for the first time.

She soloed for two of the verses, and he discovered she had one of the purest, highest soprano voices he'd ever heard. The pews on which the congregation sat literally vibrated with her high notes. Alex was still taking it all in when Marcail returned to sit beside him.

In his confusion, Alex didn't enjoy the sermon nearly as much as he'd anticipated, or the lunch with the family at Rigg's parents' farm afterward. In fact, Alex spent the day under a painful cloud, which he tried to hide by smiling until his face hurt.

Marcail, who was having the time of her life now that she was home, didn't notice that the smile didn't reach Alex's eyes. Not until they returned to the house in the late afternoon and Alex told everyone he was going to take a walk did Marcail stop to think about how quiet he had been all day.

❏ ❏ ❏

Rigg usually put the kids to bed, but tonight he and Marcail were alone in the kitchen. Katie felt it was best to leave them. Sensing the need for privacy as well, Sean and Charlie put the children to bed with their cousins and stayed in the living room with Katie.

The talk beyond the kitchen door began very lightly, but Rigg's heart was so burdened by what he'd seen on Alex's face during the morning service that he had determined to have a serious talk with his young sister-in-law.

"Was it good to have the school year end?" Rigg asked some minutes into the conversation.

"Yes and no. I'm ready for a break, but I can't think what I'll do to keep busy for the rest of the summer."

Rigg's brow lowered on Marcail's words. She noticed and had the good grace to looked ashamed.

"Tell me something, Marc," Rigg began again, "did Alex know you were going to sing this morning?"

Marcail gave a small, apologetic shrug. "I guess I didn't bother to mention it."

Again Rigg frowned. Things were worse than he first believed.

"Would you be mad at Katie if she hadn't told you?" Marcail asked, seeing his disapproval.

"Not mad, just hurt."

Marcail was not comfortable with that and tried to change the subject, but Rigg would not be swayed. Even though she was growing angry, he kept at her.

"Tell me something, Marcail, did you really get married?"

"What's that supposed to mean?"

"Only that nothing has changed. You still act like the single woman who left here over a year ago."

These words made Marcail furious, but Rigg believed someone had to tell her. "Has he ever seen your anger, Marc? Do you open your heart to him at all?"

"You don't know what you're talking about, Rigg," Marcail said to him, but knew it was a lie. Rigg had guessed perfectly how closed Marcail was to her husband.

"I do know what I'm talking about," Rigg stated emphatically. "Alex Montgomery is a man, with feelings and needs, not some toy for you to play with when your family isn't around."

Marcail jumped to her feet in one angry move.

"Sit down, Marcail!" Rigg commanded.

"Don't you order me around, Rigg. I'm a grown woman!"

"Then act like one." Rigg's voice turned so gentle on those words that it was almost Marcail's undoing. "I realize a person can't force feelings that aren't there, but I've been watching Alex. Marcail, he's in love with you."

Marcail slowly sat back in her chair and stared across the table. "You don't understand, Rigg. I've done something, and I don't know how to undo it."

"Talk to Alex about it," Rigg told her.

"I don't know how."

"Then I'll pray that you'll know, because you're selling him short, honey. I was impressed when I met him last year, and then when your father came back from Willits, he told us he thought Alex was as fine as they came, a real man of God. Give him a chance, Marc; in fact, give him your heart. I can see he would treasure it all the years of your life."

Marcail didn't know what to say, but then she didn't have to. Alex chose that moment to come in the back door.

"Am I interrupting anything?" He glanced at Rigg, but his eyes turned to his wife's strained features.

"Have a seat, Alex," Rigg invited.

It took a few moments for Rigg to bring Alex out, but they eventually began to talk about where Alex had been on his walk. This time it was Marcail who was quiet.

# fifty-two

Alex, still half asleep, reached to wipe the hair from his face. It took a moment for it to register that it was not his own. Marcail's back was to him, but she must have just been asleep on his shoulder since his arm ached and her hair was spread across his face and chest like a fan.

Alex stretched, in no hurry to leave the warmth of the bed. It had taken only a few days for Alex to learn that Santa Rosa nights and mornings were cool. The heavy quilts on the bed made it a hard place to leave. That, and knowing that little Donovan was going to join them any minute.

Alex reached for his Bible. He was reading through the New Testament and just finishing the book of Mark. Not many minutes after he'd begun reading he heard the now-familiar thumping on the stairs outside the room. He knew what would come next as the bedroom door crashed back against the wall.

Donovan appeared beside the bed and grinned as soon as he saw Alex's face. Alex reached for him and put him on his chest. His big, dark eyes went to his Aunt Marcail's sleeping form and then back to Alex.

"Shhh," he said, one pudgy finger held carefully to

his lips. Alex nodded in approval. Donovan had felt it was his job to wake Marcail the first two mornings they were there, but Alex had taught him that they must be quiet.

Katie came down the stairs and peeked around the corner to check on her small charge. When she left, Alex knew she would head to the kitchen and start breakfast.

Alex let Donovan sit on his chest and chatter softly to him until the smell of fresh coffee floated through the air. Alex rose, pulled on enough clothes to be decent, and went to the kitchen with his nephew.

No one was around, so Alex helped himself to the coffee. He kept an eye on Donovan to see that he didn't get hurt, but at 18 months old, the boy was bent on destruction. He had emptied two cupboards and was started on a third while Alex sipped his coffee.

Alex had just put everything back in the first two when Katie came out of the bedroom right off the kitchen. An experienced mother, she tapped two of the blocks together that sat on the floor near the table. Donovan took the bait. After he'd plopped down on his well-padded seat, Katie helped Alex right the kitchen.

"I used to sleep as well as Marcail, but that was before children," Katie began conversationally.

"She scared me before I knew how hard she slept," Alex replied. "I checked her repeatedly, thinking she'd stopped breathing."

Katie laughed. "Before Rigg and I were married, he carried me from his parents' living room all the way upstairs. I didn't know about it for some time, but being such a sound sleeper can be very embarrassing."

"Marcail tells me that Sean held her upside down one time and she never woke."

Katie laughed again. "You know, I'd forgotten about that. Older siblings can be pretty awful."

"I never was," Rigg said as he came from the bedroom.

"Of course you weren't." Katie's voice was patronizing. "Tell us Rigg," she continued sweetly, "was it Jeff or Gilbert whom you lowered from the hayloft by the ankles and threatened to drop?"

"Oh that." Rigg was as calm as if it were an everyday occurrence. "It was Jeff, and he asked for it. If you don't believe me," Rigg said to Alex, "ask Bobbie—she has to live with him."

Alex grinned at the light banter. They were really a delightful couple. Alex had never had a marriage like they shared. Linette had been so serious and unhappy, and Marcail kept a carefully erected wall between them at all times. Alex had watched Rigg kiss his wife, hug her, tickle her, and even give her backside a playful smack when she walked by. None of this was offensive to him; it just caused him to yearn for the type of love they shared in his own marriage.

As he sat contemplating the mistakes he'd made in the past weeks, along with the indeterminable future before him, he was forced to ask himself whether Marcail was worth his efforts. Before the question could fully form in his mind, he knew the answer. As the Riggs' kitchen began to fill with people, Alex only half listened to what was going on around him: His heart was silently deciding to court his wife once again.

❑ ❑ ❑

Marcail noticed the change in Alex even before breakfast was over. She was a little unsure of how to take this new Alex, with his attentive manner and gentle touch.

He was acting as he had when they'd first wed, but Marcail, still a little bruised from the weeks of silence, was not sure how to respond.

She was sure of one thing, though. She did want to respond. Rigg had been correct about the way she hid her emotions, and Marcail knew that if she kept it up, it was going to be at her own expense. Right now she was looking forward to a time of new beginnings with her spouse.

Alex was spending the day at the mercantile with Rigg, and Marcail took advantage of the time to pray and ask God to help her love her husband unreservedly. Why she'd never prayed for this in the past was a mystery, but Marcail knew the time for waiting was over. She knew her feelings were not going to change overnight, but at least she was on the road and headed in the right direction.

The morning flew by, but a little before lunch, while Donovan was still taking a morning nap, Katie told Marcail that now was as good a time as any to cut her hair. Katie was wearing her hair a little differently these days, and Marcail wanted the same style.

"I meant to ask you to cut my hair when I was home for Christmas, but now I'm glad I forgot. I want you to take about ten inches off the back, Katie, and I want my bangs just like yours."

"You haven't said anything, so I wondered if you liked the way mine looked." Katie's hand went to the dark thatch of hair that covered her forehead, stopping just above her brows.

"They're darling. I want mine to be the exact length of yours."

Nodding her agreement, Katie knew how easy that would be. She combed and parted Marcail's hair in front, and for a time Marcail couldn't see through the fall of hair covering her eyes. The mirror was handy, however, and as soon as Katie was finished, Marcail checked her work.

"Oh, Katie," she exclaimed.

"Do you like it?"

"Yes!"

"I do too. I can get away with it because my face is round. And they're darling on you because they bring out your beautiful eyes."

Katie was behind Marcail now, brushing her hair straight. She was poised, scissors in hand and ready to cut, when Alex's incredulous voice broke through the air.

"*What* are you doing?"

Katie froze. Her gaze, along with Marcail's, flew to Alex. He stood in the doorway of the kitchen, his face clearly showing his displeasure. Rigg stood just behind him, and over Alex's shoulder he exchanged a look with his wife.

Just the night before Katie had been saying how she genuinely liked Alex, but she'd always believed Marcail needed someone with a firmer hand.

Rigg and Katie slipped quietly out of the room while Alex took a place at the kitchen table. He picked up a long strand of hair from Marcail's lap and fingered it for a moment. She was still behaving as though she were a single woman. At some point he had to make her understand that he cared enough to be included in every part of her life.

"Why were you cutting your hair?" Alex's question was simple, but it depicted just how complicated their relationship had become.

"Because of the headaches," Marcail explained, still watching his face. She'd never seen him this angry before.

Alex had completely forgotten about her headaches and said as much. "I wish you had talked to me," he added.

"I do too, *now*. But Katie knew I wanted it done and said she had time, so we just—" Marcail shrugged rather helplessly.

Alex reached and brushed his finger through her bangs. "I like the front."

"I'm sorry I didn't talk to you, Alex," Marcail said softly.

"And I'm sorry I was angry."

Alex reached for her face again, this time to brush his finger down her cheek.

"We'll just keep at it, Marcail, until we get it right."

The comment might have seemed cryptic to some, but Marcail caught his full meaning. She nodded ever so slightly, and for the first time in weeks Alex moved close and kissed her softly on the mouth.

# fifty-three

The remainder of the days in Santa Rosa were spent in idle pursuits. Marcail's family came to love Alex and approved of his tender care of Marcail. Sean and Charlotte had people they needed to visit, so some of their days were spent moving about, but Alex and Sean did get to have some time together, and got along famously.

The most memorable of their times together came on an afternoon when Alex and Sean ended up alone with the kids. All three of the women had gone shopping, and after the younger children were down for naps the men began to share. Alex was amazed to learn that Sean's marriage to Charlotte had been forced.

"I didn't even have the luxury of knowing her ahead of time. I saw her, and about ten minutes later, we were married."

Sean went on to explain the entire story about his run-in with the law, and Alex simply stared at him in amazement. When he was through, the room was silent as Alex digested all he had heard.

"But you have made a marriage of it," Alex finally commented, thinking how happy Sean and his wife seemed.

"Yes," Sean told him. "It was not without its pain, but God never gave up on either of us. I love my wife deeply, and I know she loves me. I hope that gives you hope, Alex."

"It does, Sean, thanks. I've made some mistakes, but it's never too late."

"You're right; it's not," he agreed. "I'll be praying for you both."

Alex thanked him just before the older children appeared, claiming to be hungry. The rest of the afternoon was spent playing with little ones and cleaning up their messes.

Marcail and Alex spent time alone together as well. They went for walks, took a boat out on the lagoon, and went out to supper a few times. Mostly, they talked. They cleared the air on many issues. Marcail explained that she had never meant to exclude Alex from her talk with Cordelia Duckworth. She also told him that it had been her lingering fear of doctors that had kept her from telling Alex of her bruises. She explained that her shock at the time had been so great, she had reacted without thought. She then admitted that, once better, the sin of pride reared its ugly head and kept her from approaching Alex sooner.

They talked about Marcail's fear of being herself with Alex, and even though talking about it didn't instantly right the situation, both husband and wife were relieved to have things out in the open. When Marcail asked Alex if he was working longer hours in order to avoid her, he confessed that he had been. For the first time a new understanding was growing between them.

The days flew, and both were surprised when it was time for Alex to leave for Willits. It seemed they had just arrived. Marcail was uncertain as to whether or not she should stay. As Alex packed she talked with him about it.

"Maybe I should come home with you."

Alex was very pleased by her offer, but now that they were once again talking with each other, he had no problem with her staying.

"You still have a few friends you didn't get to see," Alex said, adding, "School begins in less than two months, and then who knows when you'll get back here again."

"That's true," Marcail answered, trying to be as logical as her spouse.

Nothing more was said on the subject, and when Alex was ready, Marcail walked him to the train station. All the nieces and nephews had hugged him goodbye at the house, each one having come to love Uncle Alex. The adults were just as warm in their send-off, and Katie had fixed a huge lunch for him to enjoy on the train.

Once at the station, husband and wife sat quietly waiting for the train to arrive. For a time, both were content to sit and watch the train station activity.

"You will come home to me, won't you, Marc?"

Marcail turned her head as they sat on a bench by the ticket office and gave Alex a quizzical look. "Where else would I go?"

"You might not *go* anywhere. After I leave, you might find you like it better here and—"

"I'll come home," Marcail quietly cut him off. She'd never seen Alex look as hesitant before and found it rather heartbreaking.

"I think," Marcail added, hoping she was not being overly bold, "that the bed will be lonely without you."

Alex wished he could take her in his arms, and his eyes told her as much. "My bed at home is lonely without you too."

Marcail nodded, finding she was unembarrassed for the first time. Nothing more was said since the train was now coming into the station. Alex stood and pulled Marcail around to the quiet side of the ticket office. Without warning, he pulled her into his arms and kissed her as he'd done on the beach in Fort Bragg.

When Alex was finally on board, Marcail stood on the platform and watched the train as it eased out of sight. She found herself wishing she'd followed her heart. If she had, she would have been on the train with her husband.

❑ ❑ ❑

Marcail closed the book she had been reading to Donovan; he was sound asleep. She knew she could carry him upstairs, but she rather enjoyed the feel of his warm little body snuggled against her own.

Rigg and Katie had gone out for the evening, and when his father had not been there to put him to bed, Donovan dissolved into tears. Both girls had gone to bed without a qualm, so Marcail took Donovan to the living room for a story.

Sean and Charlotte had left the day before for Visalia, to spend some time with Patrick, Duncan, Lora, Sadie, and the church family there. The house was very quiet. Marcail thought she could sit there for hours, holding her nephew and praying.

She ended her prayers by praying for Alex. Marcail couldn't believe how much she missed him. She was scheduled to leave in two days, and the idea of going early was tempting. Since two weeks was barely enough time to exchange mail, they had not tried to communicate, but he had been in her thoughts almost constantly.

After Alex left, Marcail thanked Rigg for his words to her. They had made her stop and think of all she was wasting by distancing herself from a man who obviously cared deeply for her. Marcail was not ready to go home and throw herself into Alex's embrace, but she *was* ready to go home and be herself.

Alex had proved that he was not going to reject her, and Marcail had finally figured out that this had been her deepest worry. There was nothing she had done to cause the death of her mother, or the way her father and then her brother had suddenly exited her life. After each departure, however, she had mentally prepared herself to be a very good girl so they would want to come back.

When Marcail was still a teen, she had done this with God, but her heavenly Father, in His perfect love, showed her that His acceptance was all-encompassing. That wasn't to say she could mindlessly sin and do as she pleased, but it did mean that full fellowship was just a prayer away. Marcail came to understand that God would never cast her aside. Now she was learning that neither would Alex.

It seemed for a time that he had decided she was not worth his effort, but all that was put aside. He had only been taking his cue from her, and Marcail realized she'd been as much to blame as he had.

Marcail hefted Donovan into her arms and took him to bed at last. She stood over his crib for a moment, her mind once again on Alex and what the future of their marriage might be and then on the adorable boy in the crib. She couldn't help but wonder if God would bless her marriage with love, and someday give them a little person like the one who'd fallen asleep in her arms tonight.

# *fifty-four*

Alex stared at the howling infant in his hands, still not fully believing he had just delivered a baby. Mother and son were doing fine, and the father was still lying exactly where he'd fallen in a dead faint some ten minutes earlier.

The morning was taking on a feeling of reality. At 5:30 Alex had awakened to the sound of the bell. He was just coming out of the barn with Kelsey when a wagon came tearing up the road. Frank Nelson was the man at the reins, and he had been too frantic to even wait for Alex to come to the office.

Frank breathlessly insisted that his wife was dying. Alex had swiftly tied Kelsey's reins to the back of the buckboard and climbed aboard. He held on while Frank drove to his farm, shouting the events of the past hours as they went.

It seemed his wife's stomach had started to hurt some six hours ago and had slowly worsened. Frank was not too keen on doctors, and since the pains came and went, he had held off coming into town. But about 30 minutes ago, his wife had started to bellow.

Frank shouted to Alex over the sound of the horse's hooves, telling him about the time he'd accidently driven a pickax right through her foot without her so much as making a sound. But after five minutes of her bellowing, he could take it no longer, certain that she was about to die.

It was fully light by the time they reached the house, but Alex would have had no trouble finding it in the dark. He'd have been led by the horrendous cries of the woman within.

Alex entered the house alone and followed the noise to the bedroom. On the bed he found an extremely over-weight woman. She gasped for breath as he entered the room and tried to speak.

"I'm Dr. Montgomery, Mrs. Nelson. Can you tell me exactly what's wrong?"

Mrs. Nelson began to do so, crying about her stomach and the fact that she was dying—but before she could finish, she was suddenly gripped with another pain. Alex stood by the bed and watched as she cried out and writhed in agony. He then bent and placed his hand on her enormous stomach.

"Mrs. Nelson," Alex spoke when the worst of the pain had passed. "The pains you're having are not going to kill you. They're perfectly normal; you're having a baby."

A loud crash sounded behind Alex, and he turned to see that Mr. Nelson had come into the room behind him. The big man had hit the floor with an awful thud, but from a distance seemed unhurt. Alex would have checked on him, but Mrs. Nelson's next contraction hit.

"Would you like my assistance?" Alex shouted above her wailing. He went to work after witnessing the fren-zied nodding of her head.

Ten minutes later he held a healthy baby boy up for his mother's inspection. Her cries this time were cries of joy, and after Alex had wrapped the baby in a shirt he found on a chair, he placed the tiny scrap of life into its mother's arms.

Mr. Nelson was coming around, and after Alex had a quick wash in the basin, he helped him onto a chair. The man seemed stunned, and Alex knew just how he felt. Some minutes passed before Mr. Nelson moved from his chair to sit on the edge of the bed. It became evident in the next few seconds that there was real love between this hardworking couple as they first stared at their tiny son and then at one another.

"Twenty-three years," Alex heard him say, his voice full of wonder. "Twenty-three years we go childless, and now in the space of a few minutes—" Frank suddenly chuckled. "I thought you were dying, Emmaline."

His wife laughed along. "I thought so too."

Mr. Nelson sobered suddenly. "Even if there hadn't been a baby, Em, I'm still glad you're here."

Alex exited the bedroom on this tender note. He waited in the kitchen for about five minutes, and then Frank called him back in. Alex was profoundly moved at the humble way they thanked him for the life of their son and then asked his fee for the delivery.

He left with the $5.00 in his pocket and a promise from them that they would bring the baby to his office in a week's time. Alex went back home to clean up and head to the office. Marcail was due in that very afternoon. Alex, anticipating her return, had believed the time would drag, but if it continued as it had begun, he had a feeling the day would fly.

❑❑❑

Marcail stepped off the train and found a fair crowd of people milling about the platform. She stood still and waited for the throng to clear, and then spotted Alex leaning against the side of the ticket office. His stance was nonchalant, belying the thunderous beating of his heart at the mere sight of his wife. She had an extra suitcase with her, and Alex was pleased that she'd brought some extra dresses back as he'd asked.

Alex pushed away from the side of the building and met her halfway. Wanting to crush her in his arms, he immediately reached for her bags, thankful for something to do with his hands.

"Welcome home," he spoke sincerely.

"Thank you." Marcail smiled at him and bit her lip. He looked wonderful, and as she took in his white shirt, dark hair, and gorgeous blue eyes, Marcail wanted to hug and kiss him for the first time.

Alex led the way as they walked from the train station platform. Marcail looked for Kelsey as they moved, but didn't immediately spot him. She also missed the way Alex turned to watch her once she sighted the horse.

"Where did you get this?" Marcail questioned Alex when her surprised visage took in the small black buggy to which Kelsey was hitched.

"A patient who hasn't paid me in the last year gave it to us. When he saw me at church alone for two Sundays, he thought you'd grown tired of riding on the back of a horse and left me."

Marcail laughed with a mixture of astonishment and pleasure. "Maybe I should go away more often," she teased with exaggerated innocence, as Alex's hands took possession of her waist to swing her aboard the buggy.

"You're not going anywhere for a long time," he growled good-naturedly, with a hint of ownership.

Hearing that tone, Marcail's smile was one of pure contentment as she settled back against the well-padded buggy seat.

□ □ □

Marcail took the next few days to resettle. She cleaned the entire house and spent one day baking, all the while thoroughly loving the feel of being home.

Seth and Allie had eloped while Marcail was away, and this news was all over town. The newlyweds were living in a place near the train station, and Marcail went to see them on her fifth day home. Since her own marriage was becoming more precious every day, Marcail was no longer envious of the happiness she saw in her friend's eyes.

Alex had not pressed her to move from her sofa bed into the bedroom, but even though she'd only been home a few days, he was more attentive and their communication was stronger than it had ever been.

They fell easily back into their routine. Some mornings she was asleep when Alex left for work; others she was up and preparing breakfast. The Monday morning of her second week back was just such a morning. Marcail was up early and had breakfast started, but her face was pensive when Alex entered the kitchen.

Alex showed his pleasure at seeing her by planting a kiss on her cheek. She never stiffened at his touch now, and Alex always felt a bit lightheaded at the lovely smiles she gave him. This morning, however, her smile was somewhat preoccupied.

"I'd like to go see Cordelia Duckworth this morning. Is today good for you?"

"What were you thinking of, midmorning?"

Marcail nodded.

"That's fine. I'll head out pretty soon and then come back for you about 10:00."

"Thank you, Alex," Marcail was deeply moved by his willingness to accompany her.

Knowing that Mrs. Duckworth might refuse even to see her, Marcail spent the morning in prayer. If she

# fifty-five

Cordelia Duckworth dismissed her maid with an angry word and turned back to the mirror. Her dress was so tight she could hardly breathe, and she blamed her son Richard for this fact. Richard and a few people from town. They were actually trying to gain control of matters that were lawfully hers to manage. It wasn't the first time the townspeople had tried something like this, and when they did, Cordelia ate.

She was a very big eater on a regular basis, but when upset, her appetite became enormous. Since Richard had been acting so strangely, she had been very upset indeed. Her eyes slid shut on her image as she remembered the argument they'd had a week ago.

"I'm thinking about moving back, Mother."

"Back where?" Cordelia had almost been afraid to ask.

"To Willits, of course. You could keep the west wing," he went on conversationally, "and Beverly, Sydney, and I would take the east wing."

"I will not live with that woman, Richard," Cordelia told him, her voice turning shrill.

"You forget whose house this is, Mother," Richard said coolly. It had taken years of living apart from his mother to finally put his own life together. He now saw

Cordelia with new eyes. "I've let you run things for a long time, but lately I've been observing the situation a little more carefully. You've set yourself up as a queen in this town." His voice had turned scornful.

"Father would never have wanted that. Sydney has not been able to speak of it until lately, so I had no idea. What you're doing here is criminal, and it had better stop."

"I will not be talked to this way by my own son. How dare you come here and threaten me—"

Richard's laughter had cut her off. "Threats, Mother? No. Promises. Where Willits and Sydney are concerned, I *will* be more involved in the very near future."

"What do you mean?"

"I mean that if you want to see your grandson, you'll watch your step in this town."

He had never threatened her before, and she was so taken aback she was speechless. It was unfortunate that she chose to remember that scene on this particular morning, since it put her in a horrid mood. She nearly shouted when someone knocked on her bedroom door.

*"What is it?"*

"The door opened cautiously, and her personal maid tentatively stuck her head in. "Dr. and Mrs. Montgomery are here to see you, ma'am."

Cordelia's brow furrowed, and the maid steeled herself for a hairbrush or some other handy object to fly at the door.

"Tell them I'll be down shortly" was all the older woman said, and the maid, from years of experience, knew enough to close the door without a sound.

❑ ❑ ❑

Alex and Marcail both looked around the huge living room with something akin to awe. Marcail, of course, had been in this house before, but at the time she had been too nervous to notice much of anything.

Alex commented that their entire house could fit in the living room, and Marcail nodded her agreement. Another five minutes passed, and Cordelia entered.

"Doctor," she greeted him with a regal nod of her head. "Mrs. Montgomery." Again the nod. "To what do I owe the pleasure of this visit?"

There was a bite to her voice, but the young schoolteacher chose to ignore it.

"I'm here to discuss my position as Willits' schoolteacher for the coming fall." Marcail's voice was quiet and respectful.

"Since you have a two-year contract, I don't believe there is anything to discuss," Cordelia told her simply. "You did break your contract by acting indiscreetly on one occasion," Cordelia went on in a judgmental voice, "but all of that's been forgiven." This last statement was made magnanimously.

"I do not feel I broke my contract," Marcail replied just as respectfully, "although I'm sure you would have preferred to find me frozen in the snow rather than safe and sound in the doctor's home. However I'm not here about that. I'm here about the fact that you and the school board broke *your* part of the contract."

"Well I *never*—" Cordelia was outraged.

"You *will* let me finish," Marcail used her sternest teaching voice. Mrs. Duckworth quieted instantly, and even Alex sat up a little straighter in his chair.

"The contract stated that I was to teach school, and yet you abused your power, and I had only six students in my room. In addition, as the teacher I have the authority to discipline the children, but your grandson was the exception to this condition and was on at least two occasions completely out of control."

Cordelia was livid, but this time was able to keep her voice calm. "Why have you waited so long to come to me?"

Marcail's voice was not accusing, but she spoke truthfully. "I was told quite plainly what your reaction would be if I approached you in any way. The consequences of my being caught in the white-out have proved the extent of your control. Unlike you, Mrs. Duckworth, I will not sacrifice the children's education for my own selfish motives."

Cordelia was now so angry she couldn't have spoken if she tried.

Marcail came to her feet, as did Alex, clearly showing her hostess that she was nearly through. Her voice was sad as she finished what she had come to say.

"Since it seems you cannot handle honest confrontation, I assume you'll now be searching for another teacher for this fall. Should you decide that you do in fact need my services for another term, I will teach on my own conditions. You have until the first day of August to inform me of your decision, and to discuss revisions on my contract."

Marcail turned toward the door but stopped at the sound of Alex's voice.

"There is one condition *I* will change on Marcail's contract should she return in August. She will dress and wear her hair in a manner pleasing to her husband and not the Willits school board."

Alex and Marcail exited then, leaving a silent Cordelia in their wake. Alex treated Marcail to lunch at the hotel before dropping her off at home and telling her he'd see her at supper.

Marcail prayed the afternoon away, knowing she'd done what was necessary, but feeling she may have burned her bridges behind her.

# *fifty-six*

Marcail's spirits were a bit low in the days following her confrontation with Cordelia, but Alex proved to be a source of great encouragement. He felt she'd handled herself and the situation very well and told her so on several occasions.

They had talked in detail that evening and then prayed together about the future. Other than mealtime prayers, it was the first time they'd prayed as a couple. When they were finished, Marcail felt closer to Alex than ever before.

Marcail's new interest in Alex's work was also bringing them closer together. She found that she enjoyed accompanying him when he made housecalls, the first of which was to the Brents.

Mrs. Brent, Alex told her as they neared the house, was a woman in her sixties, whose frail, sickly body had never dulled her wit or the sharpness of her tongue. Marcail smiled at his description as she took in the neighborhood. The houses on this street were set farther apart than some, but were all quite small. Some of the homes were in disrepair, but most were well kept and welcoming.

The Brent home was one of the loveliest on the street. With yellow paint, white shutters, and a white picket fence along the front yard, the house was very well maintained. Alex held the gate for Marcail's entrance and then followed her up the path to the front door.

The door was opened by a woman in her mid-forties. Her name was Freda, and she was Mrs. Brent's spinster daughter. Freda looked very pleased at their arrival, and once inside she spoke in low tones to the doctor.

"How is she today?" Alex wanted to know.

"The same; certain that you're coming to cure her every ill. She—"

"*Freda!*" A strident voice cut into Freda's sentence. "Who are you talking to?"

Freda's features, already drawn and tired, seemed more so on the sound of that voice. Alex patted her shoulder when she would have answered her mother and then took himself off to the bedroom. Marcail stayed in the kitchen and had coffee with the younger Brent. They chatted easily, but Marcail prayed silently for Alex, since she was certain he was having to deal with an absolute shrew.

"I hope you've come to cure me" were Mrs. Brent's words the moment Alex stepped through the door. They both knew very well that she would never get out of her bed, and Alex had no trouble with the fact that she took her bad humor out on him.

"Well now," he spoke easily, "we'll see what we can do for you today."

Alex was bent over Mrs. Brent, listening to the sounds in her chest, when she noticed Marcail's and Freda's voices. He had just pulled the stethoscope from his ears when she bellowed with outrage and curiosity, "*Who is Freda talking with?*"

"My wife," Alex answered absently, his fingers searching for the pulse in her bony wrist.

"Well, bring her in here. I want to have a look at her." It was an order that Alex ignored. He found her condition just as usual, and regretted the scene he knew would follow when he told her she didn't need a change in medication. Mrs. Brent always took a change in medication as a good sign, but today she was too preoccupied with Marcail's presence to question the doctor's judgment.

"Are you going to bring her in here, or do I have to get out of this bed?"

Alex was putting his things away when she issued this final ultimatum. Still very much in control of the situation, he stepped to the door and called Marcail's name.

Mrs. Brent craned her neck to see around Alex's broad back as Marcail entered the room. Her eyes narrowed when Alex walked her to the side of the bed, her hand held within his own.

"Mrs. Brent, I'd like to present my wife. Marcail, this is Mrs. Brent."

"Hello, Mrs. Brent," Marcail said with a smile, only to have the old woman scowl at her.

"That brown dress is terrible on you," she finally said. "Do you take good care of this man?"

The change in subjects stunned Marcail for just a moment. Not that it really mattered. Mrs. Brent went on to talk of several things, giving Marcail no chance to speak. Neither she nor Alex said a word, and when Mrs. Brent had had her say, she informed the quiet young couple that they could leave now, since she was tired.

"It was nice meeting you, Mrs. Brent," Marcail told her and received a grunt in return.

"I'll see you in a few weeks," Alex added and moved to follow Marcail to the door.

"Doc."

Alex stopped, his hand on the door frame, and looked back to see Mrs. Brent sporting the most unselfish look he'd ever seen on her face.

"You take care of that little girl you've got there," she said seriously, "because you won't find a sweeter wife in all the county."

Alex grinned in her direction and took his leave. Once in the buggy, Marcail questioned Alex about what Mrs. Brent had wanted. Alex didn't give her a direct answer; he was too busy thinking that Mrs. Brent couldn't be more correct.

❑ ❑ ❑

The month of July, although slow-paced for Marcail, was hectic for Alex. There were days when they barely caught sight of each other. It seemed the bell rang for Alex nearly every night, and if he spent too much time at home for lunch or left the office early on Saturday, the bell would again seek him out.

On the rare evenings they were not interrupted, Alex often fell asleep in his chair. Marcail never minded. It was a simple pleasure to sit and watch him. It was during one of those evenings that Marcail recognized the first stirring of true love for her husband.

The first of August came and went. Marcail had known deep in her heart that she would not be asked back for the fall term. But when the day actually passed with no word from Mrs. Duckworth, it was harder to take than she anticipated. She found herself praying for the teacher who would replace her. God blessed her willingness to trust Him for the future, and soon Marcail saw His hand when she received a surprise visit from Sydney.

It was August 4, and Marcail hadn't seen Sydney since she'd arrived home from Santa Rosa. She had missed him terribly and prayed daily that he would continue to yearn after God. He came directly to the house, and Marcail was a bit concerned when she noticed he had walked rather than been driven in the Duckworth coach.

"Hello, Sydney," she greeted him, joy filling her at the shy smile he bestowed upon her. "Did you walk all the way from home?"

"No, just from downtown."

"Does your grandmother know you're here?"

Sydney nodded, but some of the smile deserted his eyes.

Marcail didn't question his look until he was in the house and seated at the kitchen table.

"How are you getting along with your grandmother this summer?"

"We were doing all right until I found out about you."

Marcail had suspected this might be the reason for his visit. "She told you I wouldn't be teaching?"

"My father came yesterday, and before he left this morning, he and Grandmother had an argument. You could hear them through the whole house. Father was very angry to learn that Grandmother was looking for another teacher. Grandmother was very angry that Father was checking on her business affairs." Tears filled the 12-year-old's eyes. "I don't know what I'll do if you're not my teacher."

Marcail drew him into her embrace. She held him silently for long moments as she chose the right words. With his face cupped in her hands, she spoke.

"I know that you will have a wonderful school year—not because you like the teacher, because you may not, and not because the work will be easy for you, because it may not be, but because you're a new person in Christ. The old Sydney has passed away, and as you learn more about our Lord, He is changing you to be more like Him."

Sydney's young heart was lifted by her words. Marcail saw the relief in his face and pressed a tender kiss to his brow. They talked through the afternoon, the time getting away from them both. Marcail had to rush to get supper on before Alex came in the door, but she did have a meal ready when he arrived. During supper she told him all about the afternoon with Sydney.

"I'm just so thankful, Alex, that the door is still open between the two of us. I was afraid she'd never let him see me again."

"It's got to be our prayers," Alex told her fervently.

"Amen to that," Marcail agreed. She rose to get dessert, and Alex spoke again, having just remembered something.

"Mrs. Nelson paid with a chicken today. I left it in the barn."

"Why would you do that?" Marcail asked as she placed a piece of pie before Alex.

"Well, I didn't think you'd want it in here; it's just in a makeshift cage."

*"It's alive?"*

Since his mouth was full of food, Alex only nodded, completely missing his wife's horrified stare. Marcail gawked at her husband's bent head and then at her own pie. Her mind ran with things she wanted to say, but she stayed silent. "Maybe I can do it" was her last thought before turning her attention to her own dessert.

□ □ □

"I can't do it." Marcail spoke to the quiet barn as she looked into the dark, inquisitive eye of what was supposed to be dinner.

Nearly 48 hours had passed since Alex had calmly announced that a patient had paid her bill in the form of a live chicken. A determined Marcail had marched out the next day, knife in hand, to do her job. After seeing the chicken, her bravado lasted only a moment before she returned to the house and made vegetable soup.

Now she was back in the barn and wishing she could be anywhere else. Katie had always done the butchering when they had been given an animal. Marcail knew that it was a way of life to kill animals for food, but she'd never been able to kill anything larger than an ant. To top it off, "dinner" was starting to look hungry. Marcail shook her head. It was no use. Even if she asked Alex to kill it, she'd never be able to eat it.

With a move born of desperation, Marcail lifted the cage. She carried it to the edge of the woods and opened the funny little door.

The moment the chicken was free, she began to peck around searching for food. Marcail, not wanting to think about how she would explain to Alex, turned and walked swiftly toward the house.

# fifty-seven

Alex stabled Kelsey and immediately noticed the chicken was missing from the barn. He licked his lips in anticipation of what was sure to be a great supper. He knew from weeks of experience that Marcail was a good cook, and he entered the house, a smile on his face, ready for whatever she had prepared.

Unfortunately, one look at Marcail's stern profile told him something was wrong. Since she'd been back from Santa Rosa, he had seen the Marcail that Kaitlin had spoken of—the Marcail whose face showed every emotion. He wasn't exactly certain, but it appeared to him that her tight-lipped silence was from anger. To Alex's mind this made no sense; they'd parted on very good terms at lunch. Alex shrugged mentally and broke the silence with what was sure to be the perfect comment.

"I thought I would smell chicken when I came in the door tonight."

His voice was friendly, and he was totally unprepared for his wife's reaction. Marcail spun to face him so quickly that her hair flared around her back and shoulders.

"I *cannot*," she stated furiously, her eyes flashing with ominous fire, "look something in the eye and then have it on my plate. The next time a patient pays you with an animal, it had better be *dead!*"

Marcail turned away to finish cutting out the biscuits. Her hand was moving the cutter so hard against the breadboard it was leaving marks. Alex was relieved she'd turned her back because his whole body was shaking with silent laughter. He was not quite under control when Marcail turned to look at him and her eyes narrowed with suspicion.

Ten minutes later Marcail finished putting the bowls and plates on the table with unusual force, and they sat down to eat. Alex kept his prayer of thanks very brief. The meal was half over before he decided that Marcail was calm.

"What did you do with the chicken?" Alex asked conversationally.

"I let it go at the edge of the woods," she told him softly. "I just couldn't bring myself to kill it."

"She won't survive, you know," Alex told her, compassion filling his voice. "Some fox or another predator will make a meal of her."

"I hadn't thought of that."

"I'd have been glad to kill it if you'd asked me."

"I wouldn't have been able to pluck it, let alone eat it, once I'd seen it alive."

Alex suddenly began to chuckle again.

"Don't you laugh at me, Alex Montgomery!" Marcail tried to sound stern, but failed.

"Honestly, Marc, my mind raced to figure out what I'd done, and lo and behold I'm in the doghouse over a chicken."

Marcail finally saw the humor in the situation and began to laugh herself.

"I was all right until an hour ago, when I sat here

trying to figure out how to tell you what I'd done. Suddenly it all seemed to be your fault, and I worked myself into a fine fury before you hit the door."

Alex was still laughing. "In the future, hang a dishcloth on the door so I'll have fair warning."

After the table was cleared and the dishes put away, husband and wife took a walk. Alex held Marcail's hand, and even though they talked some, most of the walk was spent in quiet reflection and the joy of each other's company. They stopped in a field and were watching the sun sink low in the sky when Marcail asked Alex a question that had been on her mind since they'd left the house.

"Are you upset with me over the way I acted before supper?"

"No."

"Are you sure?"

"I'm sure," Alex told her as he pulled her over to sit next to him on a huge boulder. "I realize it wasn't personal."

A peaceful smile passed over Marcail's face at his words of understanding.

"What does that look mean?" Alex wanted to know.

"I'm just pleased at how comfortable I am with you now."

"I'll admit it's very nice, just as long as you're not too comfortable."

Marcail looked at him with no comprehension whatever. "I don't know what you mean."

"I don't want you to view me as a brother, Marcail, or as a father figure."

Marcail was still not entirely sure what he meant. "Do I do that?"

"I don't think so, but I can't really be sure." Marcail was still looking at him strangely, and Alex knew it was time for some straightforward honesty.

"I'm in love with you, Marcail," he told her without apology, "and I'm not at all ashamed of the desire that love stirs within me. I am glad that you're comfortable with me, but I pray that at some point we'll have an intimate, passionate marriage. That's why I said what I did."

Marcail studied his face in the gathering dusk. "Are you afraid that I'm not a passionate person, Alex?"

Alex chucked softly and cupped her face in his hands. "After witnessing you in the kitchen an hour ago, not in the least."

Marcail smiled, and Alex bent his head. He pressed his lips to her forehead and the tip of her nose before finally claiming her lips. His kisses were tender, yet growing more insistent, and Marcail was taking longer to pull away every time he held her. But pull away she did, and much to his credit, Alex did not rebuke her or so much as frown in her direction.

He took her hand, and they walked back to the house in silence. They retired as usual to their separate beds, but even then Alex knew no frustration. That she was coming around was very evident in her response to his touch. Knowing this, and believing she was well worth the wait, Alex could bide his time.

# *fifty-eight*

A week later Marcail walked into town just before lunch, a picnic basket swinging from her arm. She still felt compelled to wear dark dresses and her hair up, so the walk was a warm one. Because she was no longer the schoolteacher, Alex had told her he preferred to see her dressed in lighter-colored clothing and with her hair down. In sensitivity to her feelings, however, he left it to her judgment as to when she would start dressing in greater comfort for her visits to town.

Alex's office was on Willits' main street, directly across from the bank and between a tiny dress shop and a lawyer's office. Her face was flushed by the time she arrived, but she knew the surprise she would be giving him would be reward enough for her effort.

Alex did not disappoint her. His eyes lit with delight, and since he had no patients, he took her into his arms and held her for long minutes. They were in the back room, and Alex would have been content to hold her for the next hour, but the outer door opened. He dropped a quick kiss on her upturned mouth and exited the room.

Marcail heard low voices, and then silence. A moment later Alex was calling to her. A man whom Marcail had never seen before stood beside Alex. He was obviously a businessman with his dark suit and shiny shoes. He held a top hat in one hand.

"Mr. Duckworth, this is my wife. This is Sydney's father, Richard Duckworth." Alex had turned to Marcail. "He'd like to speak with you," Alex added.

"It's a pleasure to meet you, Mr. Duckworth." Marcail's smile was pleasant, but her mind was abuzz with reasons why he might wish to see her.

"The pleasure is all mine," Richard told her, and meant it. Sydney had told him that his teacher was beautiful, but Richard, remembering his own hero worship of many of his teachers, had taken his son's words with a pinch of salt. He saw now that he should have heeded them; Marcail Montgomery was a beauty. She also seemed as sweet as she was lovely.

*Well, no matter,* Richard told himself. *She could have the face of a horse, and I'd still think she was beautiful for the changes she's made in my Sydney.*

"Why did you wish to see me?"

The sound of Marcail's voice made Richard realize he'd been staring at her like a man who'd taken leave of his senses. He cleared his throat and began.

"First, I'd like to thank you for the time and attention you've given Sydney. It's made a tremendous change in him, and his mother and I appreciate it."

"It really wasn't me, Mr. Duckworth. Hasn't Sydney shared with you—"

"Oh, you mean this God stuff," the older man interrupted. "It doesn't matter how it happened, Mrs. Montgomery, only that something *did* happen. Now," he went on before Marcail could correct him, "I understand that there has been some disagreement over your contract. I'm here to tell you that I want you as Sydney's teacher. Name your terms for this fall, and I'll have the contract typed up this afternoon."

"Is your mother feeling ill?" Marcail asked softly.

Richard stared at her, completely nonplussed. "No," he spoke, his voice filled with confusion. "I just left her, and she was fine."

Marcail nodded. "I do not wish to undermine your mother's authority. I've always dealt with Mr. Flynn or your mother; I can't say I'm very comfortable in doing something without them."

"Oh, well," Richard replied, thinking he understood, "I'm taking over some of Mother's responsibilities, and since I want you as teacher, I'm here in her stead."

"With her approval?" Marcail went on serenely, and Alex had to fight a smile. He knew her well enough to know she was not as calm as she appeared.

Richard was tempted to lie in answering that question, but the direct, dark-eyed gaze of this diminutive teacher made him feel as though she could read his very thoughts.

"I can see my answer in your hesitation. Please do not think me rude, Mr. Duckworth, but unless your mother contacts me personally, I couldn't consider returning in the fall."

"But Sydney needs you." Richard hoped to appeal to the teacher within her.

"I love Sydney dearly, but I would say that what he needs most is to be living with his mother and father. Surely you've a competent teacher where you live."

"We're moving here," he told her simply, as if this solved everything.

Marcail was surprised, but it did not change her answer. "I'm sure Sydney will be very pleased about that, but as far as my teaching is concerned, I've given you my answer."

"I'm willing to pay you—"

"Please, Mr. Duckworth," Alex cut in, his voice not overly loud, but firm. "My wife has given you her answer."

Richard had nearly forgotten the other man's presence. He looked between the two and felt a little ashamed of how pushy he'd been. The doctor was very protective of his wife, and Richard was the first to know the feeling. His mother hated the mere sight of his Beverly.

"I apologize for my rudeness. I'll let my mother know what you've said, and hopefully I can persuade her to reconsider."

Goodbyes were said all around, and Richard went out the door. His shoes could be heard on the boardwalk for some moments.

Marcail turned to Alex, her eyes wide with disbelief. "Did that really happen, or did I dream it?"

Alex shook his head in wonder. "It happened all right, but I'm not sure when it will really sink in."

"What do we do?" Marcail wanted to know.

"We do what we've been doing all along; we just keep praying." Alex pulled her into his embrace and held her once again.

"For right now, however," he spoke after a moment, "I'd like us to forget about Mrs. Duckworth, her son, and the school long enough to see what my wife brought in her basket."

Marcail smiled and opened the top to reveal a splendid picnic lunch. Alex's brows rose in delight, and he eagerly put his "out to lunch" sign on the door. He then took his wife to a private, shady glen, where he could enjoy her company and her cooking for the next hour.

❏ ❏ ❏

Cordelia Duckworth's entire body trembled with the emotions running through her. Richard had gone home that day and tried to persuade her to reconsider. Their argument lasted more than a week; it had been a nightmare. Cordelia had stood her ground, even amid threats of never seeing Sydney again.

On the last day, mother and son had had a huge row, whereupon Richard had stormed out of the house. Cordelia had looked up to see Sydney in the doorway. She really scrutinized his face for the first time in days, and knew that what was going on in his own house was tearing him apart.

Richard and Beverly had never visited much before, and Sydney's home with her had been a peaceful one. Now it was one fight after another, and the feud was over a woman Sydney loved with all of his heart.

At first Cordelia had been so jealous of Marcail that she could hardly see straight, but lately Sydney had begun to give more of himself to his grandmother than ever before. She knew it was time to put aside her pride and admit that Marcail Montgomery was the best teacher Willits had ever had, not to mention the best thing that ever happened to Sydney.

Now, because of her love for her grandson, she was in her carriage and headed for the Montgomery home. School was scheduled to resume in three days, and all Cordelia could do was hope that Marcail would reconsider.

Marcail heard the approach of the carriage and looked out, thrilled to know Sydney had been allowed to come for a visit. She took a moment to recover her poise when the black-garbed figure of Mrs. Duckworth emerged from the carriage.

"I'm sorry for coming without an appointment," Cordelia began, "but I hope you'll agree to see me anyway."

"Of course," Marcail told her warmly. "Please come in."

Marcail held the door open, and then followed Mrs. Duckworth inside. With the older woman's back turned, Marcail took a moment to wipe her damp palms together. She then realized with a start that she was wearing a pink calico dress and her hair was hanging down her back. Mrs. Duckworth was taking in the small house and didn't notice Marcail's look of chagrin.

"Please," the young hostess said, suddenly remembering her manners, "won't you have a seat in the living room?"

Marcail had to force her hands to her sides. The temptation to wring them and flutter about was nearly overwhelming. What did this woman want? A sudden thought came to her, and Marcail's heart thundered with concern.

"Mrs. Duckworth, is everything well with Sydney?"

Cordelia took in Marcail's suddenly pale features and felt the first stirrings of warmth for this woman. She also noticed the way the living room was set up like a bedroom and felt guilt—not a comfortable emotion. Into what had she forced this young couple?

"Sydney is very well, Mrs. Montgomery," Cordelia finally answered her. "I thank you for asking."

Marcail was so relieved she sat down in a chair. A moment later she was up again, mentally chastising herself for her breach of manners.

"May I get you some coffee, or something else to drink?"

"No, I won't be staying—" Cordelia stopped midsentence, realizing how thirsty she was. "Some water, please."

Marcail hurried to serve her. After she'd watched Mrs. Duckworth refresh herself, she sat once again and waited, this time in silence.

"I'm sure you must be curious as to the reason for my visit," Cordelia started, and Marcail determined to listen. "I realize we are many days past August 1, but I wondered if you might consider teaching again this fall."

Marcail bit her lip. This reason for the older woman's visit had passed through her mind, but she had dismissed it as impossible.

"Why?" was all Marcail could think to say.

*Why* Cordelia seemed taken aback.

"Yes. I mean, you must have looked for someone else, and I know you really don't want me as your teacher. Quite frankly, I don't think I could take another year like the last, another year of not having the whole town behind me. It was so hard to teach that way."

Cordelia looked ashamed. Richard was right; she had set herself up as a kind of queen in this town, and everyone hated her because of it.

"Last year is behind us, and I promise you it will not happen again. Richard is taking some of the properties off of my shoulders and—"

"Is that what you want?" Marcail knew she'd interrupted and been impertinent to boot, but suddenly this invincible figure was showing feet of clay, and Marcail was not as intimidated as she'd been before.

Cordelia sighed, seemingly not at all offended by the question. "It's taken some time, but, yes, it is what I want. I'm going to be traveling, and in truth, I'm tired of carrying the full weight on my own." The admission so surprised both women that they were silent for the space of a few heartbeats.

"I would love to come back and teach," Marcail said after some moments. "But it would have to be under the terms I mentioned to you previously, including my hair and dress."

Cordelia's eyes roved over Marcail's trim figure. "I'm sure that will be fine. I'll tell Stanley to work out the details with you. Neither Richard nor I will be on the school board, and I know that Stanley Flynn and the other men have only the town's best interests in mind."

Cordelia stood then, and Marcail followed suit. She moved toward the door, and Marcail thought she seemed defeated. At one time the thought might have pleased her, but not now.

"Thank you for coming, Mrs. Duckworth," Marcail said when it looked as though she would leave without a word.

"I don't suppose we'll be seeing much of each other in the weeks to come, but Sydney keeps me informed." The older woman paused and looked Marcail in the eye. "He thinks the world of you, did you know?"

"I realize that. I think quite of bit of him too."

"Yes, I can see that you do" was all the older woman said as she moved out the door, pulled herself into the carriage, and went on her way.

As the coach pulled away from the house, Cordelia contemplated the serene loveliness of Marcail Montgomery's face. Her home was small and a bit run down, but she seemed as content as a queen in a palace. Cordelia thought about her own home with its servants and beautiful furniture, and knew in an instant that it had never given her an ounce of happiness or peace.

"Her happiness comes from another source," Cordelia whispered as the coach moved along, and for the first time she forced herself to think about all Sydney had told her of his faith in Jesus Christ.

# *fifty-nine*

"I'm worried about this sudden depression you've fallen into," Alex teased Marcail as she nearly danced around the kitchen. It was the first day of school, and she was so excited she could hardly eat. In fact, she hadn't even sat down. She'd had a piece of bread in her hand at one point, but had laid it down and now couldn't find it.

With only three days to prepare, she kept thinking of new items she wanted to take back to school. Alex hadn't seen her standing still since he arrived home after Cordelia Duckworth's visit.

"Is my dress too low?" Marcail asked suddenly, her huge eyes watching her husband's face with concern.

"Simply scandalous," Alex answered with a mock shake of his head. The fabric of the lavender dress was nearly to her throat. "You really should try to eat."

"I will," Marcail called as she darted back into the living room for yet another missing schoolbook. Alex decided to sit back and let her run.

Marcail insisted they leave an hour early so none of the students would arrive and find her not in attendance. She had thoroughly cleaned the room two days earlier, but the first thing she did upon arriving was reach for the broom. Alex sat at her desk and watched her, a myriad of emotions running through him.

He was nothing less than thrilled that she had regained her teaching position, but they had been growing so close, and this was one more thing to take her mind from her husband.

*Lord,* he prayed silently, *I really believe she loves me, but the time hasn't been right for her to say the words. Please help her. Please help her to see that I would never reject her.*

This continued to be Alex's prayer that day and in the days to follow. As before, he did not know the Lord's timing, but as Alex continued to surrender his will and trust in Him, he found God to be sufficient.

❑ ❑ ❑

The end of the second week of school was upon her, and Marcail waved the children off before straightening up her room for the weekend. Class was going very well, and Marcail couldn't have been more pleased. The students, all but Sydney, were still staring at her hair and clothing, but she knew they would eventually grow accustomed to the different dresses and hairstyle.

Each morning Alex drove the buggy as far as the school, and then left it at the side of the building until he returned for Marcail. For some reason, he was late this day. Marcail didn't mind since it gave her some time to sit and pray.

She poured her heart out to the Lord over her spouse. She now knew she was in love with Alex, but she didn't have the faintest notion as to how to tell him. She knew he would welcome the words, but they simply would not leave her mouth.

She also knew that when she told him, Alex would make her his wife in every way. There was no fear within her at the thought, just a little breathless anticipation. Marcail was finally in a position to heed her sister's words of long ago: "Marc, when the man you marry takes you in his arms, you won't feel fear. You'll desire him as much as he desires you. That's the way God meant it to be."

Marcail now understood those words, but she also knew she was the person who would have to initiate something, and here she drew a blank. She prayed until Alex came for her, but was no closer to a decision than before.

Alex saw that she was very quiet when he picked her up, and assumed she was tired. She was as sweet as ever through the evening, and he even found her watching him on several occasions. When he questioned her, she only shook her head. Alex wished she would share what was in her heart.

Once in bed for the night, Marcail found herself with the same wish. She knew she'd had several opportunities to tell him, but she had stayed silent. Now she wondered how she would feel if he was called away and something happened and he never came back? She would never have had the joy of telling him of her love.

Her tortuous thoughts did not lead to a good night's rest. Within two hours of falling asleep, Marcail awakened in the midst of a vivid nightmare. For the first time in their marriage, Alex woke to find her moving about the house in the middle of the night.

"Marcail?" he called softly to her as he came to the bedroom door. He found her standing before the window, hugging her arms around herself.

"Marcail, are you all right?"

"I'm sorry I woke you."

She sounded breathless, and Alex realized she was

crying. He came forward and put his arms around her. She let her back fall against his chest.

"Bad dream?"

"Yes." Her voice was little more than a whisper.

"Want to talk about it?"

Marcail turned in his arms, "I wouldn't have let you fall," she told him, the light from the full moon catching the tears on her face.

"In your dream I was falling?"

"Yes," she said, her voice catching. "You were falling from a cliff, and I was at the top. You kept begging me to catch you. You said if I loved you I would catch you, but I couldn't reach you. I wouldn't have let you fall, Alex—I wouldn't have!"

"Shhh." Alex pulled her against his chest. "It was only a dream. Of course you wouldn't let me fall."

"You don't understand." Marcail pulled away from him, feeling desperate to make him understand. "What if you really did die, and I never told you I loved you. I couldn't stand it, Alex; I just couldn't stand it! I do love you, Alex, more than I can say. I wanted to tell you all evening, but I couldn't find the words."

Alex continued to hold her and spoke softly. "I'm sorry you had the dream, but I'm not sorry about what you told me."

"You don't seem very surprised," Marcail whispered to him and hiccuped.

"I've known for some time that you were in love with me."

"Why didn't you say anything?" This question accompanied yet another hiccup.

Alex chuckled and admitted. "There are some things a man likes to hear voluntarily."

The word "voluntarily" hung between them. Alex's greatest desire was to lift Marcail in his arms and carry her to the bedroom. But just as he had waited for her admission of love, he also needed to give her time to desire their physical union. In his own mind, the two went hand in hand, but he realized that Marcail probably did not feel that way. He knew he'd done the right thing when Marcail stepped from his arms.

"Better now?" he asked softly.

"Yes, Alex. Thanks."

They moved of one accord then, back to their own beds. Marcail settled in quickly on the sofa, but sleep was miles away.

*What did I do wrong? Did he not understand?* Marcail didn't know when she'd experienced such confusion. *I think he's taking his cue from me as usual, but I don't know how to do this.*

An image rose in Marcail's mind of Alex taking her in his arms, and she knew real fear that swiftly turned to anger. After turning over uncomfortably on the sofa, she scolded herself.

*You're such a coward, Marcail. Afraid of everything including your own husband. When are you going to grow up?* Marcail carried on in this vein for the better part of an hour without a single thought of sleep. She remembered much later than she should have that she needed to pray. She had barely said ten words to the Lord, when she realized she *had* to talk with Alex about the way she was feeling.

*You know he'll listen*, she told herself as she rose from the bed. *However, he might wish you had waited until morning.* Marcail sat up on the edge of the sofa in a moment of indecision. When she finally moved soundlessly through the living room, she had decided on a plan.

The house was very dark, but Marcail moved with purpose toward the bedroom. The door was open, and she stopped on the threshold. Very softly, Marcail called

Alex's name, knowing that if he was already asleep her voice wouldn't disturb him.

To Marcail's surprise he stirred instantly. She peered through the darkness as he rustled around and lit the lamp on the bedstand. When the room was illumined in soft light, Marcail saw that Alex had come up to rest on one elbow to watch her in her simple, sleeveless nightgown with its deep V-neck and buttons down the front. Her own eyes went to Alex's bare chest above the sheet and then back to his eyes. After taking a deep breath, she spoke.

"Katie told me a long time ago that when a man and woman are in love, there is nothing to fear. I seem to be struggling with believing her right now. I know I must seem like a child to you, but really I am afraid."

Alex's look was more tender than Marcail had ever seen. She watched him draw the covers back from one side of the bed in invitation. Of their own volition, Marcail's feet propelled her forward. She crawled onto the bed and knelt just a few inches from her husband.

"Katie is right." Alex's soft voice was deep, and Marcail felt a chill down her spine. "There is nothing to fear because we do love each other. I've never thought of you as a child. If you were a child, you wouldn't be ready to be my wife—and you've proved that you are by joining me tonight."

Marcail took great comfort in his words and found that all cowardice had melted away. She leaned forward until her lips found Alex's. She kissed him tenderly and when that wasn't enough, she reached to hold his face in her small hands and kiss him some more, hardly aware of the way Alex's strong arms had come up to hold her.

Alex's own heart threatened to thunder from his chest at her touch as well as the softly spoken words of love she whispered again and again. He knew this was a beginning for them, even as he knew she would spend this night and every night in his arms. Again Alex found himself asking if she had been worth the wait, and without a doubt, he knew that she had.

# *sixty*

Willits, California
April 21, 1882

Alex arrived at the schoolhouse a little early, so he stood and watched his wife play with the children in the schoolyard. It was a beautiful spring day, and the entire class had joined hands and was moving in a circle. A sweet song rose in the air, and Alex was content to stand and listen.

Alex watched his tiny wife from 15 yards away. Her skirt was dark, but her blouse was snow white, accentuating the dark color of her hair and eyes. He heard her laughter drift through the air and smiled. She was such a delight.

They had been married over a year, and Alex could say in all honesty that it had been the most joy-filled year of his life. The start had not been altogether easy, but now they were as close as a husband and wife could be, and Alex believed that with God as the head of their home, the future would hold many more years of love and joy.

The group broke up some minutes later, and the children greeted Alex as they filed past him up the steps to retrieve books and sweaters. Marcail did not follow them inside, but stood opposite Alex at the bottom of the schoolhouse steps. One little boy, on his way up the stairs, stopped to speak with Alex before going inside. When the child was gone and Alex finally looked up, it was to find Marcail's eyes on him.

"What are you thinking?" he questioned her softly.

"That I love you." Her voice was equally soft.

Very aware that the children would be reappearing at any moment, Alex pointed a finger at her. "That's not fair, Mrs. Montgomery. You're not allowed to say that when I can't kiss you."

Marcail's smile was impish, and Alex's look told her he'd collect that kiss another time. The children did appear just seconds later, and both Marcail and Alex talked with each one as they saw them off for the weekend.

"Mr. Flynn came to see me today," Marcail told him as soon as they were alone.

"About?"

Marcail hesitated. "He wanted me to sign another two-year contract."

Alex's brow rose. "I take it you didn't tell him about the baby."

Marcail frowned, and Alex laughed incredulously.

"Marcail," he said, laughter still filling his voice. "I'm your husband and a doctor. When are you going to believe me?"

"But I don't *feel* pregnant," she protested.

"I assure you, darling, all the signs are there. If it would make you feel better," his voice became very dry, "write Katie and describe your symptoms to her. Having four children makes her the expert."

Now it was Marcail's turn to laugh. She moved close and put her arms around his waist. "I do believe, Dr. Montgomery, that your feelings are hurt."

"No, but when you start to rival Kelsey for size, I'll just say I told you so." Alex hugged her back, and dropped a kiss on her head. "It's certainly a compliment that the board wants you for two more years, but now you have a decision to make."

Marcail leaned back in her husband's embrace, allowing her to see his face.

"Do you really think I'm expecting?"

"Absolutely."

Marcail smiled at the surety in his voice.

"Well, then," she spoke as a smile of pure contentment came over her face, "I believe the decision is already made."

# *epilogue*

*Visalia, California*
*May 18, 1884*

Pastor Sean Donovan stood at the front of the church and watched as his father came in from the side door, Rigg just behind him. He smiled down into those eyes that were so like his own until he let his gaze travel out over the congregation. He reflected for a moment on how much he liked having a wedding immediately following the sermon on Sunday. It had been Sadie's idea, and an excellent one at that.

Minutes passed and the organ played, allowing Sean to look out at his family and friends. Kaitlin stood with her four—Gretchen, already so tall, Donovan, a sturdy four-year-old and next to him, Molly, still a picture of her Aunt Marcail. Katie held 18-month-old Zachary in her arms.

Charlotte also stood with their own four rascals. Ricky was showing signs of being tall, and Callie was as lady-like as they came. Little Sadie, now three, was such a combination of both of them that Sean smiled at the sight of her. His youngest, Micah, in his mother's arms, was working on his thumb as if he no longer had need of it.

Alex and Marcail stood together, and resting contentedly on Alex's arm was their Megan. She was an adorable dark-haired toddler, and a sign to the family that their beloved Marcail and Alex had found a love to carry them through the years.

Precious friend, Lora Duncan, was in a front pew, alone for the moment. A change in the music drew Sean's attention back down the aisle. Lucas Duncan had entered the back of the church. On Lucas' left arm was Charlotte's aunt, Sadie Cox.

Sadie was dressed in cream-colored linen. Standing poised and serene, she looked straight into the eyes of the man she loved. Sean felt an unexpected rush of emotion when Sadie came to the front, and he saw the look of profound love that covered his father's face for the woman who stood beside him.

They'd both been alone for so very long, and now God had seen fit to bring them together. Sean watched as Duncan kissed the bride's cheek and took his seat next to Lora. Patrick and Sadie joined hands and turned to face him.

"We are gathered today . . ." Sean began the service, his voice confident, yet tender with emotion. Rigg was on hand to provide the rings and sign as official witness. The room cheered at the end of the service when Patrick kissed his wife. Family and friends alike filed out behind the bride and groom for a reception to be held at Duncan and Lora's.

As Sean came down the aisle, he plucked his niece Megan from Alex's arms and carried her outside. Alex and Marcail were the last to leave the building. Once alone, Marcail looked up at her husband, her eyes shining with happiness.

"That was beautiful, wasn't it?"

"Yes, it was," Alex agreed. "But then I've noticed that beauty tends to run in your family."

Marcail grinned at the compliment, and Alex bent to give her a long, loving kiss.

"Hey, you two," Rigg's voice broke in, teasing them from the door. "Break it up. The wagon won't wait all day."

Marcail laughingly jumped out of her husband's arms, pulling her most innocent face to the fore. Alex grinned at his brother-in-law, but pulled Marcail back into his embrace.

"It was a hard wait before I had this woman in my arms, Rigg. You go ahead with the wagon, it'll be worth having to walk."

Rigg stayed on the scene only long enough to see that Alex was kissing Marcail once again. *Yes, I imagine you would say it was worth having to walk*, Rigg thought as he climbed into the wagon next to Kaitlin. He leaned to kiss her and then slapped the reins, putting the vehicle in motion.

"What was that for?" asked a pleasantly surprised Katie.

Rigg smiled, but didn't answer. *Yes indeed*, he repeated to himself. *Worth the walk, and a whole lot more.*